C

By

Mark Stonecipher

Badgley Publishing Company

ISBN

978-0-9854403-7-4

Copyright © Mark Stonecipher
2012
All rights reserved

Dedication

With love and gratitude and a big thank you for her patience I dedicate this, my first book, to my wife Debbie. I told her I wanted to write a book and she said, "Go... write it!"

Contents

Prologue 1
  Near Today's New Jerusalem, Ohio 1

Chapter One 1

December 24, 1773 3
  Virginia 3

Chapter 2 7

Around 1380 7
  The Mayan city of Balamku, Present Day State of Chiapas Mexico, The Yucatan Peninsula 7

Chapter 3 13

Present Day 13
  Antioch University, Yellow Springs, Ohio 13

Chapter Four 21

Present Day 21
  Zane Shawnee Caverns, Bellefontaine, ... 21
  Logan County, Ohio 21

Chapter 5 25

1390 25
  Gulf of Mexico, Along the South West Coast 25
  of Florida, near present day Tallahassee 25

Chapter 6 29

March 1772 29

- Fort Dunmore (Pitt) 29
- Chapter 7 35
- September 20, 2012 35
  - Zane Shawnee Caverns, Bellefontaine, ... 35
  - Logan County, Ohio 35
- Chapter 8 41
- July 1, 1521 41
  - On present day Pine Island, Florida 41
- Chapter 9 47
- Late April, 1774 47
  - The Settlement of Wheeling 47
- Chapter 10 55
- September 20, 2012 55
  - Zane Shawnee Caverns, Bellefontaine, ... 55
  - Logan County, Ohio 55
- Chapter 11 57
- 1707 57
  - Suwannee River, Georgia 57
- Chapter 12 61
- September 20, 2012 61
  - Yellow Springs, Ohio 61
- Chapter 13 67
- April 28, 1774 67

Chief Logan's Camp	67
Chapter 14	77
September 27, 2012	77
Zane Shawnee Caverns, Bellefontaine,	77
Logan County, Ohio	77
Chapter 15	83
May 5, 1774	83
Ft Henry, Wheeling	83
Chapter 16	91
September 29, 2012	91
Antioch University, Yellow Springs, Ohio	91
Chapter 17	101
1738	101
Shawnee Village of Pequea in present day Lancaster County, Pennsylvania	101
Chapter 18	107
June 16, 1774	107
Mouth of the Scioto River	107
Chapter 19	121
1738	121
Chalahgawtha Mid-November	121
Chapter 22	123
September 29, 2012	123

Yellow Springs, Ohio 123
Chapter 21.. 131
June 17, 1774 131
  Chalahgawtha on the Scioto River 131
Chapter 22.. 143
October 4, 2012 143
  Zane Shawnee Caverns, Bellefontaine, ... 143
  Logan County Ohio 143
Chapter 23.. 151
June 17, 1774 151
  Chalahgawtha on the Scioto River 151
Chapter 24.. 163
October 4, 2012 163
  Zane Shawnee Caverns, Bellefontaine, ... 163
  Logan County Ohio 163
Chapter 25.. 169
Summer, 1774 169
  Chalahgawtha on the Scioto River 169
Chapter 26.. 183
April, 1789 183
  Apple Creek, Missouri 183
  (Present Day, Perry County) 183
Chapter 27.. 193

October 4, 2012 193
    Zane Shawnee Caverns, Bellefontaine, ... 193
    Logan County Ohio 193

Chapter 28 205

October 1789 205
    Amogayunyi, Running Water 205

Chapter 29 213

September 28, 1792 213
    The Creek Crossing Place near Nickajack, TN 213

Chapter 30 229

April, 1798 229
    Near Present, Old Town, Ohio 229

Chapter 31 237

October 5, 2012 237
    Zane Shawnee Caverns, Bellefontaine, ... 237
    Logan County Ohio 237

Chapter 32 247

August, 1812 247
    Old Town, Ohio 247

Chapter 32 253

October 5, 2012 253
    Zane Shawnee Caverns, Bellefontaine, ... 253
    Logan County Ohio 253

Reference Notes..263

Prologue
October 10, 1813

Near Today's New Jerusalem, Ohio

"This will be his final resting place. It was our fortune that the man named Kenton purposely did not identify him. In his respect, he identified the body on the battlefield of another, so that his body would not be mutilated. This Kenton is an honorable man."

Thick Water, Tecumseh's first cousin, best friend, first warrior and personal bodyguard, along with several others under his direction, had removed the body under cover of darkness from the battlefield. Fortunately, there were few whites, few Americans, who could identify him. He had been shot in his left breast, just below his heart. Two bullet holes were identifiable and his shirt was stained with the dried blood of his wounds. He was dressed in his deerskin leggings and hunting shirt, with a sash around his waist. His face was painted black and red. He had a bandage around one arm from a wound he had gotten at Chatham. He still had a British medal around his neck. There was little that would have identified him from any of his fellow Shawnee.

"Lay him there," said Thick Water. They had finished the small platform. Thick Water looked at the body. "My brother, you have been a great man. History will remember you. I am sorry that we cannot give you the burial of your people. You will always and forever be in our hearts. One day, mankind will understand your heart. "

"We will seal this place forever and none of us will speak of this place."

Chapter One
December 24, 1773

Virginia

Caesar ran. It was cold, dark, windy and raining hard. He had waited for this night ever since he had decided to make his break for freedom. He knew that it wouldn't be easy going in the cold wind and rain. He had thought about waiting for the warmer weather of Spring, but his new master was less likely to chase him in this weather and more than likely, he wouldn't even know that he was gone until sometime Christmas day. He was confident that his master wouldn't chase him on Christmas day and that with a whole day's head start and the rain covering his tracks and his scent from the dogs, he would have a good chance of not being caught.

Caesar hadn't had it too bad as a child and into his early adult life. He had been raised by his mother, but he had never known his father. No one spoke of his father, except to tell him that he had died when Caesar was only one year old. He was now thirty-two, just over six feet tall and muscular, with no body fat. His eyes were light brown and his curly, dark hair was short, with a slight tint of red. He had a light complexion in comparison to many of the other slaves. But now, he was bequeathed to his master's son, who had taken him from working in the family's fields and put him in their tobacco factory under the authority of an unfair, hypocritical overseer. The overseer was a colored man, and the conditions were prison like. He and the other slaves had to sit under a large table filled with tobacco and tie lugs all day long except for the short time they were allowed for breakfast and the same time allowed for dinner. Like all the slaves, he ate "one-pot" meals, such as vegetable stews with pork fat. He hadn't been subjected to much physical violence in his experience as a slave, but he was not content to remain a slave. To him, being a slave was no longer bearable. It wasn't just this...though it helped him make the decision to run for freedom. In September, his new master had sold his wife and two children. Their new master took them to North Carolina and he knew he would never see them again. His heart was broken. They were all that he had that he could call his own. With them gone and in his despair, he realized that he could no longer live this life. If he were caught and killed it would be better than the life he now had. He had to be free. He had to escape. He couldn't go after his wife and children, as the risk of capture and the punishment they would have to endure were too much to consider. If they were captured together, he doubted that he would ever be returned to his master. He would probably just be strung up in a live oak and buried in a hole in the ground and his memory gone forever. His choice was to run for freedom and with it, whatever lay ahead.

That night, Caesar kept off the roads as he alternately ran and walked through the rain. He was wet and cold. His wool coat and wool shirt were soaked. His woolen pants were so wet they clung to his muscular legs. The wetness of the wool, which he thought would help him keep warm, just weighed him down to the point that just walking was difficult, let alone running. To make matters worse, He didn't own a pair of sox and his black leather shoes, with holes in both of the soles, didn't provide his feet with much protection. They were wet and cold as he slogged through the leaves and mud near the small swollen stream that he was following. His feet soon became numb as he struggled along, stumbling over logs and through the underbrush. He had left the main road a few miles back and knew that the stream he had come to, and was now following, would lead him to an old trail that wasn't much traveled anymore. It was longer, but it would be safer to follow it than any other road. He knew that the trail went north and as long as he could keep going north, he would be ok.   As he kept moving, his mind, however, was not on his wetness or how cold he was or even on what he was escaping from. His thoughts were on where he was heading to and what he would find on his quest for freedom.

Caesar knew that if he was not recaptured in the first two or three days he would have a good chance of making it to what folks called Braddock's Road. It started in an area called Maryland, at the mouth of Redstone Creek. It was an old Indian trail between two big rivers, the Susquehanna and the Monongahela. He was told it was once called [i]Nemacolin's Trail, after an Indian, and was now wide enough for a wagon to pass down. Once he got to it, he could follow it West, through the mountains all the way to Fort Duquesne. The Fort was at the head of a great river formed by two other smaller rivers flowing into it. This river was called the Ohio by the whites and flowed on the southern edge of what he had heard was called the Ohio wilderness. That's where he wanted to go, as far away from the whites and their cruel society as he could get.

He wasn't quite sure if he could do it, or even if he could get there, but he had heard that there were a lot of Virginians in the communities that surrounded the Fort and that there were lots of blacks with them. He was told that there was a place called Lower Town and that he would be able to hide there with free blacks. Some of the Virginians were artisans. Some were building boats for the settlers to enter the Ohio Country. He was strong and his old master had taught him to etch silver and gold and he had worked part time away from the tobacco fields in their small store. If he was lucky he might earn some money working for a smith. If not, he could help build boats and he would then have a good chance of getting on a boat and heading down the big river that started there. He had heard that the folks that were setting off down the river were searching for freedom from their lives in the East in their own ways and that they always needed help. More importantly, most of them were running from their own pasts and demons and wouldn't question his freedom or where he came from. He knew it was dangerous and that he might not survive, but for him it was his only chance to be free and to just disappear from his miserable existence as a slave. To leave his old life behind and to journey into a new life...as uncertain as it was.

Chapter 2
Around 1380

The Mayan city of Balamku, Present Day State of Chiapas Mexico, The Yucatan Peninsula

Balam was seated in the House of the Four Kings. He was ruler of his city-state. He was short. His eyes were slightly crossed and his skull was somewhat flattened. Large silver earrings dangled from his ears. His teeth had been filed into a T shape and were inlaid with small, round plaques of jade. His face, chest, back, arms and legs were covered with tattoos. His tunic was made of jaguar fur. Seated before him was Tepeu, ruler of Calakmul. Several priests sat beside the both of them. Others had been invited from several other cities, but they had just not come. There were few left now as many had already left their homelands. They had begun leaving over the last several years in search of land where they could live without fear of the Toltec warriors and where there were not mighty storms that would come from the ocean and leave so much destruction. Balam and Tepeu were two of the remaining rulers of what was once the vast Mayan Civilization.

The room they were in represented the surface of the Earth. There were several images such as the jaguar, that symbolized war, aquatic elements that represented fertility and masks of the Monster of the Earth, Cauac, separating the underworld, or the kingdom of the dead, from the upper world, the kingdom of the gods. Also, emerging from the aquatic surface were animals...two toads and two crocodiles with their mouths opened 180 degrees, representing the Earth in its vegetative and fertile state. The kings of the upper world were responsible for the abundance and wealth of their subjects. There were three doors that opened into the room they were in. They symbolized the entrance into the underworld.

Balam, to his people, was believed to be a descendant of the gods. He had faithfully practiced personal bloodletting over the years, as was his people's custom. His blood was considered sacred and an ideal sacrifice. For him and his people, there was a time for everything and everything had its place in time. It was he who controlled the daily lives and activities of his people.[ii]

He was king. He was chosen by the gods and his son would be king because of their blood. When his son was born, he had performed a blood sacrifice by drawing blood from his own body as an offering to his ancestors. He had also taken a captive in war and this enemy warrior was sacrificed at the time of his installation as king. Up to now, this had been the most important point in his life. It was the point at which he inherited the position as head of his lineage and the leader of the city. It had been necessary for the continuance of the Universe.

Balam was seeing it all change now, and many of the people from the Kingdoms whose lands were near and far away had already abandoned their cities and their monuments. Over the years, their resources had been strained and their food sources had become scarce mostly because of a prolonged drought that had depleted their water supplies. Some years the storms from the sea would come and would bring the floods that would destroy the crops. The last few years however there had been no storms, and little, if any rain. With no water, their food sources had diminished and many people had died of starvation and thirst. Many of their social services had unraveled and many of the common people had lost faith in the abilities of the leaders to transact favorably with their gods. They had turned more and more to blood sacrifices, but in the end, many clans just left and returned to the villages of the jungle and the highlands. He knew that other brothers had left the area and traveled far to the South and to the North. They had sent individuals back to keep in touch, but they were gone.

As he thought about all of the changes over the years, his mind wandered back to his younger days. He could see the crowds at the base of the enormous blood red pyramid. He had been standing for hours in the dripping heat of the jungle. No one moved...every eye was fixed on the building's summit, where he, the new King, his head adorned with feathers, his scepter a two-headed crocodile, was about to emerge from a sacred chamber with instructions from his long-dead ancestors. The crowd saw nothing of his movements, but it knew the ritual. Lifted into the next world by hallucinogenic drugs, Balam would take the obsidian blade and pierce his own penis. He felt no pain. He would then draw a rope through the wound, letting his blood drip onto bits of bark paper. Then, he took the bark and set it afire. Out of the rising smoke a vision of a serpent would appear to him. As he was about to collapse, he would reach under his bloody loincloth, displaying a bloodstained hand and announce his ancestors' message. It was the same message he had received so many times in the past: "Prepare to go to war!" The crowd below him erupted in wild cheers.

Balam, sweaty, snapped back to reality. It was hot, and the sound of rain could be heard through the door openings. All things were different now. He rose and put a pipe to his lips and puffed. As he exhaled, the smoke rose. He did this four times, in four directions, facing the Four Corners of the universe, to appease the gods.

He spoke slowly and deliberately.

"We who are born out of the mouths of the frogs that sit upon our sacred mountain welcome our brothers from Calakmul. We respect you as one of our most powerful cities. Brothers, it is with a heavy heart that I have welcomed you. We have lived and prospered in this area for generations that are too many to count. The bones of our ancestors rest among us. Many of our people have abandoned us over the years, and those of us that remain must make a difficult decision today. Just to our North and only a few days from us, an army of warriors is approaching. They are from the city they call Tolln.[iii] They are mighty and their fierce reputation has reached us. In past times, we could defend our cities and our families, but today our numbers are few in comparison to these people that approach. Our time as leaders has been good. We have accomplished much, but now we must decide all of our futures. We cannot defeat our enemy. Our choices are two. We can stay and fight, but it will only be a matter of time before our defeat. In doing this, upon the death of our last warriors, our women and children will be torn to pieces and sacrificed. Our people will no longer exist. Our second choice is to leave our homes and this land. I present these two choices to you for your discussion and vote. My choice however, is to leave. I will take my family and go across the great clear and blue waters in the direction where the sun greets each new day. I have heard that there is land across these waters that is full of animals and fruits and that the peoples of this land will welcome us as brothers. Those of you who choose to journey with my family and I are welcome. I know that this is not easy, but we will survive and raise our children. They will continue in our ways as a people. It is for you to decide, however. If you choose to come with us, we will leave in the morning taking only our clothing, some food and much of the treasure that we have, including our silver, silver stones and gold, with which to trade."

Chapter 3
Present Day

Antioch University, Yellow Springs, Ohio

Professor Stevensen shuffled his notes and cleared his throat as he stood behind an old wooden lectern, and began his lecture to the 28 students in his History and Myths 101 class.

"Today we are going to begin a study into two unrelated, but I think possibly related, little known legends. One is the Legend of Swifts Silver Mine. The other is a legend that is rather close to home...that of the Great Cavern of the Shawnee and their mythical silver. As with all legends that involve treasures, we can find some truth in the surrounding circumstances of the legends at least enough to give credence to them...enough to have generated numerous treasure hunts over the years. But...like all legends, no one has been able to find any of the mines, the caves or any of the silver that is to purportedly exist. One author, a James A. Dougherty, in is paper, "The Legend of Swift's Mine," asks the following questions and ends with a poem from Southeastern Kentucky folklore:

Who was John Swift? Did he really live, mine silver, and coin money? Did he have a mine? If so...where? What is the origin of the different and conflicting accounts of the mine? Is there still buried in the Southern Appalachians a vast lode of treasure? Were the many people who were "taken in" by swindlers selling treasure maps completely fooled or is there some truth to the story? What part did the

Shawnee Indians play in the mine story? The Spaniards? The French?

> *"The Silver Mine of Swift,*
> *A fine will-o-the wisp*
> *Left in a heroic age*
> *For a vision of the sage*
> *With reason bereft."*[iv]

The same evasiveness evoked in the poem and the questions asked by Dougherty can be applied to the evidence surrounding the mine and the cache of silver that the Shawnee Indians were supposed to have. One theory in regards to the Shawnee silver and that of Swifts mine...that links the two together, and there is substantial, though not proven information that does link the two together, is that the Shawnee did in fact have silver and that the legend of Swift's mine and that of the great Shawnee cavern were both fictitious stories created by the Shawnee to keep the white man from the real truth...that the Shawnee did in fact have a silver mine and vast amounts of silver and that it was in Ohio, not Kentucky.

I want to read to you a short excerpt from an article that appeared in the Louisville Courier-Journal on December 18, 1922. It was written by James W. Lutz. One last thing before I read this...one finds it interesting that there is even a discrepancy in what the name Shawnee means. In the Algonquin language, the name means Southern People [v]. However, if you go to the Ohio Department of Natural Resources State Parks web site, under Shawnee State

Park, you will find a statement that "Historians note that the Shawnee name means "those who have silver," as the tribe conducted considerable trade in this precious metal."

"I'm not sure where this information came from and can't find any other documentation that this is what the name means. But obviously, it had to come from somewhere."

Stevensen smiled with a quizzical look upon his face. Shuffled the papers behind the lectern and began:

"1790 Pine Mountain, Virginia

The last thing that Shadrach saw was the shining silver nose ring of the Shawnee guide Caesar as he felt the axe hit the middle of his forehead splitting his head open. He was dead within seconds. The last thing that John Swift saw was the axe splitting his partner's head open. A hand was on his mouth and his eyes stung. Whoever had hold of him had forced something into his eyes. It burned, but he could do nothing as he felt the knife blade at his throat.

Whoever had him had come up behind him so quietly that he had not heard them at all. This person, whoever he was, was very strong. They had one of his arms pinned behind his back.

He was afraid to move...his couldn't open his eyes...his legs began to shake uncontrollably and as fear overcame him, he felt his bladder empty, soaking the front of his pants.

He could hear the commotion around him...the screams and dying moans of the others in his party. It seemed that as quickly as he was grabbed, he was let go. As he was let go, he felt something thrust into his chest. He reached for it and felt the handle of a tomahawk.

As he tightened his grip on the handle, he could feel the warm blood from the steel face drip onto his hand.

Laughter erupted as he heard the footsteps of two individuals running from the camp. The moans of the dying around him lasted a few moments and the woods were then deathly quiet.

With his eyes closed and burning, he stumbled and crawled until he found one of the men in his party. The body was motionless. He felt for the man's head. He could feel the warm, sticky blood on his fingers as it oozed from the deep gash in the man's head. He could see nothing. He cried out, "Anybody here?"

There was no answer. He stood up and stumbled across the campsite tripping upon another body. He knelt down and felt the man's head. It too had been split wide open and he could feel the man's warm blood on his hands. The bloody axe he had been given was in his hand and his arm hung down to his side. He sensed that he was alone and knew that those who had done this had fled.

He cried out again, "Is anybody here?"

There were only the normal sounds of the night and the crackle of the embers of the dying fire.

He had to assume that all of the 6 members of his party had been murdered. What was he going to do? He collapsed to his knees...unable, for the moment, to stand. He eyes were burning and his mind raced with the thoughts of what had just occurred. What could he do and where was he. He only knew that he was in the mountains of Virginia and was a few days from the Sandy River, where they had gone inland to find the entrance to the Shawnee cavern that was supposedly rich in silver. It was the reason he had led his party to the mine with the two Shawnee guides that Blue Jacket had provided for him. He had promised during his meeting with Blue Jacket, that they would only collect as much of the silver as would be necessary to cash in and get the weapons that the Shawnee desperately needed and that they would take only enough to cover the expense of their travel and a little for their families. Blue Jacket knew that Swift was lying. His intention all along was to have two of his warriors lead Swift and his men into the mountain wilderness, kill them all and make it look like it was Swift who killed his party.

The location of the cavern was known to very few and had been kept a secret among the Shawnee who frequented it often and kept it well hidden. Tradition said that it existed on or near the Red River, which is one of the head branches of the Kentucky. Swift however, from his recollection of living with the Shawnee, thought that their mine and the source of their silver lay somewhere between the Breaks of the Sandy and Pound Gap in Pine Mountain. The Lower Pigeon Creek drains from the north face of Pine Mountain, just east of Elkhorn City, KY. Its forks converged on the mountain and entered Elkhorn Creek. Elkhorn Creek meets the Russell Fork of the Sandy River at the village of Elkhorn City, immediately north of the Breaks of the Sandy. He had heard of a large cave in this area that went from one side of the mountain to the other. The cave's entrance however, was said to be no larger than the size of a barrel...a sinkhole, covered and impossible to find unless one knew its exact location.

Swift had always questioned where the Shawnee had gotten their silver as he was living among them and had befriended Blue Jacket. He had first come to Virginia and then moved on to North Carolina. As a fur trader, he traded with the Shawnee in the Ohio River Valley before 1750 and lived most of 1750 – 1769 with the Shawnee in what is now Ohio. He married the daughter of a chief and fathered a few children. While trading with the Indians, he was captured by the French, but escaped through the help of two Frenchmen he knew. After his escape, he went to Virginia, and later had fought in the army of Braddock and Washington at Fort Duncannon.

While on Braddock's ill-fated expedition to the French fort, Swift had met and came to know well some men from North Carolina; James Ireland, Samuel Blackburn, Isaac Campbell, Abram Flint, Harmon Staley, Shadrach Jefferson and Jonathan Munday. All of these men had lived about the head of the Yadkin, the South Yadkin and the Catawba Rivers in North Carolina.

In 1790, all of the men met at Fort Pitt, procured tools and bought some maize from the Indians in Ohio. Swift and the others, after leaving Fort Pitt, traveled to what is now Charleston, West Virginia and then on to the forks of the Great Sandy Creek. It was on this trip that the Indians, two Shawnee warriors provided by Blue Jacket, took Swift and his party into the mountains to find the silver ore.

No one knows exactly what happened, but Swift was thought to be a murderer because he was found wandering with a bloodied axe. Somehow he had found his way back to civilization blinded, and to this day, all searches for the mine and the Shawnee silver have been to no avail.

There are a lot of legends about Swift and the location of the secret silver mine. One legend even says that there is a carving of a "feather" that is visible at the cave entrance. It is claimed to have been put there by the Shawnee Chief Cornstalk who is claimed to have assisted Swift in his silver mining in Eastern Kentucky.

It is also claimed that over the years Spanish coins and English Crowns have been found, as well as silver ingots in one cave. Interestingly, along with some of the coins, it is said that other silver artifacts had been found that appeared to be Mayan.

As Stevensen finished, John Hawk, a Junior History major, turned and whispered to Bill Brown, one of his classmates and closest friends.

"This should be an interesting class, but I have heard a lot of this before. Both of these myths or legends, as he calls them, are just that. Swift's mine, the Great Shawnee Cave and my peoples' silver mine never existed. "

"What? I'm sorry. What d'ya say John?"

"Bill. None of that's true. The truth is that our women were very good at stealing silver from the white man."

"You gotta be kidding."

"No. I'm not. There is no silver mine. Never was. Everything that the women stole was taken and kept hidden and used as needed. Some was melted down and made into jewelry and some was just used to trade with."

John was a pure blooded Shawnee. He was one of the few who could actually claim to be full blooded. Most were matis, or mixed. The Shawnee, like most Indian's, had crossbred over the years with the whites, blacks and others and had incorporated themselves into American society. John was 23, 5'9" tall and had long, shoulder length, straight black hair. His eyes were dark brown and his dark complexion had a slight bronze cast to it. With no facial hair, he looked somewhat boyish.

As the class started to get up to leave Stevensen stopped them.

"Hold up a minute please. Next week we are going to discuss both of these legends further. I want you to read up on both of the legends and find out as much as you can about each. I want each of you to put together a short paper on "Are there any truths to these two legends? If so, what are they?"

"See you next week."

Chapter Four
Present Day

Zane Shawnee Caverns, Bellefontaine, Logan County, Ohio

John Logan had just finished giving a tour of the museum that is attached to the cavern's gift shop when Emma Bluejacket came in through the door[vi]. Emma was the Mother of the Nation of the URB. She was a short woman in her early 50's with long, straight, graying black hair that reached to the middle of her back.

"Can I talk with you for a minute? John said respectfully.

"Sure. What's on your mind?"

John glanced at the tourists as the last of them was heading out the door.

"In my history class on History and Myths, the professor is having us take a look at the legend of our people's silver and if we had a great silver mine. He wants us to write a paper on what we can find out about any truths to the legend. He also read to us about a mine that is supposed to be in Kentucky called Swift's Silver mine. He said that this guy supposedly came to Blue Jacket to ask for permission to take some of the silver from the Shawnee and in return, he would buy the guns that Blue Jacket needed. He also said that Blue Jacket sent two scouts with him and some other men and that one of the scouts led all of the men into the mountains, and then killed them all, except the guy named Swift. They blinded him, gave him a bloody tomahawk and left. Swift somehow made his way out and was found. They say that lots of people have searched for our people's Silver mine and Swift's but have never found it. Is any of this true?"

Emma put her hand on John's shoulder.

"Kakawipilathee"... Tame Hawk. She called him by his Shawnee name.

"There are many rumors that have come down over the years. I do not know the source of all of them, but I can tell you that as far as I know, our people did not have a silver mine. I have heard the stories of our people's silver. If they were true, we would be a rich people. I don't think that we would have left the silver hidden all of these years. Yes, our people have had silver. We had understanding on how to melt it and form it into beautiful necklaces, earrings and armbands and it was used to buy many things in the past. It is my understanding though that there was not a mine or a great cave where we had a great treasure of silver stored. Our women were very good at stealing the white man's silver. Besides that, much of it was gotten from settlers who came down the Ohio River and who were killed or captured in the late 1700's. They brought all of their belongings with them on the boats. Our warriors brought many of the white man's things back to our villages. I suppose that it is possible that the silver items could have been stored because we knew of the value of this material. As I said, it was easy to melt the items down and make them into jewelry.

My Grandmother gave me a necklace that was made for my great grandmother by her grandfather. If you would like, I will show it to you. I would love to know what the stones are and how they stay in the necklace. They look like tiny shaved pieces of blue, red, yellow, white, pink, orange and black, and are set in silver.

For your paper, I would just write what I have told you. You can say that there is no doubt that our people did have silver, but there is no evidence that there ever was a large cave or silver mine. It is all just romantic folklore."

"Thanks Emma."

John looked at his watch.

"I better get going. It's almost 2:00 and I have to conduct the cave tour. Thanks again. See you in a little bit."

Chapter 5
1390

Gulf of Mexico, Along the South West Coast of Florida, near present day Tallahassee

"Look. There are strange boats coming!" [vii]

The five boats were just becoming visible from the shore as they rounded the long point and entered into the bay. They had been hugging the coast of the Gulf waters for just over 6 days after leaving their native lands near Kankun in the Yucatan Peninsula. Balam had decided to stay along the coast, with land in sight, rather than risk going across the open water. Many of the women and children had never been in boats before and he had felt that this would be safer and less fearful for them.

The children had been collecting shells on the beach when they spotted the boats and began shouting to the women that were with them. Within minutes, men, dressed in deerskin loincloths and with their bodies painted with red ochre appeared. The men had feathers in their long black hair. They moved quickly to pull their canoes to the water, and quickly their boats glided through the small surf headed towards the approaching boats.

"Remain calm" Said Balam.

"Do not alarm these warriors. No one is to speak. We know these people from our people's trade with them. I will tell them who we are and why we have come."

As the boats approached, still some 400 meters away, Balam raised his right arm and waved. One of the men in the lead boat raised his right arm and waived back. As the boats got closer, Balam could see that the men in the boats showed little emotion. Their dark skinned, muscular bodies glistened with perspiration from their efforts in quickly paddling from the shore. But in these men's calm, Balam could also sense a resolve and readiness to strike swiftly if they felt threatened in any way. Balam's men were warriors too and he knew that they would fight fiercely to the death to defend their women and children. Their purpose however, was not to fight, but to be accepted by this people and allowed refuge. They were a people with no land now...a people who had no home.

Balam's people now numbered only 53... eighteen men, twenty-three women and twelve young children. That was all that had decided to leave Balamku. His heart was still saddened that they had to leave the land where the bones of their ancestors laid. But, he was certain that if they were to have remained they would have been defeated. The men and boys would have been killed and cannibalized. The women and children would have been taken into slavery. It was better to survive and begin anew in a new land.

He knew of these people who approached. They called themselves Apalachee.[viii] He knew of their city, Anhaica.[ix] Even though they spoke a different language than his people, his belief was that they would accept his people. They were an agricultural people, but their warriors were known to be fierce defenders.

The dugout cypress canoes of the Apalachee people were large and held 20 men each. They were much different than the reed boats that Balam's people had paddled and sailed in. As the canoes approached, they split off to either side of Balam's boats. The sun was hot. The water was a deep blue reflection of the cloudless sky and both the boats and canoes floated quietly on the calm waters.

Balam watched intently as one canoe separated from the others and slowly approached his boat. A man stood. He was tall in comparison to Balam's people... almost one head higher.

"Who are you? Balam did not recognize his speech, but knew this greeting and the question that was asked. He knew its' tone. Balam slowly stood and bowed forward toward the man.

"We are from across the waters and mean you no problems."

He knew his answers must be kept short and that his tone must not reflect fear or be menacing. The man's brow rose as he squinted his eyes. It was evident that he did not understand what Balam had said. Balam watched as the man slowly and deliberately searched the boats with his eyes. The man was looking intently at these strange people whose bodies were covered in tattoos, and who had pointed teeth. He saw the saddened looks on the women's faces as they kept their children silent. He could since their fear. He saw in the men's dark brown eyes uncertainty. Certainly these people were not a threat.

He raised his hand upward and pointed to the shore. Moments later, the boats and the canoes were gliding though the water headed towards the white sand beach. Most of Balam's people's fear had vanished, but not their apprehension. They were a brave people, but Balam knew that any man's journey to the unknown was one filled with wonderment, but also with the fear of what lay ahead. It was not the fear of harm or being afraid of danger, but just a fear of the unknown. If these people would accept his people, he knew that they would soon lose their fear in the activities of their everyday lives. The children would go about playing with these people's children. His warriors would prove themselves as men and hunters. He knew that in a short time, their lives would return to normal and that their decision to leave would prove correct.

Balam's boats pushed ashore in the surf and his people stepped out onto the white sand and into a new life and a new future.

Chapter 6
March 1772

Fort Dunmore (Pitt)

Caesar had arrived in early February to the Fort[x] and he had quickly assimilated into the small community of Virginians and blacks that had grown south of the palisades of the Fort. As most men who had come to the fort, he looked bedraggled, hungry and tired. No one had questioned him as to where he had come from or where he was going. He was still cautious however and was constantly aware of those around him for any sign or word that he had been discovered, but every day he was able to relax more and more. It seemed to him that out the on the edges of the Ohio Territory, men were just intent on surviving.

Caesar had found Nemacolin's trail easily. He traveled mostly at night the first few days and in between napping during the day, he stayed far from the trail, paralleling it as he worked his way west. He had stolen food from some of the scattered houses that he had come across and had even picked up some socks, a flannel shirt, a slouch hat and a wool blanket. On the Nemacolin Trail he had stopped at a place called Will's Creek, where he found a storehouse that was owned by the Ohio Company. He stopped and spent a short time among a large camp of men who were headed toward the Ohio Country. They didn't pay much head to him and he was able to scrounge some food from them before setting off again down the trail. He really didn't know much about distances, but the men said that it was only 140 miles to the Fort. He figured that it couldn't be much further. The trail had taken him through tree covered, sweeping valleys, over rocky, rugged mountains, across swollen creeks and fallen trees and through heavy Laurel underbrush.

The winter had been somewhat mild and there were early signs of spring. He had seen a few Robins and the buds on the trees appeared as though any day new leaves would spring forth. He had quickly found work at the fort felling trees and helping to build the log rafts that were being readied for the spring. Soon, there would be an exodus of men, women and children down the river. They were always looking for a hand and he was hoping to catch a ride, the sooner the better.

At night Caesar would sit around the fires that could be found in the off alleys. He mostly kept to himself and listened to all of the talk about the dangers of traveling down the Ohio and about all of the land that was to be claimed on the South side of the river. He learned that a few years earlier, the British had signed a treaty with the Iroquois. The treaty was said to establish the Ohio River as the permanent boundary between the whites and Indians. The Ohio was to mark forever "Indian country". He heard that the broad open country west of the Ohio River was perfectly suited for farming and that in less than a year after the signing of the treaty, small parties of hunters, settlers and land speculators had spread over the land west of the river. The settlers had started laying claim to the land. The problem was that the Indians north of the Ohio River did not recognize the treaty that the Iroquois had signed. He heard that the Iroquois claimed the land south of the Ohio and that when the British claimed the land according to the treaty that the Ohio Indians, who had hunted the land, refused to sign the treaty.[xi]

Over the last few years there were lots of settlers, including British explorers and surveyors going down river to claim their lands. But, it was now more bloody and dangerous than it had ever been. Caesar heard that not only were the Ohio Indians ambushing the boats that came down the river and massacring the settlers, but they were mutilating and torturing to death any surviving men, and taking the women and children into slavery. Now, small parties of whites were also roaming the lands and ambushing and killing Indians. All of the Ohio Valley was covered in a cycle of revenge and bloodshed with both sides blaming the other for all of the violence.[xii]

The Ohio Valley was a struggle between two contending races, both warring for supremacy. One wanted land and the other was protecting the land that they lived on. The Indians saw the march of the white man's civilization coming symbolically down the Ohio. They had heard the voice of Christianity from the white man's missionaries, but they had also heard the sounds of war and the scenes of blood and cruelty from a race that felt they were superior.

Caesar had heard around the fires that late winter talk of a hunter from the area by the name of Boone, who had led a group of about 50 emigrants in

September into the area south of the river called Kentucky. The story was that Boone's oldest son and a small group of men and boys left the main group to retrieve supplies and were attacked by a bunch of Indians. Boone's son and another boy were captured and brutally tortured to death. Boone had returned to the Fort after the attack, but was now back in Virginia.

Caesar had thought long and hard on all that he had heard, but he had already come this far, and no matter what would or could happen, he was settled on going down the river. He was going to get as far away from the whites and any chance of being captured that he could. He was free now and was going to remain free at all costs.

As winter disappeared, he continued to work building boats and rafts through March and into April. One day, as he was helping to attach a large rudder to one of the rafts, he overheard one of the settlers talking to a small group of men. The others called him Captain. They were well outfitted with supplies and weapons and he supposed that it was because he heard in the conversation that the Captain owned a trading post at a fort in Pennsylvania up the Monongahela River. The Captain was discussing the land that he had claimed at and below the mouth of Middle Island Creek and that he was going to settle his holdings there. [xiii]

Caesar decided that this was his opportunity and approached the man the others called Captain. It was not a time to be shy.

"Mista Cap'in."

"Yeah...whatcha want?"

"I cain't help but overhear what ya'll bin talkin' bout. Going down the riva. I wanna go on down the riva and if'n ya need some hep, would ya let me go with ya?"

"Whatcha good at? I seen ya helping build these here rafts, but what else can ya do?

Well. Cap'n, sir....justa bout anythin' ya want. I'm strong and good with my hands. Don't fear much o' nuttin."

"Can ya shoot a gun? I need every man going down river to be able to shoot."

"Never tried afore, but I's a quick learner. Just wanna chance."

Caesar and the Captain were interrupted by another tall, lanky man with long, shoulder length, curly brown hair.

"Captain Cresap?"

"Yeah...that's me."

"Got a couple more barrels of powder for ya. Where you want em?"

Captain Cresap looked at Caesar.

"Now's as good a time as any to start workin' for me. Take that powder and secure it over with the other barrels. Make sure ya cover 'em all up. We're leaving in two days and you're coming with us. What's your name?"

"Caesar...sir."

Chapter 7
September 20, 2012

Zane Shawnee Caverns, Bellefontaine, Logan County, Ohio

"Welcome to the Zane Shawnee Caverns. My name is John Logan. I am a member of the United Remnant Band of Shawnee and I will be your guide on this tour. The tour will take approximately one hour. Our cave is small in comparison to some you may have been too. However, it's the only live cave in Ohio. It is a natural cave that is nearly 290 meters in length. It was supposedly discovered by a white man named John Dunlap in 1892 when he rescued a boy and a dog from a sinkhole. The entrance to the cave we will be using is not the original entrance that was a sinkhole. I'll show that entrance to you, as we're going to pass right under it in the cave. I don't know if the Indians in this area knew of the sinkhole and the cave, but my people used all of the lands next to the cave and in this immediate area as a passageway. It was a portage between the Great Miami River and the rivers feeding into Lake Erie...particularly, the Maumee.

A small boy standing next to his parents interrupted John.

"Are there any secret passageways in the cave?

John smiled at the youngster.

"That's a really good question! But, I'm not aware of any secret passageways. The cave has three levels. We will be on the first level. I will show you a couple of entrances to the second level that runs parallel to the first. The third level is full of water. On the second level there is an entrance to a cavern or tunnel that runs perpendicular to this cavern and extends all the way back to the main road at the entrance to the park."

"Has that been explored?" said the youngsters' father.

"I've never been down it, but I was told that some scientists have been down it. From what I was told, it is not an easy trip. As far as I know, after the cave was discovered, it was explored extensively, including the section that goes to the main road. All of the tunnels end or are not passable. The section on the second level that runs to the main road is supposed to be very tight and low in some sections that you would have to crawl on your hands and knees and then on your stomach just to get through."

As John quickly glanced through the small group, he happened to notice Professor Stevensen standing in the back.

"Professor Stevensen. I'm surprised to see you here. "

"Well John, I live nearby and have always wanted to go through the cavern, but I just never took the time. I had some time and thought I'd come over and take the tour."

"Have you been through our museum?"

"No. I was going to do that after going through the cavern."

"That's great. I conduct the museum tour too. Just let me know if you have any questions."

John leaned over and half-whispered to the Professor, "Professor. Don't worry about paying for the tour of the museum."

"Thanks John. Don't think that this will get you an A," the Professor said jokingly.

John smiled back. "I'm not worried."

John opened a door in the back of the gift shop and immediately everyone could feel the draft of cold air from the cavern.

"Let's head down to the entrance now. If you would, please watch your steps and follow me. If you have any questions, just ask and I'll try to answer them as best as I can."

John led the way down a wooden, manmade tunnel containing a flight of steps. They went down only about 12 feet to the small cavern entrance. John stopped at the bottom of the stairs to allow everyone to get down to the actual entrance to the path into the cavern.

"I would like to remind everyone to please not touch anything in the cave. As I said, it is a living cave, and contains stalactites, stalagmites, soda straws, flow stone, draperies and rare cave pearl nests on some ledges. Everything is very fragile."

"This entrance was enlarged so that it is easier to get down into the cavern. Further in I will show you the original entrance. It was a small sinkhole originally. The opening was just large enough to crawl and squeeze down through. Once through the opening, it dropped about fifteen feet to the floor. They improved the opening and lowered people down one at a time in a large basket. Without a rope, ladder or the basket, it would have been almost impossible to climb back out."

John led the people across a steel grate that went over a hole that was about 15' deep. As the people crossed the grate, John shined his light down, explaining that this was one of the two entrances to the second level of the cave. Off to the left on the far side of the grate he showed a series of steps that had been carved out that led in the reverse direction down to the second level.

"Are there a lot of sink holes around here?" asked a middle-aged man.

"I'm not really sure, but I think that there are. This cavern and the Ohio Caverns were both formed by the glaciers that covered most of Ohio at one time. Both of these caverns are part of what is called an aquifer. They held an underground river of melted glacier water. The river eventually receded to lower levels underground and is no longer visible. The sinkholes are just holes that were caused by the removal of the soil or what is called bedrock, by the water. This whole area is made of limestone and as the water from the river kept eating away at the limestone under the ground, the ground would collapse and form a sinkhole. Over time, the water table or river would continue to lower and the caverns or a cave would form. The river here has disappeared way below the surface and is on the third level. We know the level exists, but no one has gone down there that I am aware of. In other caves or large sinkholes, such as what you find at Mammoth Cave, the river is still visible."[xiv] Usually in the spring and sometimes after we get heavy rainfalls, parts of this main level still flood. The water level will rise very quickly and it goes down almost just as quick. I'll show you near the exit to the cave the different water level lines, as that is part of the cave that still floods often.

The group stopped about 50 feet further as John pointed out the second level off to the right and said that on the second level was the entrance to the rift that ran east to west and went all of the way back toward the main road and the entrance to the park where it supposedly dead ended.

"That's a long way," said a young man. "Has that been explored?"

"As I mentioned earlier I've been told that it has, but that it's a real difficult trip. It's really wet and there are places that you have to crawl through to keep going. I've always wanted to go, but I'd need someone to go along that was an experienced caver and I just haven't taken the time to go."

John led the small group slowly through the cave, stopping at times to switch the lights on ahead of the group and off behind them. The passage was only around 3/8th of a mile and was not really that spectacular. It was notably devoid of any large formations, but all along one could find areas of soda straws, and a few small stalactites and stalagmites. John stopped at a pocket of cave pearls. A few yards passed the cave pearls; he shined his flashlight off to the left and pointed out a large pile of good size rocks that appeared to have fallen from the ceiling. He explained that the rocks were evidence of the cave's instability and that at any time rocks could fall, as cracks in the cave's ceiling enlarged over time. About two thirds of the way through, John focused his light on a rather large rock structure on the left wall that did have the appearance of an alligator's head. This head, to him, was an assurance that his people were meant to be the owners of the cave. There were no questions, so John continued to lead the group down the cave another thirty yards or so towards a flight of steps back to the surface.

Emma Bluejacket was behind the glass display countertop as the small group from the tour mingled in the gift shop. John and Professor Stevensen had gone into the museum. There were Native American and Shawnee artifacts everywhere. The display cases were filled with arrowheads, axes, and pipes and included a display showing the evolution of Native American weapons from throwing stones to the trade gun. There were stuffed forest animals, a display of the evolution of corn...Zea maize to modern corn. There was an interesting display under glass of handmade Shawnee jewelry, including several large silver, coin like medallions. One display was life size replications of Shawnee women and children in everyday activities and another was a 1/16-scale model of a 1700 Shawnee Village. There was a display dedicated to the life of George Drouillard, the mixed blood Shawnee who was the chief hunter, guide and interpreter for the Lewis and Clark expedition. In the corner of one of the glass display cases however, was a stuffed alligator's head.

Chapter 8
July 1, 1521

On present day Pine Island, Florida

De Leon and his small group of 200 had been struggling in the late spring heat for almost six weeks. The fort and church that they had been building were almost complete, but the sweltering heat and the damned mosquitoes had kept his men tired and on edge. In addition to the heat and the mosquitoes, De Leon knew that they were being watched by the natives in the area and had instructed his men to keep their weapons close at hand and to continually be alert.

De Leon had been to this area eight years before, but this time had returned with 200 men and 50 horses. He was determined to colonize what he had named Pascua de Flores. It was Spanish for Easter. On his earlier trip to Florida, he had been privately financed to find Bimini. He had set out from Puerto Rico in March 1513. He did not find Bimini, but had arrived on April 2nd at a site north of present-day St. Augustine. He had named the land Florida in honor of the recently celebrated Easter holy day. He had believed that he had discovered an island, and while attempting to circumnavigate it, he sailed as far south as Key West and then north as far as what would become Tampa. During this trip, he had encountered fierce opposition from the natives and had returned to Puerto Rico in the fall. He returned later that year to Spain, where he was named the governor of Bimini and the "island" of Florida. He returned to the New World in 1515 and had served as a soldier for several years in attempts to suppress native rebellions, but his dream of being the first to find the mythical "Fountain of Youth" and the fame that would come with it had continually played in his mind. Now, he knew that this permanent settlement must be established as a base for his explorations.

Thoboquebah, "Hole in the Day", laid flat on his stomach behind the large cypress tree. His bow was in his left hand and an arrow was in his right. Its tip dipped in poison. Even without a direct hit, it would cause certain death. He was waiting for the signal to attack. During the night he had crept silently with the other 800 warriors to the edge of the woods that surrounded the small buildings that had been erected over the last few weeks. Years before, they had attacked these men and had driven them from their land before they could even come to the shore. Now, they had landed and by their actions it was clear that their intentions were to stay. This would not be allowed and they were to be driven from this peoples' land.

Over the last few years, Thoboquebah and his people, who lived among the Calusa peoples, had boldly attacked any of the people who called themselves Spaniards. The Spaniards had appeared up and down the coast and the Calusa warriors had fiercely resisted them. They had killed many and the few that were captured, were scalped and dismembered as human sacrifices. The Calusa that Thoboquebah and his clan lived among, had plundered and killed without mercy all of the crews of any vessels that had come near. They had amassed large amounts of the Spaniards gold and silver, in the form of both bar and coins, from the many wrecks and deserted ships that were left behind by those who were killed. The Calusa people, who were now ready to attack the Spaniards, were tall and well-built with long hair. In their language, their name meant "fierce people."

Thoboquebah and his clan had lived among these people for his entire lifetime. When he was a small boy, his father had brought their clan of some 80 people south from the mouth of a big river with black water. The Timucuan people, who lived on the Eastern side of the river, called it the Suwani. He had heard that his grandfather, Balam, had brought his people from a land far to the west. They had been accepted by a people to the West, the Apalachee. Over the years they had adopted the language of this people as well as their life styles. Thoboquebah's father and his people had slowly migrated with these people to the western edge of this river, and eventually crossed the river to live among the Timucuan. His people had moved down the river and now lived along the coast. They still farmed some of the land with their precious maize, but had also learned to fish on the coast, bays and rivers. Thoboquebah's father had also told him that their people had split when he was around 4 years of age. His father didn't explain why, but only that a part of their clan had left and headed toward the North following the Ochlocknee River. Through traders,

Thoboquebah had heard that these kinsmen were a great distance away now living in the North near a great river called the Warioto.[xv]

Carlos, one of the outer sentries for the Spaniards, had spent the early morning trying to keep his eyes open. For the past six weeks he had found it difficult to stay awake most nights, especially in the early morning as the sun began to rise in the east. He, as well as the others, worked most of the day in the hot sun to build the buildings that they had erected, and then took their turns through the night standing guard for the uncompleted fort they had been feverishly working to erect. Carlos stood to stretch his legs and began to slowly walk over to relieve himself in a small ditch that they had dug. As he reached to unbutton his pants, the arrow sliced through the front of his throat and stuck halfway out the back of his neck. He tried to yell to alert the others as he brought his hands to his throat. As he fell, no one heard his moan.

Thoboquebah and the other warriors swarmed upon the Spaniards that were unfortunate enough to be caught outside the confines of the fort's walls. Several other Spaniards felt the sting of their arrows. The sounds of the morning's stillness disappeared with the demonic screams of the Indians as they attacked the Spaniards from all directions. The charge was so quick, that few of the Spaniards outside of the fort were able to fire their muskets. Those that did, however, because of the close range, found their mark.

As he looked to his right, Thoboquebah saw one man fall backward as the back of his head exploded from the round ball that had entered just above his right eye.

More musket shots rang out from within the fort. Smoke from the musket fire hung low in the morning mist as several of the Indians had now gotten close to the opened gate of the fort. Thoboquebah watched as these Indians fell from the volley of shots that exploded from the roof of the fort. He saw several more of the Indians fall as he ran towards the entrance to the fort.

There were no Spaniards on the outside of the fort any longer and the gate to the fort had been closed. With this realization, the Indians began to turn and run to the cover of the tree line. The surprise of the attack was over and any advantage that the Indians had, was now gone.

The tree line where the Indians hid was just over 80 meters from the wall of the fort. While the Spaniards could shoot at the Indians, their muskets were not very accurate at this distance. The Indians could continue to send volleys of arrows into the fort, hoping to catch one of the Spaniards who was caught out in the open. Aside from the initial assault, the remainder of the day was a stalemate. For De Leon however, the day had proved fatal. During the initial charge of the Indians in the early morning, he had caught an arrow in his thigh. Although not one dipped in poison, it had caused a severe wound.

The Indians called off the attack and retreated under the cover of nightfall realizing that their attack was now futile against the Spaniard's muskets and protection within the fort. Many of the Indians went back to their villages, but a few remained forcing the Spaniards to spend the next few days within the fort with continual harassment coming from the Indians. De Leon's wound had become gangrenous and the decision was made to abandon the colony and return to Havana.[xvi]

Chapter 9
Late April, 1774

The Settlement of Wheeling

Caesar was now in a settlement on the South side of the Ohio. They had past the lower point of two islands[xvii] and had gone ashore on a level plain that rose to steep hills along the river. On the riverside, there was a difficult, steep incline from the river landing up to the village. On the south, the hill fell off abruptly to the lower levels of the bottomlands towards the creek. On the north and east there was a gentler slope from the highest point of land between the river and the hills.

The trip from Fort Dunmore down the River had been uneventful. Captain Cresap had the men keep the broad-horn rafts and canoes to the south side of the river the entire trip. On the broad decks of the rafts several pens had been built that held several milk cows, one huge sow and several goats. One raft held 10 horses. One raft also was built with a large structure that had sleeping quarters and storage for many of their provisions including clothing, utensils and cookware, flour and salt and preserved meat as well as staple supplies of all kinds, tools, coils of rope, and importantly a few guns and kegs of powder and ammunition. They had seen several canoes of Indians on their descent. Cresap's men had fired potshots at the Indians from long range, laughing. Caesar thought that the Indians would attack, but they had kept their distance. Captain Cresasp's men had strict orders not to chase the Indians.

For Caesar, it was the first time he had actually seen Indians. Up to now, he had only heard about them. He had heard that some were friendly and that some were just evil, heathen savages. Although he hadn't encountered any before, he couldn't imagine how they could be any worse than many of the drunken whites that he had been subjected to his entire life. How could they be crueler than the slave masters who had forced themselves upon the black women who cooked their meals and raised their children and those who beat or hung a black man if he even looked upon a white woman...those who went to church on Sundays and whose lives were one hypocrisy after another the other six days of the week. He couldn't imagine that they could be any more evil than the whites that had enslaved his people. In fact, most of the men in Captain Cresap's party were intoxicated most of the time and from their conversations he had learned that most of them hated the Indians. They were full of prejudice and their thoughts were to kill any Indians that they saw. In his eyes they were filthy, cruel, treacherous, immoral men who could not be trusted. To Caesar, the whites were repulsive. He found it ironic that even though he was thought to be free, he was still treated by the whites as unequal, but it was he who was now using them to free himself from their tyranny against his race.

On the trip down the river, Caesar had heard the men talking about a settlement called Wheeling. This is where they had stopped and off loaded. Like Captain Cresap, who had land claims in the area, the Wheeling site was claimed a few years back by a Colonel Ebenezer Zane and his two brothers, Jonathan and Silas. They had come from the south branch of the Potomac Valley in Virginia and had marked trees to establish tomahawk claims to the land. Caesar also heard that someone named Connolly was up at Fort Dunmore and was preparing to send a force down the Ohio to build a small fort "at the mouth of Wheeling,"[xviii] and that the building of the fort was approved by some governor, who was recommending that a Captain William Crawford come down the river with about 200 men to help erect the fort and to carry on a campaign into the Indian country from the fort. Caesar was told that he and others would help build this new fort on Cresap's site and that the logs from the rafts would be used to help begin the construction of the fort's blockhouse. [xix]

Since Caesar's escape, his arrival to Fort Dunmore and the float down the river, he had learned to be quiet and listen. He worked hard, but by being quiet and listening to the other men, he could learn a lot. In fact, the more he knew about the white man and the struggles between the Pennsylvanians and the Virginians, the British and the French and the whites and the Indians, the more he realized that he wanted his freedom more than ever, not just from the white man, but from the civilization that the white man was trying to impose upon the Indians. The whites could not agree upon anything themselves and constantly fought for land. They were arrogant in their belief that the land was to be owned. He had heard that the Indians respected the land and believed that it was given to them to live on. It couldn't be owned any more than the air. The white man's greed and feeling of superiority was wrong. Didn't the Bible teach that the white man believed that God created all men? This is what his mother had taught him. But like almost all things that the whites did, they said that they believed one thing and their actions were just the opposite of what they professed.

Caesar had heard Captain Cresap's men talking about the tensions between the Virginians and the Pennsylvanians. He heard about the tensions between the colonists and the British, and the more he heard, the more he knew he must get as far away from the white man as possible. He had heard that just before he had gotten to the fort, that an agent of the royal governor of Virginia, the Earl of Dunmore, had taken possession of the Fort. He had renamed it Fort Dunmore, and started attacks against the local Indian settlements. The men said that these Indians were Delaware, and that they were under the influence of some missionaries. They said that the Delaware were friendly and kept the peace. They said that it was some Indians called the Shawnee that wanted war. They said that it was the Shawnee that were causing the Indian troubles all along the western frontier of Virginia and especially along the river. He heard them say that to them it made no difference what kind of Indian was causing the problems. They were all the same. No matter what they had heard, the savages couldn't be made Christian. "One dead Injun nigger was no different than another." Caesar often questioned how these men could call themselves Christian.

Caesar and Cresap's men had been at Wheeling for almost three weeks helping to cut timber and fortify the small community that was beginning to grow along the Ohio. The talk in the settlement was of war. There was an excitement and expectations that any moment there would be a breakout of hostilities. The men had heard that a Major Connolly, who was a Virginia militia officer under Lord Dunmore, and second in command at Fort Dunmore, had sent a message to the Indians. That message was not received. He had also sent a letter to Captain Cresap and now, as the men stood in the early morning of April 21, Captain Cresap read Major Connolly's letter. The letter communicated Major Connolly's apprehensions and belief of an immediate Indian war and gave orders for the men to prepare for it. The letter concluded with a state of war being formally announced. Later that same evening, two Indian scalps were brought in by some of Captain Cresap's forces.

The next day Caesar was up just before daylight. They had been given orders the night before to go downstream and check on any Indian activity first thing in the morning. It was a cool morning. They had had strong storms the evening before, and Caesar was sure that the River would be running high. As he and the other 15 men shoved off from the muddy bank in the four man canoes, the current quickly grabbed the canoes and shoved them silently downstream. Shortly after leaving, they saw several canoes of Indians descending the river just ahead of them on the same side of the Ohio, and began to chase after them. They were out of gun range and the Indians had seen them. They paddled hard with the current and had chased the Indians some fifteen miles down the river, finally driving them to the shore as they started to get within gun range. They had fired half a dozen shots as they got closer, but none had reached their target.

The Indians had quickly scattered into the trees along the small sandy bend in the shoreline and as Caesar and the others approached the shore, arrows suddenly began to fill the sky. Next to Caesar, one man grimaced as an arrow struck him in the right shoulder. As he grabbed his shoulder, he dropped his paddle and slumped forward in the canoe. As Caesar's canoe hit the shore, he helped to grab the wounded man and drag him from the canoe to the cover of a fallen log. The men were firing into the tree line, but the Indians remained hidden, only briefly showing themselves to shoot an arrow. The few Indians with guns started to return the gunfire and kept up an equal fire with Cresap's men. One Indian exposed himself for too long, as it appeared that his gun had misfired. Caesar had glanced at him and saw him get hit. He grabbed his left leg as he spun and fell to the ground. Another Indian attempted to reach him, but Cresap's men fired at him as he tried to get to the wounded warrior. Two shots just missed him. The bark of a tree exploded from a rounds impact just next to the warrior and another kicked up the sand just before him. He turned and ran back into the cover of the trees.

Just as quick as the firing had begun, it stopped. The Indians had thought better of the fight and had silently disappeared. When the all-clear signal came, Cresap's men rushed to the downed warrior and quickly subdued him. Both of his hands and feet were bound. Caesar watched as the men taunted the warrior, spitting in his face and kicking him in his wound. The young warrior, realizing his fate, said nothing. Caesar could see that he was in pain, but watched as the warrior's only show of emotion to his captures was his clinched teeth.

These white men treated the young warrior as though he was not a human being, just as Caesar had seen many slave owners treat their slaves. He was free and living amongst these white men, but he still felt a separation from them. His emotions were mixed, but he felt kindred to this young Indian. He knew what this young man was fighting for. It was more than just the land that the whites were taking from him; it was his freedom and his way of life.

Caesar was told to help bind the young warrior's hands and feet and to secure him in a canoe, for their return trip upstream to their camp at Wheeling. They had only traveled a short distance up the river when in the canoe just ahead of his; Caesar saw one of the men grab the young warrior by his hair. He took his knife and quickly cut just below the man's hairline, running the blade from the left to the right side of the young man's head. The brave screamed out in pain. The man stretched his arm high, raising the young warrior's bloody scalp up into the air in a show of pride. As the blood dripped down his arm, he let out a scream to let the others in the party know of his triumph. He then shoved the bloody faced warrior out of the canoe into the fast moving, muddy water. The young warrior couldn't struggle. He had no chance of swimming with his hands and feet bound. He was quickly caught up in the current, rolled and thrashed for a moment, and just disappeared beneath the surface. Caesar could do nothing but watch. His mind wondered how many Indians, and whites for that matter, had just disappeared in this wilderness... into the river... no trace of them to be found... families never hearing from them again. It wasn't the wilderness that was claiming them. It was the evil of men. Caesar had seen men hung by the whites before for doing nothing. Maybe it wasn't any different out here? In some ways these men were worse than the whites back where he had come from. If you were black, they accepted your help out here, but you certainly weren't treated fairly or equally. Just used. If you were Indian, you were nothing more than an animal...a heathen, as they would say. Caesar wondered who the heathens really were.

That evening, back in Wheeling, a resolution was adopted to march the next day to attack Logan's camp, at Mingo Bottom, which was situated on the Ohio about thirty miles above Wheeling.[xx]

Chapter 10
September 20, 2012

Zane Shawnee Caverns, Bellefontaine, Logan County, Ohio

Professor Stevensen looked at the alligator head in the display case.

"John, what is...?"

John interrupted him. "The alligator head! First, it is the symbol of our tribe and yes; I know that it is out of place here in Ohio. It's an interesting story though. You see, my people were originally Mayan, from the Yucatan Peninsula."

"Really! I've read that the Shawnee had come from down in South Georgia and North Florida but would never have imagined that they were Mayan. I guess it doesn't really surprise me though."

"From what I have been told, our ancestor left the Yucatan Peninsula hundreds of years ago. We don't really know why, but we are told that they ended up in Florida."

"How did they get to Florida, John?"

"They left from somewhere near Cancun in boats and went across the Gulf of Mexico to somewhere in Florida. Over the years they assimilated into the local Indians. The local Indians taught them how to live in this area. They learned to hunt Alligators and killed so many that they kinda felt guilty. As they migrated north, because they felt guilty for killing so many alligators, they took some with them and let them go in the Okefenokee Swamp in Georgia, and adopted the Alligator as the totem symbol for our tribe."

"The Suwannee River in South Georgia is the river that flows through the swamp and it's named after the Shawnee.[xxi]

Emma Bluejacket was behind the counter in the gift shop while John was with Professor Stevensen in the museum. Standing just across the counter from her in the gift shop was a tall, dark haired man with brown eyes. He was wearing a faded pair of Levi's and a blue and white patched, flannel shirt. The only thing that set him apart from the many visitors to the museum and cave was his knee length, beaded, leather moccasins.

"Emma," said the dark haired man. "Who's that in the museum with John?"

"It's his professor from Antioch College. He showed up today for the cave tour. I heard him say that he had always wanted to go through the cave but he just never took the time to come over. I think he lives over near Bellefontaine."

"Oh. All right...just was wondering. Well, I've gotta get going. I'll probably see you around later this afternoon. I've gotta run into the city and get some lumber and nails. We've gotta replace some of the boards on the stage."

"Alright Will," said Emma. "I'll see you later."

Chapter 11
1707

Suwannee River, Georgia

"My brothers, we have traveled a great distance to give you information about your brothers to the North and to the East. We are a people that is scattered across this land. Many years ago, our friends to the North, the Delaware accepted one of our clans as their own. We adopted their language and we became as one people. Over many seasons, our wars with the Iroquois peoples of the land were many and we were forced from our lands in the valley of the Spaylawetheepi. Some of our people traveled west to the valleys of the Cumberland. Some to the East to the valley of the Delaware and some further to the South across this great river to the land the white man calls Carolina. As you know, many years ago, and even to this day, our people have marched. We have no one land that we can claim as our own. Our Grand Chief, as has been our custom, has decided to move our people rather than engage with our enemies who have superior strength. We are not a cowardly people, but we have withdrawn from our lands. We will now, once again, move north and east along the great river called the Cumberland toward the Spaylawetheepi, the Ohio.[xxii] It has been many years and many of our Grandfather's sons from the time we were one people. We have encountered others who claim to be our brothers from the South and who have scattered across this land. They have moved, settled in areas and have moved again to avoid the warriors of other tribes whose numbers were much greater than our scattered peoples. Our peoples have roamed our hunting grounds, hunting and fishing and whenever our need has arose, we have stopped long enough to plant our maize and raise a crop. We know that the land along the valley of the Great Spaylawetheepi and to its' North is a land of much beauty. While you have led good lives in this Southern land, our fathers have traveled separate roads and have lived in this land. We have lived in this land that the whites call Kaintucky. We have lived and hunted in this land from the Cumberland to the Scioto, North of the Beautiful River.[xxiii] Our enemies, the Chickasaw have now allied with the Cherokee and as I speak to you now, our people have moved from the Cumberland Valley toward the lands of the Spaylawetheepi. We ask you to join us in this Ohio land. We ask you to join us and be one people again. Our people have wandered for too long. Our women and children have suffered much hardship. Together, as one people, we can grow strong again. Many sticks that are separate have no strength alone and can be easily broken. Joined together, they cannot be broken."

As Thoos finished speaking, Soapqua rose. "My brother, I thank you for your words. We know that you have traveled far and that the Master of Life, the Good Spirit Moneto is traveling with you. We have always known that our peoples would one day occupy the center of the earth and bring harmony to the universe. The objects in our sacred bundles possess powerful medicine that Moneto has used for good to assist his chosen people. We have remained faithful to our laws and now understand by your words that it is time for us to travel to this homeland of your fathers and become one people again.

Let us rest on your words and our thoughts tonight. Our village is yours for food, drink and rest."

Thoos smiled as he left the small village behind in the morning. He hoped that he would one day greet Soapqua and this people again in the Ohio country. After a short council, Soapqua's people decided that those who wanted to leave would head north toward the Ohio valley. They would cross toward the north and the east into what was called the Carolinas and join with other clans from the north there. They would then travel with them to the Shawnee village of Pequea, in what was called Pennsylvania. They would meet with the Chief of Pequea, Opessah and his people and from there they would pass through the mountains to a river that ran north and emptied into the Spaylawetheepi. Many understood the reality of the move. They knew that it would be a long journey and that many of the elders of the tribe would not survive the journey north. However, Thoos' words of unity and of being one people again echoed in their ears. Those that wanted to remain could remain, but the Shawnee had wandered for too long.[xxiv] This would be their last journey. It was time their voices became one again...no longer a scattered people, but once again a strong nation. They were a nation of people who believed like Mother Nature, their provider that they were only going through a cycle of change. They were a people experiencing the effects of change. Mother Nature was like a mirror, and she was now inviting them to step inside the circle and experience the ceremonial dance of reunion. The time of their disruption was over. Moneto was shining upon them. They were the Alligator people.[xxv]

Chapter 12
September 20, 2012

Yellow Springs, Ohio

"Dad, I went to the Zane Shawnee Caverns today." I took a tour of the caverns and their museum. A young man in one of my classes at school guided us through the cave and gave me a personal tour of the museum. It was interesting, but there is nothing in the cave or in the museum that would lead me to believe that the Shawnee had any silver mine, at least not in that cave. I even have my class studying the myth of Swift's Silver Mine and the myth of the Shawnee silver mine to see if there is any truth to either myth and if there is any link to the two myths."

Professor Stevensen was speaking to his father, William Stevensen. His father was 93 years old and living in a nursing home. He was stooped over and walked with a cane and had all of the normal ailments of a man in his 90's, but his mind was still sharp. Not too good on the short-term memory, but crystal clear on the long-term.

"Rob. I know that the Shawnee have a sliver mine and I know that it is around here somewhere. Like I told you, it's not in Kentucky. All of that is a lie just to keep people from knowing where it really is. I know that young Shawnee boy in your class may not know anything. I wouldn't think that he would, but those Indians didn't buy that cave and the land back for no reason. It's not just tribal land as they might claim."

"Dad, there's really not much to the cave. The museum is interesting, but other than an alligator head and an interesting story of their ancestors being Mayan, I really didn't see anything that would lead anybody to believe that they have any cave with silver, lost or not. They don't appear to have any money. In fact, what I saw are campgrounds with a lot of potential and a pioneer and Shawnee village that was in disrepair. If they had any money, you think that they could have fixed everything up really nice so that they could attract campers. If they had money, they could put in full hookups. The grounds have lots of potential, but needed a lot of work. That's money and they don't appear to have any. If they had a cave with hidden silver, they sure haven't spent any"

"Rob, there is something I've got to show you. Reach over there on the nightstand and grab that old Bible for me. It was your great grandma's, you know."

Rob or Robert walked over to the nightstand and picked up the old Bible. It was well warn. The black leather cover was cracked on the front, and had a long tear on the back. The pages had turned yellow and a few of the pages were loose and out of place.

"Be careful with it son! It's seen its better days."

"Sure looks like it dad," said Rob as he picked it up and handed it to his father. His father opened it and removed a small piece of folded, faded white paper, which was stuffed into the back of the book. He slowly unfolded it and handed it to his son.

"Read this! It's from your great-great grandmother. I'm not quite sure where she got it from, but supposedly it came from your great- great-

great grandfather, William Stephensen. He died in November of 1820 and is buried in the Old Massie's Creek Cemetery. It used to be called the Stevensen Cemetery. In fact, James Galloway is buried in that cemetery too. He's the Galloway that's mentioned in this letter."

"I wanted to write this here letter to let everyone know that God has blessed me and that I done my best to bless any man that come my way. Living here in Ohio, I want you to know that I'm ashamed of being a white man. God said that he created all men the same. Most white folk around here and those in Kaintucky hate the injuns. They treat the injuns around here like they were some kind of animals, worse than the white folks back east treat the slave niggas. Ain't had no feelings about killin' 'em...women and children too...stole their land. There ain't many round here no more, but I met a few that come round Galloway and his wife's place.[xxvi] They were smart as I could tell. One of em said he taught hisself to read and write English. He hated the whites though. Heard he got hisself killed in the war up there in Canada fighting for the British against the Americans. Name was Tecumseh. The whites also treated the niggas no different than the Injuns. I met a few of em that had joined up with the Injuns. They didn't talk much, but one of em told me and James that he was a runaway slave from Virginny. Said he went by the name of Caesar. Said for a while when he was a slave, before he had to work in the tobaccy fields, that he worked for a silversmith. He and that Tecumseh gave James and his wife a medallion made of silver.

Caesar had carved an Indian on it and told James the medallion was special because it was a key to where all of the injun's silver was hid. He said that the Injun on the medallion pointed the way. All they had to do was place it on the Feather Rock in Turkeyfoot Creek Ravine. The marked tree pointed to the rock. Caesar said that the Galloways were some of the first whites that he had ever trusted. He wanted them to know where the silver was hidden. He said that it was hid well and that the Shawnee had left it when they left the Ohio country. He wanted the Galloways to have as much of it as they wanted, but that if they got it, he wanted them to help any runaway slaves with it."

"Wow. This is amazing. Why didn't you show me this before? This letter mentions a runaway slave named Caesar that the Shawnee must have adopted. I've got an article that I read to my class that was written by a guy named Lutz in 1922. It's about the legend of Swifts Mine. In it, he mentions a Shawnee guide named Caesar. When I read it, I thought the name was a little strange for an Indian name. I wonder if it's the same Caesar. That would make a lot of sense about his name."

"Could be...I can't imagine there would have been more than one Shawnee named Caesar."

"I wonder if it's the same Caesar that the State park is named after. Wasn't he an Indian?"

There was no answer from the Professor's father... just a blank stare.

"Dad! It's too bad that medallion's not around anymore" said Rob. "Any idea what happened to it?"

Rob's father's head turned back toward Rob. The blank stare was gone. "No...none whatsoever. I reckon that like most things it just got lost over the years. Don't even know if the Galloways ever got any of the silver, or even figured out where it was. I just don't know. I can tell ya though that deep down in my bones, I know that silver is out there, and it's here in Ohio."

Just as William Stevensen was finished talking, there was a knock on the door.

"Mr. Stevensen. It's time for your medications."

"Come on in, Stevensen replied.

The door opened and a tall, slender man with slicked back, black hair entered the room. He was wearing white pants and a white short-sleeved shirt. The shirt had a patch just above the breast pocket. John Parker, Sunshine Gables.

"Sorry to interrupt, but it's time for your medications."

"No problem, replied Stevensen. John, have you met my son Rob."

The Professor shook John's hand and smiled at him.

"No. I don't believe I have."

John handed William a cup with several pills in it, and a glass of water. William took the pills and tossed the cup into the trash.

"Thanks Mr. Stevensen...I'll be back later to check on you... nice to meet you Rob."

Chapter 13
April 28, 1774

Chief Logan's Camp[xxvii]

Tahgahjute wasn't really a Mingo chief, he was a war leader[xxviii]. And yet, like his father, Shikellamy, he had maintained friendly relationships with the white settlers who were pouring into the Ohio Valley. Kiashuta and White Mingo were the Mingo chiefs. They had visited him at his village the day before to discuss the continuing influx of white's onto their land and the disturbing violence from both Indian and White's. It was a cool morning and a surreal mist hung close to the ground encompassing his small village. He had gotten up early with a troubled mind and as he sat near the fire in his lodge, he was silent. He was pondering the reports that Kiashuta and White Mingo had brought to him. His memory of his years crushed in upon him. He remembered the days of his youth, on the banks of the Susquehanna and in the Juniata Valley, and pictured the colorful scenes of his entry into the valley of the Ohio. He visualized the two contending races that were now warring for supremacy in America. His life, his world, had been a part of both. He thought on the teachings of his youth, the struggles and trials of his manhood, the humanity of Indian teachings and the teachings of the missionaries in his father's wigwam. All of these thoughts pressed upon him. He wondered how long this struggle and conflict would last. How could his people survive? He saw the white man's civilization steadily approaching and knew that it was not good for his people. He heard the voice of Christianity, but also the sounds of war and his eyes had seen the blood and cruelty. He also saw the wild drunken shouts of his own tribe, who had fallen under the demons of alcohol that was given freely to his people.

As he thought, Logan felt a confusion of his thoughts and feelings, as they reflected both his Indian values and those of the Christian missionaries. How could he continue to express and embrace the Christian sentiments of kindness and humanity while he watched the whites, who were supposedly Christian, act hypocritical? Their preachers professed a love of a God for their people. A God that said in His commandments to love your enemies and yet these Christians hated and killed those of his race for no reason other than that they were Indian. His mind was a state of confusion. He found himself struggling with remorse at times, beleaguered by the wood-demons that followed him. He could feel their influence wherever he went. They pursued him constantly, in his cabin, in the woods, the trees and the air. All were filled with demons. They seemed to haunt him by day and by night. He could not escape the paradox that Christianity had brought to him. How could this loving God send a man called Jesus to the earth as an example for all men...a man who taught that it was wrong to kill...who taught that you should love your enemy? And then this God, who created all things, and all men, and was sovereign over all men and all things, would create different races to collide in time, having men kill each other and also sending men to a place that was called hell, where they would be consumed by a fire for eternity if they did not accept this Jesus.

Logan was caught between two races and the cultures that they represented. He thought of his appreciation for the knowledge and arts of both the Indians and the white man and yet, he struggled to see the sense of justice in the transactions between the white man and the Indian man, as well as between his own tribe and others. He stood by his word when once given, but saw many that did not. His was a high moral sense of justice between all men and a tenderness and sensibility for his family and his clan.

As Logan sat alone contemplating, little did he know that only a short distance up the Ohio, under the command of Captain Cresap, a party of Whites that was headed with hostile intentions for his camp had stopped and reconsidered the actions they were about to commit. Fortunate for Logan, the party, including George Rogers Clark, knew that the Indians of Logan's village had no hostile intentions – that they were hunters, camped there with their women and children, and all of their belongings, and were in no condition for war. They felt a detestation and guilt over what they had thought to do and had decided to return to Wheeling. Caesar who had been in this party was confused as to why they had headed out toward the Indian's camp, and was now even more confused as to why they had turned back.

Back in Wheeling, Caesar had overheard from a group of Cresap's men that a settler named John Baker had sent word that he and his family were in grave danger and that they needed help. Baker lived on the western Bank of the Ohio across from the mouth of a small tributary named Yellow Creek on Captina Creek.[xxix] It was forty miles above Wheeling and about 40 miles west northwest of Fort Pitt. Baker and his family operated an inn or tavern and sold a cheap, strong form of liquor, named grog, to both the whites and Indians. Baker had heard from an Indian woman that the Indians were preparing to murder him and his family. The tension between the settlers and the Indian tribes had increased and even with the friendliness of Logan in the area, there had been killings on both sides. The rivalry between Pennsylvania and Virginia over the site of Ft. Pitt only inflamed the unsettled circumstances in the region. Scouts returning to Ft. Pitt had repeatedly reported that war was inevitable, and John Connolly had sent word for the settlers in the outlying settlements to be on their guard for an attack at any moment. Many of the settlers in the area had already evacuated due to Connolly's warning, but Baker had decided to remain with his family. However, after learning of the threat from the Indian woman, he had sent word that he and his family were in danger and to please send help.

On the following day, Captain Cresap had the men up at dawn and headed up Grave Creek on a scout of the creek and the Wheeling area. The day had been uneventful and on the return, Cresap intentionally stopped about a mile from Logan's house. He had told the men that he didn't want to camp closer because he was concerned that some of his men might disturb Logan. He told his men that Logan lived nearby and that Logan had always been friendly to white men and gave orders that the men were not to disturb Logan.

In late afternoon several of the men in the camp, in particular, a man named Greathouse[xxx] began to talk of sneaking away from Cresap and going to help Baker and his family. If Captain Cresap wasn't going to go help them, he would. Another man, named Askew, said he would go and soon there were about 20 men who said they would all go. Askew had said that his brother had been killed by the Indians the spring before and any chance that he had to get any revenge he was for. They decided to sneak away and head to Bakers. Caesar wasn't sure what to do. The Captain had treated him well, and he didn't want to be a part of Greathouse's intentions. He thought it best to however to not get involved and just keep quiet. Captain Cresap would find out and would deal with these men.

Later that afternoon Caesar watched as several more of the men slipped off pretending to go hunt for some food. Several others slyly slipped off two or three at a time. In a few minutes after the men had gone, Cresap gathered a few men, including Caesar, and was about to start to go to Logan's house. He wasn't sure if Logan was at home, but Mrs. Logan spoke English, and he hoped to speak with her even if Logan was gone. Suddenly, the stillness of the woods echoed with gunfire. Cresap and the others immediately took off running towards Logan's house. On coming up to Logan's, they could see two men near the front of the house lying on the ground. As they got closer they could see the blood staining the ground from the two motionless Indians. They had been shot, but not scalped. They heard noise coming from inside the house. Inside the house, two of the men that had slipped away from the camp, were rummaging through Logan's belongings. Cresap and his men startled them and after the two put up a brief struggle, they were quickly subdued and bound. They wouldn't talk and who ever had been with them and participated in the killing of the Indians had already fled. Logan and his wife and family were not around, so Cresap was not able to find out exactly what had happened. He hadn't taken a head count of his men to know who was in the camp when he had started to Logan's village, so he wasn't sure who had been missing and didn't know who had actually done the killings. He and his men returned to their camp with the two men that had been caught at Logan's, fearful and alert for any signs of trouble. Cresap knew that when the word of the two Indian killings had spread that this would bring more problems to the region. Within an hour or two, the other men drifted back to the camp pretending to have been hunting. They were questioned, but denied any knowledge of the killings.

On the morning of April 30, Caesar and the others under Cresap's command were up early. Cresap had picketed men throughout the night in case of trouble, but the night was silent. As they were breaking camp, Cresap took a head count. Greathouse, his brother, Askew, a man named Sappington and 17 others had silently left during the night. Cresap had no proof, but was now certain that Greathouse and a few of the others were the ones that had gone to Logan's house and killed the two Indians.

Caesar decided that he would tell Captain Cresap what he had heard. That the men had discussed going to help Baker and that they were probably out for revenge. Upon learning this, and in anticipation of the troubles ahead, Cresap decided to head back to Wheeling as quickly as possible. He was not the one who was going to be the cause of, or the start of a war.

Greathouse and his group reached Baker's around mid-morning. Shortly after their arrival, Baker noticed two canoes starting to make their way across the Ohio toward his place. Indian's frequently came over to trade and to drink. Baker had no problem getting the Indians drunk and taking advantage of them in trade when they were drunk. Baker and Greathouse had a short conversation and Greathouse told several of his men to hide themselves in a back room of the tavern. A few others quickly went outside and hid in the undergrowth near the edge of the creek where it emptied into the Ohio.

The Indians reached the eastern shore of the Ohio and pulled their two canoes up onto the bank, totally unaware of the hidden men. The eight Mingo that came up to Bakers place included Toonay, Logan's daughter, Logan's mother, his brother, nephew, sister, cousin, and a small child. Baker and Greathouse greeted them on the porch of the building and quickly invited them inside. Inside, they were offered some drink and Baker and Greathouse began to drink and quickly encouraged the Indians drink with them. It didn't take long for the effects of the alcohol to begin to be felt. The only ones that had not taken a drink were Logan's daughter, as she was pregnant and nearly ready to give birth, and the young child. Everyone one else, was quickly intoxicated.

Greathouse had been joking with one of the Indians; not knowing it was Logan's brother. Logan's brother went over to a coat rack in the corner of the room and took down a military coat and hat and put it on. He then began to swagger around the room jokingly swearing, "I am a white man!" Everyone was laughing and moved to the outside on the porch. As they did, Greathouse gave a signal to the concealed men. One of the men, named Sappington, rose and shot Logan's brother. A bright red spot appeared on the Indian's chest. He looked at Sappington as the blood began to pour forth from his wound and then just collapsed, falling down the steps of the porch to the ground. He lay motionless at the foot of the porch steps.

The gunshot brought all of the men from the back room out. As Logan's brother lay on the ground in a pool of blood, Toonay, the child, and the other Indians hearing the shot, ran out the front door to the porch. Toonay was grabbed by Greathouse. All of the others, including the child were mercilessly gunned down.

On the other side of the river, several other Mingo who had been camped with those who now lay dead at Bakers, heard the gunshots and quickly set out in two canoes. These Indian men were painted and armed for war. As they came across the river, and neared the shore, Greathouse's men fired on them, killing most of them in the front canoe. The Indians in the second canoe quickly dropped down and headed back out of gunshot range.

Two of Greathouse's men, waded out in the waist deep water and grabbed the canoe and pulled it to the shore. They quickly drug the bodies of the Indians out of the canoe onto the shore, cheering loudly, proud of what they had done. Askew, grabbed one of the dead Indians by the hair and with his knife cut deeply along the edge of the Indians scalp in a complete circle around his skull. He then put his foot on the Indians shoulder and pulled on the Indian's hair and with a sucking sound, the hair pulled from the man's skull. Askew then lifted the scalp high into the air. The others shouted in triumph and then one after the other, scalped all of the Indians, including the young child. The men then dangled the bloody scalps from their belts as prizes.

While this was happening, the Indians in the canoe had reached the far shore, out of gun range and could only watch the massacre of their companions and their bloody scalping. They took the scalping as a declaration of war. Realizing that they could do nothing to help, they quickly headed back to Logan's to report what had happened.

Greathouse's men, now full of liquor, bloodied and with nothing but revenge on their minds, drug a kicking and screaming Toonay to the back of the tavern. They took her clothes off of her and two of the men tied her hands and feet to a small tree. As she screamed, they took turns making small slashes with their knives on her arms, her legs and her breasts. Blood beginning to pour out of her cuts, and Greathouse's men, now bloody and shouting deliriously, watched as Greathouse, seemingly in a trance, slowly walked up to Toonay and stuck his knife into her abdomen just below her breastbone. She screamed as he slowly slid his knife down her distended belly, disemboweling her. Blood poured from her. He then reached in and ripped the fetus from her body, pulling it out from her abdomen. He took his knife and scalped the baby, removing its dark black hair and raising the small scalp into the air, blood dripping down his arm. The men cheered again. Toonay was no longer moving as Greathouse pulled her head back, grabbing her long black hair he ran his knife in a rough circle completely around her head just at the hairline. He body was limp and the blood poured from the wound. Greathouse then pulled on her hair and with a sucking noise, the scalp lifted from her skull. Holding the bloody scalp by the hair, he let out an animal like scream as he raised it for all the men to see.

Chapter 14
September 27, 2012

Zane Shawnee Caverns, Bellefontaine, Logan County, Ohio

Professor Stevensen was at the Caverns again just before 11:00am on the Saturday after he had spoken with his father. Driving on his way home after he had left his father, he thought that he remembered seeing several silver medallions with carvings on them in one of the display cases at the museum when John Logan had given him his tour. He wasn't sure, but with what his father had told him, he had to get back to the museum and look more carefully at some of the displays. What if there was a silver medallion with a carving of an Indian on it, like his father had said? What if it really did exist? What if it was in the museum? Would it mean that the information in the letter from his long dead ancestor was really true? That the Shawnee did have a mine, or at least a cave with a cache of silver stored in it. Maybe the myth of the Shawnee having silver really wasn't a myth at all.

Emma Bluejacket was behind the counter in the gift store when Professor Stevensen came in. There were several people in the store browsing through the souvenir gifts, waiting for the start of the 11:00 am Cave tour. Several more came in, including a family or four who went to the counter to pay for the tour. As they were approaching the counter, Emma waved to Professor Stevensen.

"Hello. Back again?"

Professor Stevensen looked over at her.

"Good morning. Yeah...I really enjoyed the museum and wanted to get a chance to take a look at it again. You know, spend a little more time. I think that you've done a really good job with it. Is John around?"

"He should be here any minute. He's guiding the 11:00 o'clock tour. I'm sure that he'll be surprised to see you again."

"I talked with him earlier this week in class and told him I might come by again."

"Oh," said Emma, as she glanced behind Professor Stevensen toward the door. She had seen John through the window just outside. "There he is now."

Professor Stevensen heard the door open and he turned to see John step inside the store.

"Hey. Good morning. How are ya doing," said John?

"Good morning to you. How are you doing?"

John looked at Emma. He leaned closer to her and in a soft whisper spoke.

"Do you think that it would be alright for the Professor to walk around and look in the museum while I am on the tour?

Emma smiled reservedly at John, and nodded her approval. She could feel the Professor's eyes watching her in anticipation of her answer.

"Sure...why not...I'm not real busy. If he has any questions, maybe I can answer them for him."

"Thanks Emma...I appreciate it."

"Professor, I should be back from the tour in about an hour. If you're still here, I'll be glad to talk with you and answer any more questions you might have. I'm sure that Emma can help you though. She really was a big help and worked hard to get the museum up and running."

"No problem," replied Professor Stevensen. "And, thank you. I would be privileged to have Emma guide me."

"Great...I'll see you when I get back."

As John was leading the guests for the tour through the door into the cave entrance, Emma went over to the museum entrance and unlocked the door.

"Come on Professor. I'll let you in so that you can walk around. I've got a couple of things that I need to do, and will join you in just a few minutes.

"Ok. Thanks a lot Emma. I really appreciate you letting me look through the museum again."

The professor entered the museum and quickly went over to one of the display cases where he remembered he had seen some silver bracelets, arm bands, ear rings, necklaces and several medallions. As he looked in the display case, there it was. In with the other pieces of silver jewelry was a large silver medallion. At first glance, one wouldn't even have noticed it, especially if you weren't looking specifically for it.

The medallion appeared to be made of solid silver. It was around 1/2 of an inch thick and approximately four inches in diameter. Carved on the side that was facing up in the display case was the figure of an Indian dressed in a breechclout with typical deerskin leggings, moccasins and with no shirt. The Indian appeared to be pointing.

The Professor looked back towards the door and could see that Emma was still working behind the counter. She appeared to be answering questions from a young man that looked like he was in his late twenties. He hadn't gone on the cave tour and had been browsing through the store earlier. The man looked vaguely familiar, but with Emma distracted, the Professor quickly reached back behind the display. It didn't appear to be locked and the glass door slid easily, opening the back of the display. With another quick glance to see that Emma was still occupied, he reached in and grabbed the medallion. From a pocket on the side of his back pack, he quickly pulled out a plastic wrapped piece of modeling clay. He brought the clay along for just this moment. He un-wrapped it and pressed the clay onto one side of the medallion. He nervously turned the clay and the medallion over and made an impression of the other side. He reached down and carefully placed the medallion back into the display case, closing the door. He wrapped the clay back in its plastic wrapper and put it back in his back pack.

The Professor was nervous now. He hoped that it wouldn't show. He decided that he should continue to look at some of the other displays and quickly moved away from the display case where the medallion had been, to a display with stuffed animals and various sizes of arrowheads and Axe heads. As he was standing in front of this display, Emma came into the museum, smiling as she approached him. The man she had been talking too had left.

"See anything interesting? Any questions that I can answer, she asked?

"No, I've found some arrowheads in the past in some of the farmer's fields around here. If you ask them if you can look just after they plow and there's been a rain, they're pretty easy to find."

The professor decided it was best to make some kind of small talk with Emma rather than to leave quickly. He thought about asking about the medallion, but thought that it would be best to continue the small talk with Emma and just let her show him around a little longer before he left. As soon as he could he would ask John if he knew anything about the medallion.

After about thirty minutes, he had moved through most of the displays. He had asked Emma a few meaningless questions to make it appear that he was still interested in many of the artifacts that were on display.

"Emma. Thank you very much for your time," the Professor said as he intentionally looked at his watch, trying to give the impression that he was somewhat pressed for time. "Please tell John that I needed to get going and really couldn't wait for him to get back from the tour. If you would, please tell him that I'll see him in class."

"Not a problem. I'm glad I could be of help. Please come back anytime. I'll be sure to tell John that you had to get going."

The professor tried not to show his eagerness to leave, but he was very anxious and excited to take a closer look at the impressions of the medallion. His mind was racing with questions. Could this be the medallion that his great, great, great Grandfather had said that Caesar had left with the Galloways? If it was, how did it end up in the Remnant Shawnee Bands museum if Caesar had given it to the Galloways? How was it a key to the Shawnee Silver? Why was the Indian on the medallion pointing? What would he have been pointing at? He needed to get to where he could take a closer look at the impressions and he wanted to show it to his father.

The professor left the gift shop and went straight to his car. He unlocked the car. Opened the back door and threw his pack into the back seat. He got in the car quickly and left the parking lot not noticing the small red Toyota pickup that had backed out of a space near his at about the same time that he was leaving.

Chapter 15
May 5, 1774

Ft Henry, Wheeling

After the death of his family, Chief Logan sought revenge. He thought, as did many others, that Capt. Cresap was responsible for the attack, as he had been one of the primary leaders of the Militia in the region. He went on the warpath savagely seeking revenge and white men's blood. All during the summer of 1774 he himself led war parties. His attacks were rapid and without mercy on men, women and children, He took over thirty scalps himself that summer.

The Indians in Ohio were quick to follow his example and soon no whites were safe anywhere in the Ohio Valley. Many influential tribal chiefs in the region including Cornstalk of the Shawnee, White Eyes of the Lenape and Guyasuta of the Seneca/Mingo attempted to reason with Logan and negotiate a peaceful resolution to the situation. The Indians did not want war, but they recognized by their custom that Logan had the right to retaliate for the loss of his family. Once the bloodshed was accelerated by Logan, with the whites retaliating in turn, the Shawnee living on the Scioto River near Circleville became inflamed and went to Logan's side as leaders in the uprising.[xxxi] The Shawnee had a deep hatred of the white man and now they had the excuse for war. Now, all of the Indians of the Ohio and the entire frontier descended upon the whites in savage, bloody warfare.

The word of war spread quickly, and even though it was started and fueled by the whites, it was the settlers all along the Ohio frontier who sought safety. They abandoned many of their settlements and went back East across the Monongahela River and the Allegheny Mountains. Those that stayed withdrew to blockhouses in fear. Others fled to Fort Pitt and Wheeling where the entire area was in an uproar, panicked by survivors of the Indian's attacks. Capt. John Connolly, the commander at Fort Pitt sent messages to all to remain calm, including messages to the local tribes asking them of their intentions.

In Wheeling, with Cresap's men, Caesar listened intently to a letter from the Shawnee that was brought to Wheeling by two young Shawnee warriors. The letter was an answer to the many speeches and messages that had been sent to the Indians apologizing for the killings. Both of the men were dressed similarly...one with a red blouse, the other with a blue. Both had buckskin leggings. Both of the men had silver arm bracelets and silver, loop earrings dangling from each ear. They both looked to be in their late teens or early 20's. The warrior holding the letter, however, was much lighter skinned than the man that accompanied him. He was about six feet tall, slightly taller than the other. Well proportioned and muscular. His eyes were large, dark brown and piercing; his forehead was high. His forehead and the middle of his head were shaved with a long lock of dark brown hair coming from just behind the crown of his head. His hair was collected into a ponytail by a metal disk with an eagle feather attached to it. His face was painted red with a small band of black just above his eyes. At first he spoke only Shawnee, but then switched to English saying that his name was Wehyahpiherhrsehnwah, Blue Jacket. He introduced the warrior that was with him as Peesotum...in English, Big Fighter. He read the letter in English.

Caesar wondered how this Shawnee spoke perfect English. Was he a white man? He had heard of many whites and some blacks being captured by the Indians. He had heard that the Shawnee, in particular, were taking a good many white prisoners and that they treated their prisoners differently depending on the age of the person that they captured and if they were a male or a female, especially if they were young when they were taken. If they were young when they were taken, there was the possibility that they would be adopted by families that had lost a member. These families would treat them very well, but first they would be made to run a torture gauntlet. Running the gauntlet was looked upon as a trial. The captives were stripped naked and forced to run between two long, parallel rows that led to the main lodge. As they ran all of the men, women and children of the village would beat them with sticks, clubs, briars and anything else that was handy for them to use, including axes. If someone fell down, they were forced to start over. Those who survived and exhibited strength and courage were looked upon favorably and were good candidates for adoption into the tribe. Most of the captured did not survive the gauntlet. Some that did survive showed that they were weak and cowardly. These were deemed cowardly and unworthy to be Shawnee, and they were put to a slow and horrible death. They were usually shaved and painted, then tied to a post near slow-burning firewood. They would be slashed, stoned, and dismembered both before and after the flames were lighted. The entire village would be involved during the ritual tortures. Caesar heard that it was the women who took the lead in the torture as a way of releasing their anger and grief over men or children they had lost or who had been killed by the whites.

Caesar was enthralled with the young man who stood proudly and almost arrogantly before them. He wondered how he had been captured. Had he run the gauntlet? What was it like to be an Indian? What was it like to be a Shawnee? He thought to himself, it couldn't be any worse than being a slave and it couldn't be any worse than a black man living among the whites, even out here on the Ohio frontier. He was free now, but he was still subject to the whites. Out here on the frontier, it wasn't as bad as back in Virginia, but he still felt the discrimination. He just wasn't owned. The whites out here in fact, in many ways, were crueler than those in Virginia and they couldn't hide behind their religion. They certainly, for the most part, were not as educated. Most of them couldn't read or write. Their hatred of the Indian was even more pronounced than their hatred of blacks. One reason, he suspected, was that they owned the blacks in Virginia and they owned the land. They were in control. The slaves were their property. Here in the wilderness, they could not own or control the Indian and the Indians fought for the land that the whites believed they owned. He wondered if the Indians were really as savage and brutal as they were thought to be or if the whites were actually worse. What would it be like living with the Indians? It sure couldn't be any worse than living with the whites out here on the Ohio frontier. If you were adopted as an Indian, at least, it appeared that you were treated as one...as a son or brother...free and equal. That sounded good.

Caesar listened as Blue Jacket spoke.

"We have received your speeches by White Eyes, and as to what Mr. Croghan and Mr. McKee says, we look upon it all to be lies also, but as it is the first time you have spoke to us we listen to you, and expect that what we may hear from you will be more confined to truth than what we usually hear from the white people. It is you who are frequently passing up and down the Ohio, making settlements upon it, and as you have informed us that your wise people have met together to consult upon this matter, we desire you to be strong and consider it well. Brethren, we see you speak to us as the head of your warriors, who you have collected together at sundry places upon this river, where we understand they are building forts, and as you have requested us to listen to you, we will do it, but in the same manner that you appear to speak to us. Our people at the Lower Towns have no Chiefs among them, but are all warriors, and are also preparing themselves to be in readiness, that they may be better able to hear what you have to say. You tell us not to take any notice of what your people have done to us; we desire you likewise not to take any notice of what our young men may now be doing, and as no doubt you can command your warriors when you desire them to listen to you, we have reason to expect that ours will take the same advice when we require it, that is, when we have heard from the Governor of Virginia. [xxxii]

"The rest you may read yourself. I am not here for a response. Until we hear from your Governor, I tell you it will not be safe for you anywhere in our land! From all quarters we receive speeches from the Americans, and no two are alike. We suppose they intend to deceive us."

Blue Jacket then handed the letter to Capt. Connolly. Capt. Connolly, looking somewhat surprised, took the letter. Blue Jacket abruptly turned and without waiting for a response from Capt. Connolly he quickly began to walk away. It was obvious that he had been instructed to discuss nothing.

As Blue Jacket and Big Fighter walked away with their backs to Capt. Connolly, a couple of Connolly's men started toward them. Capt. Connolly raised his hand, brushing it to the side as a signal to the men to let them go.

"Leave them go, said Capt. Connolly." The men stopped. Blue Jacket and Big Fighter did not turn or hesitate with Capt. Connolly's words.

Caesar was amazed as the two walked off. A black man would have never spoken the words that Blue Jacket had read and spoken, especially to Whites. In such a short time, and even at his young age, he had commanded respect. While Capt. Connolly was obviously not afraid of the young Shawnee, he certainly respected him.[xxxiii]

Chapter 16
September 29, 2012

Antioch University, Yellow Springs, Ohio

John Logan lowered the paper that he had just read. His expression was one of amazement. Professor Stevensen had asked him if he could stay after his class for a few minutes that he had something that he wanted to show him. After the class, the professor had taken an old black bible from his backpack and removed a folded, yellow paper from the bible and handed it to John. His only words were that it was his fathers and to please be careful as it was very old.

"I've never seen anything like this before. You said that it was your fathers?

"Yeah...he showed it to me last week. In fact, it was the real reason that I came back to the museum. I thought that I had seen a silver medallion like the one described in the letter, in the museum. John, there is one there in a display case. I saw it. I wanted to share this with you. I wanted to let you know about this. What's the possibility of getting to take a close look at the medallion in the museum? Would anyone know how it got there?"

"I don't know, Professor. But if this letters real and if there is a real medallion, I'd like to look at it too.

I think I know where Turkey Foot Ravine is too. I think that the name of the creek that is down the hill from the cave used to be called Turkey Foot Creek. I think that the ravine's about a mile and a half long. It starts just off the road near the entrance to our grounds. I don't know anything about a Feather Rock though."

"Are you doing anything this afternoon professor?"

"No...not really...I've got to stop by and see my father."

"Why don't you come over to the caverns after you visit with your father and we'll see if we can talk with Emma and take a look at the medallion you're talking about? Can you be there around 4:00?"

"No problem, John. I'll make a point of being there. What about going down to the creek?"

"Yeah...we can do that too."

"Alright, I'll see you then."

As John walked out of the lecture hall, the professor was holding back his anxiousness. It was exactly the reaction that he had hoped for from John. Now he would have a great chance to look at the medallion more closely and maybe to even find out how it got to the museum. The ravine existed too.

The professor went straight to see his father. He was excited. He had seen the medallion and was positive that it was the one mentioned in the letter that his long dead ancestor had written. He had shown the impression of the front and back of the medallion to his father. His father wasn't sure what the impressions meant, but was now convinced more than ever that it all had to be true. Both he and his father were more than convinced that there was Shawnee silver and that the medallion was the key to finding it. What he needed now was to take a close look at the medallion and to get someone involved at the caverns and the museum. If someone knew about the medallion and the silver, why was it not talked of? What was the secret? Certainly the tribe could use the money. If no one knew about the medallion and the silver, then perhaps they would now take an interest in the medallion, the silver and the key to finding it and help to see if it could be located.

As he came down the hall at the nursing home to see his father and to let him know what he had found out, he noticed that the door to his father's room was closed. It was only around 2:00 in the afternoon, and his father was usually up and about with the door open at this time. He tapped lightly a few times on the heavy wooden door, but there was no response, so he slowly opened the door and peered inside.

He called out in a whisper to his father, "Dad, Dad are you here?"

He got no response, so he went on into the room. His father was lying on the floor and not moving. He bent down to his father quickly and felt for a pulse while yelling for help at the same time. His father was unconscious, but alive. There was a large, bloody gash on the back of his head and a small pool of blood had collected on the floor under his head. The blood was fresh on the tile floor and had not been smeared.

Within seconds a nurse's aide was at the door. It wasn't the same one that the professor had met in his father's room a few days earlier. As the aid bent down to the professor's father, the old man groaned and moved.

"Ooh!" The old man said as he reached to his head. What happened?"

"Bill...don't try to sit up just yet, "said the nurses aid, "You've got a really nasty cut on your head."

He looked over to the professor and said, "Can you help me move him to the bed?"

"Not a problem."

They took care in getting him up on his feet and over to the bed. As they finished, the doctor on call showed up. The professor and the nurse's aide stepped back away from the bed and let the doctor begin to take a look at the professor's father.

"Does anyone know what happened, said the Doctor."

The professor told him that he had just come to check on his father and found the door closed and when he went in, his father was lying on the floor.

"Dad...do you know what happened? Did you fall?"

"Bill...what happened?" asked the doctor.

William Stevensen just stared, glassy eyed, and didn't answer either his son or the doctor.

"This had to have just happened," said the Professor looking at the nurse's aide and the doctor. "But I don't see anything around where my dad was laying that he could have fallen and hit his head on...especially to cause a cut like that."

"Well, I'm going to take him down to the clinic. I'm sure that he'll be OK, but I want to get him stitched up and give him a sedative so he can rest a bit. We'll keep a good eye on him overnight."

The professor stayed with his father for over an hour to make sure that he would be OK. The doctor put eight stitches in the gash in the back of his father's head and his father had fallen asleep quickly as the sedative took effect.

"When he wakes up, we'll try to see what happened to him, said the doctor."

"Ok, said the professor. Thank you so much for your help. I'll be back in a couple of hours to check on him. Once again, thanks."

The doctor told him not to worry and that they would call him on his cell if there were any problems.

The professor left the nursing home, upset and confused about what had happened to his father, but excited to get to the caverns. When he arrived at the caverns, he parked and went directly to the gift shop and museum. As he opened the door to the museum, he saw John and Emma talking to another man that he didn't recognize. John waved at him and motioned him to come over.

"Hey professor."

"Hi John."

"Professor Stevensen, this is William Walker... Greyfeather...he is the head of our tribe. I was explaining to him about the letter that you showed me and about the medallion. We were just getting ready to go into the museum to take a look at it."

Greyfeather extended his hand to the professor. The professor took it.

"Nice to meet you Greyfeather."

"Nice to meet you professor...I have heard a lot about you recently. Please, call me Will."

"My pleasure." the Professor said.

"Let's go take a look at this medallion," said Will, as he opened the door for the Professor.

The Professor, Will, Emma and John headed straight to the display. Will reached back behind the glass counter, slid open the back glass of the display and grabbed the medallion. Let's take a look at this.

"Wow," he exclaimed, as he picked it up. "This is a lot heavier than I expected. It's definitely silver."

The medallion appeared to be made of solid, pure silver. It was around 1/2 of an inch thick and approximately four inches in diameter. Carved on it was the figure of an Indian dressed in a breechclout with typical deerskin leggings, moccasins and with no shirt. The Indian's right arm was extended with the index finger pointing, as one would point in giving directions to someone.

Will turned the medallion over and on the reverse side was a feather. The quill of the feather formed a deep groove that went from one side of the medallion to the other.

"Can I see it?" said John.

Will handed the medallion over to John. John took it and looked closely at both sides. "This is amazing. But how would we know if it was carved by Caesar? I don't think anyone even knows how it came to be here in the museum."

"Well," said the Professor. "I think you're right. We can surmise all we want, but we certainly don't have any proof or any real confirmation that this was made by Caesar, or any indication as to who it was given to or of what its significance is."

"Unfortunately...no," said Will.

John started to put the medallion back into the display case. As he reached forward, the Professor grabbed his arm.

"Hold on a second please. Can I see it again?" John handed it to the Professor.

The Professor took the medallion and looked at the front again.

"Wait a second," he exclaimed. "Look...I might be imagining, but look at the face of the Indian. How many Indian's have those features? I would swear that those are Negro facial features."

"Let me see that again," said John. The Professor handed it to John. As John and the Professor continued to examine the image, Will's eyes caught Emma's. His look was one of surprise and bewilderment. She knew not to say anything and that they would talk privately later.

"I have to agree with the Professor," said John. "That carving has Negro features. No Indian back then would have carved this image and given it Negro features. Only a black man would have done this. Leads you to think that it was carved by a black man and there certainly weren't many around then. It's not like there were whites and blacks roaming the countryside back then. I would think that if an Indian carved this that it would have Indian features. The features carved here are distinctly Negroid. There may have been other blacks living with the Shawnee back then, but I haven't seen any documentation other than the references to Caesar. I would think that this was carved by Caesar. What do you think Professor?"

"Well, that would make sense...but why would he put Negro features on the medallion? Why would he carve the Indian pointing? Why would he put a feather and groove on the back side." Wait a second, the feather lines up and points in the same direction as the way the figure is pointing. What if..." The Professor put the medallion on the counter top and turned it slowly on the glass.

"What if the figure is pointing at or toward something? What if the groove of the feather's quill is an alignment groove? If the medallion's groove was placed on something, then the finger may just be pointing at something. Or maybe even the way to something?"

Will and Emma watched and listened...neither commented.

The Professor sighed. "No! Even if what we're thinking is true. Where the heck would we even begin to look for something to set this on?"

"Talk about the proverbial needle in the haystack," said John. "Where would you even start?"

The Professor glanced at his watch. "Ooh...I need to get going. My father fell and hit his head back at the nursing home. He had to get a few stitches and was resting, but I need to get back to check on how he's doing. I'll think about this some more, but off hand, I have no idea if we're right about this medallion. I don't know."

John looked at Will and Emma and said to the Professor, "We'll discuss it and see if we can come up with something or any other ideas. We'll talk with you if we think of anything. Oh, when you get some time to come back, we'll head down to the ravine and see what we can find."

"All right...thanks a lot...I gotta get going. I'll talk with you later." said the Professor."

Chapter 17
1738

Shawnee Village of Pequea in present day Lancaster County, Pennsylvania

Wapatha, or Opessah as he was better known, had greeted his brothers from the South with a warm heart. They had arrived on a sunny, cool, early October day. The sky was a brilliant deep blue and he couldn't help but notice the wonderment in the eyes of the Southerners as they beheld the reds, yellows and burnt orange leaves of the trees. As the people had finished crossing the river, and entered the village, a silent, unseen, gust of wind rippled through the trees and sent the leaves of many colors floating to the ground.[xxxiv] He wondered what these people from the South must have been thinking as they beheld the beauty of the changing of the seasons for the first time. For him, it was his favorite time of the year. He knew that Weshemanitou, the maker of all things, the master of life, had created this beauty and peace for his people to be happy. He had the strongest confidence in his maker and believed that he was sovereign as he governed the world and all things in it. It was only by his power and goodness that each moment existed and as such, Opessah found joy in the fact that Weshemanitou had brought this people from the South safely to his village and that the Shawnee were going to become one people again. He would not go with them to the Ohio Country, but any of his people could join them if it was in their heart to do so.

Later in the evening, Opessah and other leaders sat with Laylashekan in the Council House. As they passed the pipe and smoked around a warming fire, a young 10-year old boy and his 5-year old brother listened intently in the shadows just outside. Hokolesqua, Corn Stalk, and his brother Wynepuechsika, Silver Heels, were doing what they had done many times before, but this time they listened more intently to the Shawnee visitors from the South.[xxxv] Laylashekan and Opessah talked of many things, but it was Laylashekan that spoke late into the night. He described how he had come to be the leader of his people over the last five years. Laylashekan explained how Soapqua and his clan had packed their village and were on the move North East within two days of Thoos's departure many years before. They had arrived at a Shawnee village located at the headwaters of the Santee River in South Carolina in less than two weeks. The Shawnee of South Carolina, who included the Piqua and Hathawekela divisions of the tribe, welcomed their brothers from the Savannah. After several meetings, in which they expressed their gratitude and extended an invitation to the South Carolina tribe to join them on their journey to the Ohio country, they pressed North along with several hundred of the South Carolina Shawnee in the early summer of 1707.[xxxvi]

They reached the Pedee River and followed the Pedee northward. Leaving the Pedee and crossing overland to what is today called the Little Pee Dee into the Carolinas, crossing into today's North Carolina near the present town of Fair Bluff. Here, they headed slightly North to the Lumber River. In the Carolinas, they had been besieged by the flat-headed Catawbans, but the fierceness and bravery of the Shawnee warriors turned the Catawbans away with little or no loss of life. After their repulsion of the Catawbans, they had continued to press northward roughly along what is today's Interstate 95, avoiding most Indian villages and staying as far away from any white settlements as possible. They befriended some tribes, escaped others and continued northward crossing into today's Virginia near Dahlia. They followed the Meherrin River to its' headwaters being warned of a growing white community which today is Richmond. They continued North between today's Charlottesville and Richmond passing though Culpeper, Warrentown and then crossing the Potomac near Harpers Ferry. They passed between Hagerstown and Frederick following the Catoctin River to its' headwaters and then turned Northeast to the Piney River, crossing into Pennsylvania near its headwaters near Littlestown, Pa. The continued Northeast, reaching the Susquehanna near today's Safe Harbor Dam and followed the River southward until they finally reached Opessah and their brother Shawnee's in Pennsylvania at Pequea.

The trip was one that Soapqua and many of the original Suwannee River Indians did not survive. Soapqua had slipped on a rock crossing a creek and fractured his leg in several places. His leg was set, but later became infected and he died from the infection.

Soapqua's replacement as the tribe leader was Laylashekan.

Laylashekan was only twenty-eight years of age when he became the leader of the tribe. He was twelve years old when the tribe had begun their journey north from the Savannah River. He was tall and lanky, but muscular. His dark hair was not quite shoulder length. His eyes were dark brown and deep set and his slender nose had a slight crookedness to it. He had a large coin shaped piece of silver dangling from his left ear and a small silver nose ring. Although he was somewhat young, he had already proven himself in battle having been wounded twice in defense of the tribe and near death from a knife wound to his left shoulder. He had also taken on a slight limp from an arrow that had hit his left knee and had partially cut into a ligament. It had healed, but had left him with the limp. He had seen battle and was fierce and yet at his young age, He also had gotten the reputation of being a quick thinking and kind-hearted man.

Laylashekan and the 280 men, women and children that he led would not stay long at Pequea. Laylashekan had explained to his people and to Opessah that they were grateful for Opessah's kindness, but that with winter coming on, they did not want to burden Opessah's people with additional food requirements. They had brought much with them and had a sufficient amount to last them for the final trip to the Ohio country. They would rest only a few days and leave while the weather was still good to make the headwaters of the Ohio. Laylashekan believed that they could reach the main Shawnee village of Chalahgawtha on the Scioto River before the end of November. As a token of friendship and gratitude, Laylashekan gave Opessah a bag of silver coins.

"Keep these my friend, the White's value this metal and these coins. We have kept these, as well as much of this metal, on our journey. It has been handed down to us from our fathers, fathers. It was taken from the dark skinned warriors with the big metal helmets, who called themselves Spaniards. And some, it is said, came with our earliest ancestors from across the great Southern waters."

"Thank you. I will keep it safe, said Opessah."

Opessah had met several times with his tribal leaders and told them that he would not be leaving with their Southern brothers to go to the Ohio country. Anyone who wanted to go would be looked upon with great respect for wanting to join with all of his or her brothers and sisters. It was each individual's choice or decision to go or to stay. One of the chiefs listened intently and later in the evening around his family's fire he spoke to his wife and children. Paxinosa or Hard Striker was Cornstalk and Silver Heals father. His daughter Nonhelema or Grenadier Squaw also sat with her brothers.

"We will travel to the Ohio Country," said Paxinosa as he stood. He was in his early 40's with long, graying hair.

"Our life here has been good, but my heart becomes heavier almost every day as I see the White men continuing to take more and more of this land.

They are like ants that have come out of their hole when they have found something sweet. While they have introduced many good things to us, they are also a curse. They have brought sickness to many. I have met with Donagan, the man they call the governor of New York years ago. He asked us to fight against our brothers the Mohawk who we joined to fight the French for the British. The whites want us to fight against ourselves so they can claim more of our land. The trees that they continue to cut down for their towns and roads and their crops and animals move the animals further from us. We must hunt further and further from our own lands. We have treated them fairly and with kindness, but they look upon us with hatred and contempt. I have been told that the ships that carry them from their homes across the great waters arrive daily and that there are too many of the Whites to be counted that have moved into this Pennsylvania country and all of the surrounding area. When we lived among the Munsee, this was true of the Delaware country as well.[xxxvii] I am afraid that we will never stop them from coming to this country. Our hope is to move far from them and to join many of our brothers in the Ohio Country. We will be a strong people again."

Chapter 18
June 16, 1774

Mouth of the Scioto River

Caesar had made his mind up to go live with the Shawnee shortly after he had heard the young Blue Jacket speak at Ft. Henry a few weeks back. Blue Jacket had impressed Caesar and stirred thoughts deep from inside that he had about leaving the White men and living amongst the Indians. He wasn't sure if it was the freedom he was seeking of being alone, or just a growing hatred and contempt of the white way of life. He had seen the cruelty back in Virginia and the blind hatred of the Indians that the Whites had. He had witnessed the evil of men like Greathouse. His decision was made. He would leave for the wilderness and take his chances with the Indians. He had heard of other Negroes living among them and of whites that had been captured and adopted. He wasn't sure if he was going to walk into one of their villages or let himself be captured. He'd work that out as it happened, but he was leaving.

Caesar had left Ft. Henry in the middle of the night in a driving rain and thunderstorm. The steep path down from the Fort to the river was mud and rutted with small streams of water. He slipped and fell down the path several times in his haste, until he reached the gravelly bank along the river where he found a canoe and set off downstream. There were no guards out in the storm and he was sure that he had not been seen. He paddled at times and at others, drifted silently down the river in the blackness of the night. The only sound being the sound of the rain on his hat and the constant spattering of it on the river and on the water that had collected in the canoe. He made it through the night and as the sky was getting lighter in the East, he recognized Captain Hands Island just ahead. He had stopped on this island once before and decided that it would be a good place to hide and get some sleep.

The Island was around 300 acres of land and covered with a thick growth of timber and grapevines. He knew that the island flooded, but didn't think that the water would rise fast enough or high enough to prevent him from stopping for a few hours. As he got nearer to the island, he remembered a big grove that had a mound of earth that was very high. Its' sides were very steep and overgrown on all sides with large trees. Some of the trees were at least three feet in diameter.

Caesar took a few last strong strokes on the left side of the canoe against the strong river current and the canoe glided right to the bank of the island. He jumped out of the canoe into ankle deep water and quickly pulled the canoe up onto the bank. He dragged it through the gravelly mud and hid it in some undergrowth. He then crawled under it to get out of the rain and tried to get some sleep. He had slept only a few hours before deciding to continue on down the river. He would stay on the south side of the river being alert to any activity on the north from Indians and if he was seen by any whites, they wouldn't bother him, as it wasn't uncommon to see a man alone on the river, black or white.

It had stopped raining during the mid-morning while he had been asleep and the river was now running muddy and high. The river had risen during his sleep at least 3 feet. He knew that he would be able to make very good time and distance himself further from the Fort. Even though he had deserted, he was confident that the men would not come after one nigger. Men wandering off from the Fort was common...they would leave him to his fate in the wilderness.

With the swiftness of the current, Caesar had made it a good distance down the river before nightfall, not seeing anyone. On the opposite side of the river he could see the mouth of a good-sized river as it poured into the Ohio.[xxxviii] It was a good 100 yards wide. He recognized this river, having been down the Ohio with the army this far before. He knew that a bigger river entered into the Ohio just a few miles further downstream.[xxxix] He decided however, to just pull over to the southern shore of the Ohio and rest for a few hours. He could then slip past the bigger river, where he knew there were a few cabins, and would not been seen. He also knew that this was the farthest he had been on the Ohio. From this point on, he knew that he would be going further and further into the wilderness and Indian Territory...particularly that of the Shawnee.

After a few hours rest, Caesar eased his canoe back into the current of the Ohio. It was a dark night, with only a fingernail of a moon. It had cooled off since the rain. The sky had cleared, but the hint of summer warmth was present even in the evening chill. He had decided that with the darkness he would go as far as he could before daylight, and then pull over and rest. It would be safest to travel at night for a few days to make sure that he wouldn't be seen by any Indians or white men. He wanted to make sure that he made it to the Scioto before he allowed or exposed himself to be captured.

After a couple of hours of quiet travel he found himself coming up to a small, forested island. He stayed to the south of the island and slowly and silently slid past.[xl] After traveling what he thought was another five miles or so he could make out the mouth of a small river on the north side of the Ohio.[xli] After another five miles he saw the mouth of a larger river opening into the Ohio on the north side.[xlii]

As morning approached Caesar found that he was having difficulty keeping is eyes open. He didn't want to chance falling asleep in the canoe and drifting uncontrolled down the river. He didn't know what was ahead on the river and his control on the river was the only thing in his life that he did have control of. Only uncertainty lay ahead and he didn't want to chance drifting into the uncertainty...much better to have some control over it...if you could call it control. He braced the handle of his oar against the left side of the canoe and pushed the paddle out turning the nose of the canoe to the left. In less than a minute he was on the shore and pulling the canoe up through the rocky mud to a small ledge where the roots of a large tree had been exposed by the undercutting current of the river. He lifted the nose up onto the ledge of the bank. Climbed up and then pulled the canoe up onto the top of the ledge. He dragged it a few more feet into a small thicket of trees and brush and sat down with his back against the canoe. His rifle lay across his lap. In only a few minutes he was sound asleep.

Caesar wasn't sure how long he had been asleep, but he was awakened by the sound of voices on the river. He belly crawled with his rifle over to the edge of the bank by the large tree whose roots had been exposed. The tree and its' roots offered great concealment. There was a thin rising mist coming off the river that somewhat veiled the other side of the river as it rose upward. But Caesar could make out almost directly on the other side of the river, not even 100 yards away, a small party of Indians. He quickly counted six who had pulled their two canoes up onto the bank. His eyes quickly and nervously scanned the opposite bank and up and down the river as far as he could see. There was no one else that he could see. As he looked back at the Indians, they appeared to be looking at a large rock that was exposed out in the river on a small bank of land. He quickly scanned the opposite shore up and down the river again for any other motion and saw none. All of the Indians appeared to be young men. All were of average height. Their heads were shaved about half way back and their long black hair was almost shoulder length. Several had single feathers attached to single braided strands of hair. They all had buckskin pants and long sleeve cotton shirts. He could also see that around their arms were what appeared to be wide silver armbands. Two of the young men had silver nose rings. All had various types of rings in both of their ears. Caesar watched them for about 15 minutes. They were talking softly and touching the rock. They showed no signs that they knew they were being watched. After a few more minutes they all went back to their canoes and pushed off heading downstream. Caesar crawled back to his canoe. He waited for over one hour before crawling back to the edge of the river. He didn't see any sign of anything or anyone.

As he drug his canoe back to the river, his curiosity got the better of him and he decided to go over and take a look at the rock the Indians had been looking at. He knew that he would be taking a chance at being seen, but he had to know what they were looking at.

Caesar put his canoe in the water. He climbed in and paddled back up stream as he angled out into the river. When he felt that he was far enough up stream, he turned the canoe and drifted back down toward the rock. When he got to the rock, he pulled his canoe up onto the bank. He grabbed his rifle and went straight to the rock. The rock had a smooth, almost perpendicular front with large carvings on it. There was what appeared to be a representation or figure of a man smoking. He was sitting with his elbows on his knees, which seemed to meet his breast. His shoulders and head were leaning forward and his pipe was in one hand. There were also a number of other engravings that were partly defaced by time and the friction of the Ohio's water.

As Caesar looked and touched the carvings, he couldn't help wonder who made them. He knew they were very old. They weren't recent carvings. He wondered how long people had lived in this area. When he was growing up, he had been taught that the white men had discovered America. He'd always wondered about that. In his mind, how could something be "discovered" if people were already living there? And to him, it was pretty obvious, that there were lots of people living here way before the white men came.[xliii]

Caesar didn't stay long at the rock and was headed further downstream. The further he was from the white man's world and influence the better he felt, but the deeper he got into the Ohio Territory, the more nervous he was becoming. Even though he was set on allowing himself to be captured and hoping that the Indians would adopt him, it was the uncertainty of how this would happen. He wanted to control when and how he would allow himself to be taken. He didn't want to be just caught and captured. The chances were if he was careless; he would probably just be killed.

As Caesar slid the canoe back out into the river's current, the mist coming off the river had disappeared. The smoky mist in the hills surrounding the river was also disappearing. Caesar could tell that it was going to be a sunny day. The temperature had already warmed and the morning chill was gone. He thought to himself what a beautiful morning it was and how blessed a man he was to be free to do what he wanted. He was alone and that was good, but at times, like most men, he found himself feeling a need for the comfort or companionship of others. But for the most part, he didn't mind his solitude. He felt an inner peace when he was alone. He was right where God wanted him to be at this time. In his mind, he knew that God was in control of his life. He created all of the beauty that Caesar could see around him. What he didn't understand was a question that rested heavy upon him at times, and that was if God had created all of this beauty and had created all men, why were some men as evil as they were? Why was their so much killing? If God had a plan, as he remembered the preacher saying, what was it? If he was in control of everything, why didn't he make everyone equal? Why did some people believe in Jesus and others didn't. He knew that the Indians believed in a Creator. Was it the same Creator or God that he believed in...the same God or Creator that he had been taught about?

Caesar's quiet thinking was interrupted by a loud splash just ahead and off to his left in the river. He turned quickly, somewhat startled but saw the ripples in the water as they moved out in a slowly expanding circle from where the fish had turned the surface. The quiet of the wilderness was something that he enjoyed. A man's senses, especially hearing, were very sharp. Any sound seemed to be amplified and could be heard from miles away. As he continued his drift and paddle with the current, he began to notice that the color of the river had changed from a murky brown the past few days, to become much clearer. As the paddle came out of the water, he could see the clearness of the rivers water.

Caesar drifted and paddled downstream, staying on the southern edge of the river the entire day. The sun had just set behind the hills to his southwest. Up ahead, on the southern side of the river he could see the mouth of another, large river. The riverbank was heavily forested but in the dimming light he could see the outline of cabins up on the hill near the river's mouth. Smoke was slowly rising from each of the cabins. He thought of stopping and seeing if he could get any food, but decided to go further down the river, and pull over and sleep for the night. He still had some provisions and the less anyone knew of him being on the river, especially alone, the better.[xliv] Little did Caesar know that in just four months, that what would occur on this point of land would dramatically change his life and begin to seal the future of the Indian's in the Ohio Valley.

As the canoe drifted, Caesar was secure in his own thoughts, what he did not know was that events out of his control were quickly spiraling toward him. He was aware of the brutal murder of chief Logan's family, but what he did not know was that Chief Logan had turned his anger into revenge and as more and more settlers came down the river and poured over the Alleghenies, that Logan had taken his tribe on the path of war, killing, scalping and taking white prisoners without mercy. Caesar knew that the clashes between the Indians and the whites had increased all along the river. This was one of the reasons that he decided to leave the army camp when he did. It was part of his reason for trying to travel undetected. He wasn't aware however, that along with the frequency of the clashes, that killing by both the whites and the Indians was becoming more and more savage. Both were guilty of increasingly vicious, unthinkable atrocities.

He was not aware however, that Lord Dunmore had been appointed governor of Virginia in 1771 and that he was ordered to discourage settlement of the lands beyond the mountains to the west. Dunmore's action was partly motivated by the British government's desire to keep the Indians content by preventing settlers from encroaching on their hunting grounds and to partly preserve a profitable fur trade with the Ohio Valley tribes. However, the westward migration was too difficult to halt as the settlers poured over the Alleghenies.

With Dunmore's appointment as Governor, he ordered the organization of a border militia and appointed Colonel Andrew Lewis, a veteran of the French and Indian Wars, to command the Virginia Troops. He thought that by carrying the fight to the Indian's that he would be able to divert Virginian's from the trouble that was brewing on the coast with England. Neither Dunmore nor Lewis knew at this time that the Shawnee, led by Cornstalk, had allied themselves with Logan's Mingo and had vowed to keep the settlers out of the Ohio valley by turning the frontier "red with Long Knives' blood."[xlv]

Caesar allowed the canoe to drift silently past the mouth of the big river. He had gone down the river for approximately 30 minutes or so, not realizing the he had drifted to the northern side of the river. In the growing dark, he noticed a high sandy bank that stretched gradually up from the river bottom. He thought about going back across to the south side of the river, but he was hungry and tired and decided that from the high point of the bank, he would have a good view and would be safe for the night. He hid the canoe and made his way up the bank. At the top, he sat down with his back to a large oak, facing the river. He ate some of his remaining jerky, pulled his blanket up around himself, and within minutes was sound asleep.[xlvi]

Caesar awoke the next morning early and set off down the river. He eased himself back to the south side of the river and traveled well into the evening not seeing or hearing anyone. During the early evening he had rounded a point of the river and headed back North.[xlvii] As the canoe slid down the river in the early morning, Caesar couldn't help but think back to that evening he had escaped from his white master back in Virginia. It seemed like yesterday and yet, he had been through quite a lot since that cold, wet December night. His thoughts also went back to his wife and children whom he knew he would never see again. He wondered if they missed him or thought of him. He had thought of them often, but as soon as he found his mind thinking of them, he tried to quickly suppress the thoughts. He knew that even if he thought of the good memories, they would only lead him to sadness. It was best to move on and not dwell on the past. It was done and couldn't be done over. He had to move forward no matter what the next day would bring. This was his life now. Each day was filled with uncertainty. His only certainty was freedom. He paddled the canoe over to the bank just past the point. He pulled the canoe out of the river and hid it in the underbrush. He lay down beside it and had a most restful night.

The next day he was up early and back on the river. Around mid-morning, Caesar noticed the mouth of a much larger river entering on the north side of the Ohio.[xlviii] Its opening appeared to be at least 70 yards across. When he was just about 200 yards away from the mouth of the river, he suddenly heard someone yelling for help and a woman appeared on the east side of the bank of the river. She was wearing a torn yellow dress and as he got closer he could see that her hair was matted with dried blood. She looked directly at him as he paddled toward her and waived her hands frantically, continuing to yell at him for help. Caesar paddled hard and as his canoe hit the bank, he jumped out, running in the soft sandy mud to the woman. The woman reached out to Caesar and fell into his arms. As she fell into his arms, Caesar suddenly heard the screams of over a dozen warriors as they scrambled out of the trees toward him and the woman. Caesar let go of the woman and his first reaction was to run. He had taken only a few steps when a stocky built young brave plowed into him with his knife drawn. Caesar struggled with the young brave, but quickly realized that this was the moment he had wanted to come. It wasn't how he had expected to be captured, but it was upon him. He relaxed and threw his arms in the air signaling his surrender. Several of the braves were quickly upon him shoving him to the muddy sand. They realized that he was not fighting them and quickly pulled his hands behind his back and bound them with wet strips of leather. They roughly jerked him to his feet.

The woman was also bound and they had quickly pushed her back up the bank into the trees. One brave had already gotten Caesar's gun and provisions and another had drug his canoe up into the trees. As quickly as they had captured him, the river was silent again and no trace of what had just happened was evident. Clearly the woman had been a decoy to draw Caesar to the shore and it worked as his compassion to help her let him throw all of his caution aside. The Indians had no way of knowing that he wanted to be captured, but their ploy had worked. Caesar, just five days from leaving Ft. Henry, was now captured and being taken upstream on a trail that roughly paralleled the northeast shore of the Ohio River tributary.

Chapter 19
1738

Chalahgawtha[xlix] Mid-November

Laylashekan, with help from Paxinosa and several of the young guides that Opessah had provided, had led their combined tribe members some 520 miles in only 30 days. Some 40 Shawnee had decided to join Laylashekan and travel to the Ohio lands from Pequea. They now totaled 340 men, women and children as they approached the Shawnee village at the mouth of the Scioto. They had traveled from Pequea through the mountains, across valleys, small streams, a large river and finally to Chalahgawtha. Their journey was finally ended as they entered into the village led by a group of young braves who had met them two days earlier. As they entered the village, the men, woman and children of the village lined the path, joyfully greeting them.

They had left Pequea on a brilliant, sunny day, following established river, valley and mountain trails, traveling almost 20 miles per day through the Pennsylvania and Ohio lands. It was some 260 miles from Pequea to Logstown, on the Ohio, just 18 miles north of Fort Pitt.[1] They followed roughly what is today's US 76, from near Lancaster, to Harrisburg, to Monroeville, to Economy. They did not cross the Ohio, but stayed on the North shore of the river, crossing the Allegheny just north of Logstown near present day Acmetonia and Harmarville, where there is a series of islands in the river. After crossing the

Allegheny, they followed down a path on the north shore of the Ohio before they were led further inland into the Ohio country. They traveled some 170 miles in the Ohio country passing through today's East Liverpool to Steubenville, and heading west into the heart of the Ohio lands to Cambridge, Zanesville and Lancaster, following Ohio State Route 22, the Lancaster Pike, and traveling south from today's Circleville, along Ohio State Route 23, which parallel's the Scioto River, to Chillicothe and on to Lower Shawnee Town or Chalahgawtha at the mouth of the Scioto River.[li]

Over the next few years, Laylashekan and Paxinosa's bands of Shawnee quickly assimilated into the village's life and into their new homes. The differences in their speech, the differences in their looks and some of the differences in their customs and traditions disappeared, as the Shawnee became one people. The silver they had traveled with and that had been a part of their dress, became an everyday part of the dress of the people that they had come to live with. Just as always, as the years went by, the old grew older, and the youth turned into adults. New children were born, and Hokolesqua, Cornstalk, and his brother Wynepuechsika, Silver Heels, grew into young men. It was now their turns to become leaders of the Shawnee.

Chapter 22
September 29, 2012

Yellow Springs, Ohio

The Professor got back to Sunshine Gables and found that his father was back in his room sleeping. The doctor saw the Professor return and came down to the room along with a nurse's aide. It was the same one that had helped him earlier in the day.

"Your father is doing fine. We watched him for a while and he's going to be OK."

"Was he able to tell you what happened to him," said the professor.

"No," said the doctor.

"All right, said the professor. Kinda looks like he'll be sleeping for a while. I'm gonna head on home and I'll be back to see him in the morning. Let me know if anything changes?"

"By the way," said the professor, looking at the nurse's aide. "What's your name?"

"Oh. Sorry...my name's Charles," said the nurse's aide.

Charles was a young, slender, black man in his early 20's.

"Well, Charles...I really appreciated your help earlier today. Thanks so much," said the professor.

"Not a problem," said Charles. "I'm glad to help."

"I haven't seen you around here before," said the professor. "Are you new?"

"Yeah...I've only been here a few days. I took the place of Parker."

"What happened to Parker," said the professor.

Charles looked at the professor and the doctor replying "No one knows. I heard that he didn't show up for a couple of his shifts. They called him, but got no answer on his cell or his home phone. He hasn't called in either. They called me, asked me to come in and offered me the job."

"That's strange," said the doctor. "I saw that Parker fellow here at the home earlier today. I was busy with your father and hadn't paid any attention to it, but come to think of it, I haven't seen him since we found your father. I better let the Nurses know. They'll need to keep an eye out for him. If he's not working here anymore, he doesn't need to be hanging around here. Especially if he just quit showing up and hasn't called anyone to let them know what's going on."

"That is kinda strange," said the professor. "He seemed like a nice enough guy. He was pretty helpful with my father. Anyway, thanks again for your help doctor."

"Not a problem professor. I'm glad to help."

"Charles, will I see you tomorrow?" the professor asked.

"I have classes in the morning. I'm going to nursing school. But I start on second shift tomorrow afternoon," said Charles. "If you're around tomorrow evening, I'll see you then."

After the doctor and Charles had left, the professor went over to the nightstand drawer and opened it. The clay impression of the medallion that he left with his father was gone. He knew that his father had put it in the nightstand. Crap. What the hell, he thought to himself. He didn't want to wake his father to ask him where it was, but he saw his father put it in the drawer and couldn't think of any reason why his father would have taken it out. He quickly looked around the room. It wasn't laying out anywhere.

He heard his father stir in the bed. As he turned to look at his father, his father opened his eyes.

"Rob. What are you doing here? Ooh...what the heck happened?"

"That's what I'd like to know Dad."

His father sat up in the bed. "Rob. The last thing I remember is that I was talking with that nurse's aide, John. He walked in when I was looking at the impression of the medallion that you had made. He kinda startled me and he saw it before I could put it away. He asked me what I was looking at and before I could even say anything, he had knocked me to the ground. Before I could get up I got hit in the back of the head. That's all I can remember."

"Oh my God Dad! That guy doesn't even work here anymore. Why would he Dad? Where's the clay impression of the medallion? It's not in the nightstand and I don't see it laying out anywhere in the room. Your letter is gone too. Do you think that guy took them?"

"He must have...but why would he take them?"

"You didn't say anything to him. Did you Dad?"

"No, like I said, I was just looking at the clay impression that you made when he barged in here."

"Dad...I'm gonna have to let the nursing home know about this and have them call the police. This guy assaulted you. I don't know why, but like I said, he doesn't work here anymore and the police are going to have to find him."

"Hold on a second son. Are you gonna explain all this about the medallion to the police? How you gonna explain getting that clay impression, how you got it and why we had it."

"Dad! I..." The old man interrupted him.

"Just hold on a minute. You better think about this. I'm OK. Maybe we should find out a little more about what's going on. I don't think that Parker guy's gonna get back in here. I suspect we ain't gonna see him around here again. My guess is that he overheard us talking about the letter and the medallion and maybe even the Shawnee silver. He's probably put the two together. If you wanna find him, I would think you're best bets gonna be over at that Shawnee cave you been visiting. I'd lay odds if he's up to no good that he'll try to get the actual medallion in his hands."

The professor just looked at his father. He was amazed how astute the old man was for his age, especially considering he just got hit in the head and knocked unconscious, let alone, the eight stitches he just got.

"You know dad...you're probably right. If he is involved with this, he's not gonna show up back here. If anything, he's gonna try to find out how the medallion and the silver are related. I better get in touch with John over at the Caverns and let him know what's happened. You're right...we don't want the police involved yet. I'll let them know over at the

Caverns what's going on and ask them keep an eye out for him."

"Don't you worry about me son. I'll be all right. You better let them folks know what's going on right now. Just let me know what you find out."

"Alright Dad...it's too late tonight, but I'll try to give John a call and I'll head over there first thing in the morning. I don't have any classes until later in the afternoon."

The professor went over to his father and gave him a hug. "Dad...I love you. Hope you feel better in the morning. I'll see you tomorrow some time. Do you want this door open or closed?"

"Just leave it open. I'll see you tomorrow. I love you too son!"

The professor called John Logan several times on his cell after he left his father and left messages, but John did not return his call. He tried once more when he got home, with no answer. It was late and the battery on his phone was low so he turned his cell off, put it on charge, and went to bed. He would just go to the caverns in the morning, find John, and tell him what had happened and take a look down in the ravine near the cave.

John Parker sat in his rented trailer home and continued to look at the copy of the letter he had taken from Robert Stevensen's bible. After he had overheard the old man and his son talking, he went into the room one evening while the old man was sleeping and took the letter from the old Bible; photo copied it, and put it back. He had also heard the old man and his son talking about the clay impression of the medallion that the professor had made, and decided that he needed to get it to try to put together where the Shawnee silver was. He didn't mean to hurt the old man, but he had startled him when he went into his room, shoved him to the ground and hit him before he realized that he had even done it. He was convinced that the two were on to a lost treasure and he was going to beat them to it. He needed the money and at this point in his life, he had decided that he had nothing to lose.

John was 26 years old, divorced twice and had two children. He had grown up in nearby Mechanicsburg, Ohio. After high school, he had enlisted in the Army at 19 and served in the Iraq War. He was wounded, taking a piece of metal in his leg from a roadside IED. When he returned from the war, he had gone through intensive physical therapy, supported by his high school sweet heart. They married and had a child, but the marriage lasted only a few years as John was having difficulty keeping a job. He had become addicted to the pain medication that the doctors had prescribed for him for his leg, as well as becoming an alcoholic. He remarried within eight months of his divorce, had another child, and in less than one year was divorced from his second wife. He had gotten a DUI and his drug dependency had worsened. He had been fortunate to get the job at the nursing home, but he could barely pay his rent, let alone the child support he owed to both of his ex-wives. If the silver treasure existed and he could get a hold of it, it would be his find, and it just may help him to get out of the mess he had created for himself.

He decided that he would go to the Caverns on the weekend, take the cave and museum tours and explore the ravine area to see if he could find the Feather Rock that the letter talked about. No one would be suspicious of him on the tours. He wasn't sure what he would do if he found anything, but he would worry about that later. If he couldn't find anything, he would just tail the professor. One way or the other, if the Shawnee silver existed, it was gonna be his.

Chapter 21
June 17, 1774

Chalahgawtha on the Scioto River

The day after he was captured, Caesar found himself alone in a small hut. His hands and feet were bound. He, the white woman and the young braves had arrived around mid-morning in Chalahgawtha after he had spent one shivering, miserable night bound to a stake. After being captured, the Indians had tied his hands behind his back with wet leather strips. He hadn't offered any resistance to them as they quickly moved on the trail heading up the Scioto River from the Ohio, but he was attached to one of the braves by a long strip of leather that was tied around his neck and attached to the brave's wrist. At first all of the young Shawnee's had hit him, shoved him and taunted him along the trail, but as the day went on, he found himself being maltreated less. He wasn't sure what to expect, or what lay ahead, but he was still alive and that was a good thing.

When the party stopped for the night, Caesar's feet were also bound and the leather strip around his neck was staked to the ground. The leather strips that bound his hands and his feet had dried and tightened around his ankles and wrists. The young men had no idea that he wasn't going to try and escape, but they were taking no chances. He had tossed and turned, sleeping little. In the early morning, his ankles were freed and the party was on the move again.

Caesar guessed that they had gone approximately 50 miles or so up the Scioto when it became obvious that they were approaching a large village.[lii] Men, women and children ran to greet them. Upon noticing him, the women began to make a high-pitched noise with their tongues. It seemed as if the whole village was in a state of commotion with his arrival and everyone crowded around him, touching and poking him as he was taken immediately to the hut he was now in.

The hut wasn't much of a shelter. It was made of young sapling trees that had been bent with both ends stuck into the ground. It was domed-shaped and covered all the way to the ground with thick tree bark. The top had a wide-open hole that was covered. The fire pit in the center of the hut looked as though it had hardly been used. The floor was bare ground and the door was barely large enough for a man to fit through. It was covered with some sort of grass mat that was made to open. He was barely able to stand in it.[liii]

In the early evening, the door opened and a young woman placed a bowl of food just inside the door, along with a skin of water. She said nothing. Caesar downed the food and water without hesitation. The afternoon in the hut had been hot. It was still spring, but it had been a sunny, warm day and with no air circulating within the hut, it had been quite hot. He had tried to sleep, but his nervousness had kept him awake. Every time he heard voices close by or footsteps, his heart would race. He wasn't afraid, but anxious as to what they would do with him.

Later in the evening, the door to the hut opened again and two young men entered. They cut the leather strip binding his feet, grabbed him by the arms, and yanked him to his feet, dragging him outside before he could completely stand. They pushed and shoved Caesar toward a large structure at the far end of the village. As they made their way, women and children and a few older men seemed to appear from everywhere in the village taunting and hazing him.

When they reached the entrance to a very large, central building, they stopped.[liv] One of the men went in. The other stood with Caesar. Caesar tried to keep himself calm, but he was more than nervous. His mind was racing but one thought came strongest to him. He remembered something from the Bible that his mother told him when he was a boy. It had always stuck in his mind. She said that the Bible said that God was in control of everything. He created you and knew when you were gonna be born. He knew when you were gonna die and if He knew these two things, he certainly knew everything in between. God was in control of our lives and everything He did was for a purpose. She always used to say "It's all parta His big plan. We ain't never gonna understand it. We's just gotta 'cept it." He used to question her asking her that if God was in control of everything, did that mean that we don't really make any choices. If God knew what we were gonna do, then why didn't He just tell us what to do? To him it seemed like we made choices every day. He made choices all the time. He chose to run away. He chose to come down

133

the Ohio. It was his choice to want to be captured. But, he could hear her voice answering him. "We's just gotta 'cept it," she would say. "God gave you your choices, but he already knew how and what you was gonna choose." Whatever was gonna happen was gonna happen Caesar thought to himself. He was sure that he had chosen this path, but if God had chosen it for him, then that's the way it was and why should he worry. He knew that when he was captured, he was going to be treated roughly, and that if he weren't killed right away, that he wouldn't be killed, at least not until later. He had made his choice and was resigned to whatever his choice and God had in store for him. He had heard that if you were ever captured by the Indians that you shouldn't show that you was afraid and that the Indians respected those that didn't show their fear. It was a sign that you were a strong man. Fear was a sign of weakness. He knew that his rough treatment, the taunting and hazing had only been a game to bring out his fear. Certainly they could have killed him at any time.

As Caesar stood with the young man waiting to see what came next, he couldn't help but notice the size of the building. It was built similar to the small hut he had been in, with poles as frames and a bark covering, but he guessed it to be at least 150 feet long, 20 feet wide and about 20 feet high. He was thinking that it had to be some sort of meetinghouse.

The man that had entered appeared in the door and motioned for Caesar to be brought into the longhouse. Caesar went through the door and was amazed to see separate rooms. He was taken into one of the rooms. In the center of the room was a fire pit. The smoke was wafting straight up and out of the roof. On the far side of the room and the fire, several Indians were seated. None rose when Caesar was thrust into the room. Caesar was brought to stand in front of the seated men. The two young men left him and left the room.

Caesar stood before the men. The man in the center was elderly. Caesar didn't know anything about Indians or their culture. He just figured that the man in the middle must be the chief. He slowly and calmly looked at the others that were seated. He thought he recognized one of the younger men. Yes, he was sure. It was the one they called Blue Jacket. He remembered the speech that Blue Jacket had given and his proud and defiant manner as he talked not to Capt. Connolly, but at him, just a few weeks ago back at Ft. Henry. Seeing this man had pushed Caesar to making his decision to leave the white men forever and to take his chances with the Indians. Now, here he was standing in front of Blue Jacket, and the other leaders of the Shawnee. The seated men, including Blue Jacket, were the Shawnee leaders, Pucksinwah, Blackfish,[lv] Cornstalk and the Mingo Chief, Logan.

The man in the middle spoke to Blue Jacket. Caesar didn't understand what he said, but Blue Jacket slowly stood up and walked over to Caesar. He looked him straight in the eye.

"Who are you?" He asked in English. "Are you a soldier? Are you a coward who has quit being a soldier? We notice that you did not fight your capture. You came to help the woman, but did not fight. Our young warriors were going to kill you, but decided to bring you here to our village. You showed compassion for the woman, but no fear of us. We do not understand why you did not fight, but you have showed no fear. Perhaps you are not a coward. I noticed that you have eyes that look at me. Do you know who I am?

As Blue Jacket was talking to him, asking him all of the questions, he had to restrain himself from blurting out the answers to Blue Jacket's questions. He thought that it would be best to wait until Blue Jacket was finished. At least it appeared to him that he was going to get to answer the questions and explain who he was, why he was here and what he wanted.

Blue Jacket continued. "Before you speak, I must tell you that what you say will determine if you live or die. I will translate for you. Understand...we have knowledge of fighting among the Whites who call themselves Virginians and Pennsylvanians. They have fought for possession of the fort they call Pitt. We have heard that a soldier chief named Dunmore has now taken this fort and is attacking the local Indian settlements. We want to know why? We have also heard that this Dunmore has called out an army from Virginia and that it is headed to our Shawnee lands.[lvi] What do you know of this? Our brothers, the Delaware, have tried to keep peace, but we are gathered here, now, for war."

"You may speak," said Blue Jacket

Caesar looked intently at Blue Jacket and then turned to look straight into the other men's eyes. He knew that it was a sign of respect to look into another man's eyes. As a slave he was taught to look down when speaking to a White. He was told that this showed that he respected the person he was talking to. He thought it was a disgrace. If a man respected you, he would look you straight in the eyes when he talked with you.

"First...I'm here 'cause I wanna be here. My name is Caesar."

Blue Jacket translated Caesar's first few words for the others. There was no reaction from any of the men. As Caesar started to speak again, Blue Jacket put up his hand and said

"Why do you wish to be here?"

Caesar continued. "I'm a slave who run away from the white man in Virginia. I's left everything behind to leave the White man's world. I wanted to be a free man. I come down the Ohia riva and was workin' for the Whites. I wasn't any soldier. It wer'nt much different than being a slave though. I seen all the bad things that the Whites were doing. A couple of weeks back, I was at Ft. Henry up the riva."

He turned and looked at Blue Jacket. "You asked me why I was a starin' at ya. Well, you and another fella came to the fort and you spoke to the Cap'n and gave him some kinda letter. I was there and saw ya. If Id'a talked like you talked to the Cap'n, they'd a kilt me sure. I was impressed at the way you were. I also wondered where you learnt to speak English."

Blue Jacket raised his hand and stopped Caesar again. He spoke to the others with a slight smile to his face. This time, there was some talk amongst the others. Blue Jacket turned back to Caesar.

"Continue."

Caesar looked back at Blue Jacket and then to the others. "Like I was sayin'...once I saw you and heard you speak, I made up my mind that I wanted to live with you Indians. I didn't want no more do to with the Whites. I figured that I would come down the riva and let myself be captured. That's why I'm here and why I didn't fight your men."

Blue Jacket translated what Caesar had said. One of the men turned and said something to the man in the center. The man in the center nodded at him and then turned to Blue Jacket and spoke. Blue Jacket smiled and turned to Caesar. He pointed to the man who had spoken.

This man who has spoken is Mkahdaywaymayqua. His name in English is Blackfish. The man he has spoken to is Hokolesqua. In English he is Chief Cornstalk. Blackfish wishes to adopt you as his son. He has seen your bravery. Chief Cornstalk has agreed with Blackfish. Tomorrow, you will stand and run before our village and be tested. You will run a gauntlet. If you survive this run it will prove your loyalty to us and to your new family. You will be accepted among us as our brother. Your past will be gone. It will remain only as a memory in you.

When Blue Jacket was finished, the two young men reappeared and took Caesar back to the hut that he had been in. They cut the leather strips that had bound his hands and pointed for him to go in. Caesar went in and sat down. In a short time a young girl brought food and water for him. He ate and drank quickly and within minutes his eyes became heavy. All of the emotion of the past few days had caught up to him. His body relaxed and he fell asleep.

In the middle of the night Caesar woke up. He had to relieve himself and went to the flap at the entrance of the hut and slowly pulled it back. As he peered out, he expected to see someone guarding the door. There was no one. He thought to himself as he stepped out, these people are very trusting. They have taken me for my word that I want to become one of them. Because of my word, they trust me that I would not try to escape. White men would have never trusted me. To the Indian, a man's word and his trust and loyalty were that man's essence. To the White man, at least those that he had been around and subjected too, these characteristics meant nothing. He had never met a White whose words he could believe, let alone trust.

Caesar stood alone now, and yet, as he stared up in the darkness of the night at the multitude of stars and felt the warm breeze of the spring night, he was not lonely. For one of the few times in his life, he felt peace. He was now in a place and with a people who would accept him as the man that he was. They did not care what his skin color was or what his past was. Perhaps his mother was right. God was in control and God, in His time, had brought him to these people. Caesar did not know what the future held but his mother's voice within him was speaking to him louder than ever. "It's all parta His big plan. We ain't never gonna understand it. We's just gotta 'cept it."

Caesar woke up in the morning early. He looked to the eastern sky and the sun was just breaking over the horizon and the trees. He was alive. He hadn't been up long, when two young braves came for him. As they led him through the village, he could see the crowd of people gathering. They had formed two facing parallel lines. The women, children and men had sticks and clubs. He wasn't exactly sure what was going to happen, but he was shoved into the line and the people began to frantically yell. He was hit on the shoulder by a club. He heard a yell from behind him in English "Run!" He ran. As he ran, he was beat on every side with sticks and branches. He ran as hard and fast as he could, slightly bent over, and caused many to miss him with their swings the entire way. As he neared the end of the line, he felt a trickle of blood on his forehead and over his left eye and could taste its warmth on his lip. He reached for his head and suddenly felt a strong blow to his head, this time from the right. He staggered forward and fell to one knee. Another blow landed on his right shoulder. He felt a sharp pain, but pushed himself to his feet. He could see the end of the line, but felt another blow to his right knee. He struggled forward, running and staggering until he finally broke free at the end of the line of people.

As he collapsed to the ground utterly exhausted and in considerable pain, he heard a simultaneous cheer from all around him. The same people who had just beat him, now carefully helped him to his feet and led him to another shelter. Not the one he had been in…in this one there was a fire and the warmth could be immediately felt as he was taken in. There were two women waiting on him who cleaned and dressed his wounds. As the women were tending to him, Blackfish entered. He looked straight at Caesar. Caesar returned his look and Blackfish nodded at Caesar, putting his hand upon his shoulder as he spoke to the women. Caesar didn't understand what Blackfish had said. Blackfish spoke again to the women. Both of them nodded to him, and he left as quickly as he had come.

Caesar, because of his wiry strength and speed had survived this test of initiation. What he did not know was that they had made it easy for him to survive. Most, who were made to run the gauntlet, were beaten so severely that they died. Blackfish and Cornstalk had made sure that Caesar's run would only be a test of the words he had spoken. That he wanted to live with them and become a part of them.

Chapter 22
October 4, 2012

Zane Shawnee Caverns, Bellefontaine, Logan County Ohio

John Parker was at the Caverns just after 9:00am that Saturday morning. He had taken the 10:00am tour along with several others and was making his way through the museum when the Professor arrived around 11:15. He had seen the professor come into the gift shop and watched as he was talking to the woman behind the ticket counter. Within a few minutes, he saw the young man who had guided his cave tour come into the gift shop. He was now talking to the Professor and the woman behind the counter. John decided to continue to look through the museum and stay as out of sight of the professor as possible. He didn't want the professor to see him. He wasn't sure if the professor would recognize him, but he wasn't going to take any chances. If the professor left, he would just tail him.

As John looked into the display case with the silver armbands, he noticed the silver medallion. Suddenly his heart began to race. Right in front of his eyes was the medallion he had the impressions of in his pocket. He hadn't seen anything unusual in the cave, but this was just a confirmation to him that the letter he had copied and had heard the old man reading to his son was real. There had to be silver.

John slipped around and took a look into the gift shop. The professor wasn't there. He must have left while he was staring at the medallion. Without hesitation, he left the museum and was quickly out the door of the gift shop. The young man was still talking to the lady behind the counter as he went by. He didn't see the professor in the parking lot, so he turned and headed toward the steps that led down to the hiking trail that went through the ravine. The sign said Tecumseh Gorge.

"That guy seemed to be in a little of a hurry," said John to Emma.

"Yeah...that was kinda strange. He was on your 10:00am tour and paid to go into the museum. He said he didn't need anyone as a guide...just wanted to look around on his own," Emma replied. "He wasn't in there very long."

"I'm gonna check out where he's going. I'll be back in a little bit," John said to Emma as he headed toward the door of the gift shop.

"Alright John...be back in time for the next tour."

"Not a problem."

The Professor was already down the steps and a hundred yards further down the trail that led toward the creek that flowed through the ravine by the time Parker was out the door of the gift shop. It was a beautiful early fall morning. The sky was a deep blue and the sunlight was trickling through the trees lighting parts of the forest floor. There was a gentle breeze coming from the Northeast that made the leaves on the trees flutter and cast constantly moving shadows throughout the woods. The leaves had just started to turn into their fall colors and for a moment the Professor stopped and enjoyed the beauty of the bottomland. It was quiet and the Professor was alone as he thought to himself. What would a "Feather Rock", if it existed, look like. The ravine stretched for almost a mile back to the road and went another ¾ or so of a mile further downstream. Where would he even begin to look? How could he find a tree that had a marking on it that would be at least two hundred years old? If there was a tree, it was probably long gone. As for a "Feather Rock", he had no idea what that would be either. He was assuming that it had to be a large enough rock to be noticed. But, just what was he looking for?

The trail he was following was well worn and easy to follow. The trail was dry, but in some spots there were pools of muddy water that he had to walk around. There were large White Oaks, whose acorns had begun to fall. There were large Sycamore trees whose white bark contrasted with the abundance of the early fall colors. There were a few Beeches and Elms. There were the grays and deep browns of the hardwood's bark and the greens, yellows and early reds on the leaves of the trees, scattered bushes and saplings. The forest floor was leaf-covered on each side of the trail as it led down toward the depression of the ravine to the creek.

As the Professor continued down the gently sloping trail to the creek, he couldn't help but notice that on the other side of the creek, the terrain rose abruptly in a cliff some 40 feet high before it leveled off to a ridge with more oaks and a few large pines. A layer of top soil was easily seen at the top of the cliff and water trickled from the between the layers of rock that had been revealed over time, cascading over the layers of rock as it fell to the creek below.

The trail split upstream and downstream at the edge of the creek. Downstream to his left, on the opposite side of the creek, was a considerable depression where the water from a small creek that had formed fell some 25 feet to the creek. The creek and the entire ravine bottom land had small and large moss covered rocks strewn randomly amidst the saplings, blackberry bushes and brushy undercover. The creek had a few fallen trees that went from bank to bank in various ages of decomposition.

As the Professor made his way around a bend in the creek, he noticed a young couple to his left, about 10 yards in from the creek, sitting on the branch of a large oak tree. The thick main trunk of the tree rose only three or four feet from the ground and made an almost 90 degree angle to the left. The trunk extended almost 8-10 feet horizontally before it resumed its upward growth. The couple was sitting on the extended branch that came off of the main trunk before it grew back upwards. This branch and the main trunk of the tree gave the appearance of a football goal post.

As the Professor slowly made his way along the path the couple waved and nodded. "Good morning."

The Professor smiled and returned their greeting.

As he continued down the edge of the stream he tried to imagine what the area would have looked like 200 years before. It was difficult. In reality he thought, it really couldn't have changed much, with the exception of back up at the gift shop, museum and cave entrance and the developed areas of the parking lot and campgrounds. He knew that there had never been a village on the grounds but that the Indians traveled through the area in route from villages. Three miles from the caverns was Zanesfield. Zanesfield was the Wyandotte village of Chief Tarhe, the Crane.[lvii] Chief Moluntha,[lviii] a Shawnee Chief, had his village a few miles to the west and Bluejacket's Town[lix] was now a part of Bellefontaine. Wapatomica Valley was within five miles and it had been a major village of the Shawnee People.[lx] In fact, John had told him that there were three "marker trees" on the property and that this had been an historic crossroads for the Indians traveling through the area. If this was true, then they would have walked along this same creek on the same side that he was now walking. If there was a "Feather Rock" it must be somewhere along this trail. But which way and what the heck did it look like?

The Professor began to look at the profiles of each large boulder that was within 10 to 15 yards of the creek trail. He was trying to picture a feather outlined as a silhouette on the side or top of a boulder. *What the heck would that look like?* He thought to himself, this *is like trying to find the proverbial "needle in a haystack" and I don't even know what the needle looks like*. He hadn't seen anything from a distance on any of the larger boulders or rocks and decided to just systematically go to each one and look on the surface for anything resembling a feather.

Parker had tailed the Professor at a distance, acting like he was just walking the trail and enjoying the scenery in the ravine. He was now leaning against a large White Oak watching the Professor as he examined a large, moss covered rock about 50 yards away. His body was turned to the side as he leaned against the tree so that the Professor, if he were to look his way, would not be able to see him. What Parker did not know was that John had been tailing him and was now watching him from a short distance away.

Parker watched the Professor, as he looked close up at the large rock. This was the third rock that he had examined. What the heck is he doing he was thinking to himself as he heard someone coming along the trail and turned to see John. As John passed, he looked straight at Parker.

"Good morning. How are you?" asked John without stopping.

Parker replied back to John, as he pushed with his shoulder away from the tree. "Fine...thank you...just enjoying the scenery."

"It is beautiful" replied John, as he continued on down the trail, trying to act as casual as possible.

John continued down the trail and saw the Professor. He called out to the Professor.

"Professor Stevensen!"

The Professor looked up and waved at John. John waved back and made his way over to the Professor.

"How's it going?" said John.

"I'm fine," replied the Professor, "I really just don't know what I'm looking for."

John lowered his voice and almost in a whisper, with his back to Parker said,

"Don't look up, but there is a guy back there that went on the cave tour this morning, went into the museum and from what I'm guessing, followed you down here. As I came down the trial, he was leaning against a tree, watching you. Keep doing what you're doing and when you get a chance, see if you can get a look at him and see if you recognize him?

"Not a problem," answered the Professor. Do you know him?"

"No...never seen him before."

John had somewhat shielded the Professor from the direct line of sight of Parker, but the Professor had just enough of a view of him as he looked up at John.

"No...I don't think I know who he is." The Professor hesitated. "Wait a minute...I think I do recognize him. I think he's the guy who used to work at the nursing home where my father is. My father said that he was the guy who hit him. He might have taken the..." The Professor caught himself almost saying that he may have taken the clay impression of the medallion in the museum.

"Taken what? John asked.

"Oh...nothing," replied the Professor.

John looked at his watch. "I better get going. It's almost eleven. I have to get back to see if anyone has signed up for the eleven o'clock tour of the cave. That guy has started to move on down the trail. I'd keep an eye on him. "

"Ok. Said the Professor, I'm going to keep looking for this "Feather Rock." Whatever it is...but I'll keep an eye on him."

If you quit looking for the rock before I'm done with the next tour, wait for me in the gift shop. I'd like to come back down here with you. That is if you're not in hurry to go anywhere?"

"Sounds good to me," said the Professor.

"Maybe together we can find this rock."

"I'll see you in a little bit then," said John as he headed back up the trail.

The Professor saw another larger boulder a little further downstream and headed over to it. He glanced in the direction that he had last seen Parker and noticed that he had left the trail and was down in the creek less than 50 yards away, almost out of view, behind the bank of the creek as it took a sharp bend to the right.

Chapter 23
June 17, 1774

Chalahgawtha on the Scioto River

Caesar was left alone and rested throughout the afternoon. In the evening, he was brought food and water by one of the same women that had tended to him the day before. After he had eaten, he stood and went to the entrance of the hut that he was in. He was not guarded so he thought that it would be ok to go outside. He went out and stood close to the entrance of the hut. The village was full of activity. There were people everywhere going about their daily activities. A few glanced at him, but most did not pay any attention to him. A few small children saw him and ran over to him. He smiled at them and they began to touch his arms feeling his skin and especially his curly black hair. As they touched him, he continued to smile and the children spoke to each other and giggled.

While the children were touching Caesar, Caesar noticed that Blue Jacket had come out of the long house that he had been in and was walking toward them. As he got closer, he spoke to the children and they all ran off. He motioned for Caesar to go back into the hut that he had been in. Caesar went in and Blue Jacket followed him. In the hut, Blue Jacket motioned for Caesar to sit.

Blue Jacket spoke to him in English. "You have passed this test of our initiation into our tribe. You have shown fortitude and courage. Blackfish was pleased. Tomorrow morning, you will go through our ritual of adoption. You will become Shawnee."

Caesar slept well during the night. He wasn't sure what would happen in the morning, but at least he knew he wasn't going to be killed and that he was going to be adopted into the tribe...adopted by one of their chiefs, Blackfish.

In mid-morning, two women came to Caesar's hut. They were carrying several bowls of various colors of paint. They spoke to him. He didn't understand them, but they motioned for him to remove all of his clothing. Caesar began to remove his clothing. The women, unlike what he was used to, did not leave or turn their backs to him. He stood naked, facing them and they began to paint his entire body in various colors. When they were finished, they motioned for him to follow them to the large, long building. When they entered, he was taken to the same room where he had stood before the chiefs. Blackfish and several other men were in the room, including Bluejacket. Blackfish got up and came over to Caesar. He looked upon him and then straight into his eyes. He began to recite an ancient Shawnee adoption chant over him. When Blackfish was finished, he motioned to the women who led Caesar back out and to the waters of the Scioto River. The women dunked him in the cold Scioto water several times and scrubbed all the paint off of him. When they were finished, they took him back to what he heard them call the msikamelwi. There they dressed him in a blouse and buckskin leggings. His face was carefully painted by one of the women, and a metal disk with an eagle feather attached to it was put in his hair. As he stood there, the villagers filed into the building and took seats on the mats on the floor. They lit and smoked pipes. Blackfish stood by Caesar and spoke. Bluejacket translated for Caesar.

"My new son...the colors that these women scrubbed from you in the river represented all of the ways of the white man and his world that you lived in. The removal of these colors means that all of the white man has been removed from you. You are now clean."

As Blackfish said this to him, he couldn't help but remember the time when he was a small boy that he was taken down to the small river near the farm he grew up on and was dunked in the river and baptized by the preacher man. The preacher said that he was now a Christian and that all of his sins had been forgiven. He wasn't sure what the preacher meant about his sins being forgiven because one, he really didn't even know what a sin was and two, he didn't think he had done any sinning. He had been a good boy, always worked hard and did what his momma said and taught him.

"You are now my son and a part of this people. You will be called Penegashega. This means "Change of Feathers". You have flown a great distance in your life, but now you have new feathers. You have the feathers of an Eagle and you are now a strong and free man. You are now Shawnee!"

Caesar wasn't sure what to do. He turned to Bluejacket and all he could say was "Thank ya. I 'm honored to be a Shawnee and to be Blackfish's new son. As Bluejacket translated, Caesar did the only thing he could think of. He went to Blackfish and stuck his hand out to shake. Blackfish smiled and clasped Caesar's hand. Bluejacket also smiled as Caesar went from person to person shaking hands.

Over the next few weeks, Caesar participated in all of the activities of a young man in the Shawnee tribal life. His gun was given back to him and he went out on hunts. He quickly began to learn the Shawnee language. Other than his skin color, every day he became more and more Shawnee. He had never felt more at peace with himself. He was treated as an equal and most importantly; he now knew that he was a completely free man.

In early July, Bluejacket told Caesar that he was going to go to the Kentucky lands with a small group of warriors. Caesar knew of Kentucky. He had heard it talked about by the Whites. He had heard that the limestone soil was rich and good for growing crops and for the grazing of livestock. That there was an abundance of clean water and timber. It was a land that the White people wanted to settle on. What he heard from Bluejacket was a different story. Bluejacket explained to him that this had been the hunting land of the Shawnee as well as several others, including the Cherokee. No one owned the land. It was a shared hunting ground. Now, the Whites were claiming the land and beginning to make settlements. The Shawnee would not allow the settlements and they were going to the Kentucky lands to attack and destroy a new settlement.

Caesar and the other 32 warriors, led by Cornstalk, had spent three days traveling from their village on the Scioto to where they were now hidden, waiting for daylight to ambush any of the settlers that would venture across the clearing and away from the cabins that had been built. Another 20 Mingo had joined them one day earlier. They had traveled silently and undetected, until yesterday morning when they had ambushed a party of four men near a spring. They had killed all four taking them by surprise, scalping them and taking their weapons. Now they were positioned in the forest on the edges of the clearing the men had made surrounding the log cabins that had been erected. They had counted 41 men the evening before. Their plan was to ambush any party of men first. When the others came out to rescue them, they would attack. Their strategy was to catch the men off guard and out in the open. They would then attack and burn the cabins.

Inside the cabins, most of the men were up, as was the usual practice, before dawn. They were eating salt pork, beans, hard biscuits and drinking coffee, talking of the day's work that they had before them. Some had been assigned to continue clear cutting and bringing the logs in to the center of the town and others were to begin the construction of a fort that had been laid out. The fort would encompass the spring, as well as the cabins they had built. The men were led by Col. James Harrod. Harrod had been part of a party of surveyors headed by Captain Thomas Bullitt who had surveyed the land the year before. He had led the men down the Monongahela to Fort Pitt and then moved on down the Ohio in early May. They ascended the Kentucky River in canoes to the mouth of what was called Landing Run and then passed over to the Salt River. On the 16th of June, they set up camp near a large spring that spewed pure, clear water. They had immediately laid out a town on the South side of the spring and built six cabins. They had named the town Harrodstown, giving each man half-acre lots in the new town and five acre out-lots out of the town. [lxi]

The Indians had spread in a wide arc throughout the tree line south of the cabins. They lay concealed behind downed trees; rocks and a few had climbed up into a few of the larger trees. From the cabins and even from within 50 feet of the edge of the clearing, they were invisible. Caesar was 10 feet to the left of Blue Jacket.

To his left was a brave named Silver Heels and to his left was Big Fighter. Cornstalk was positioned almost 50 yards to the left of Silver Heels. He wasn't like the White commanders, who stayed back behind the fighting men; Cornstalk was one of the fighting men. Caesar was concealed behind a large downed oak and had his gun trained toward the clearing. His eyes were heavy with the little sleep that he had over the last few days, but he was more nervous than he had ever been in his life. He had never been in a battle before and now he was set to fight alongside Indians against the whites. He had been praying earlier that God would protect him. He wondered if the men in the cabins ever prayed. If they did, did they pray for God's protection out here in this wilderness? If they were both praying for God's protection, how did God choose who he was favoring? Or, did He even care at all. How could God be in control of everything like his momma had said? He wondered what the other braves were thinking at this moment. Were they as nervous as he was? Were some of them scared?

Caesar heard the sound of a dove cooing from almost the opposite side of the clearing from where he was positioned. He glanced to the east, gazing at the lightening sky that stretched between the horizon and the blackness of the night. It was now light enough to clearly see the cabins. They were no longer just dark cabins with the yellow lights from the oil lamps within breaking the darkness through the small windows. He heard Silver Heels coo in response and noticed that six men had just appeared on the far side of one of the cabins. They were headed in Caesar, Blue Jacket and Silver Heels direction. Caesar could feel his heart begin to race. It was pounding hard as the men made their way through the clearing. Caesar's grip on his gun tightened and his palms had begun to sweat. He had never felt like this before. He was afraid to move as he sighted down his gun's barrel. He had it aimed directly at the chest of one of the men as they came closer. Blue Jacket had told him and the others to pick out a man that would be headed in a line directly at them and to keep their gun trained on him. No one was to fire until he fired. They were to make each shot count and to reload as quickly as possible, but not to rush into the clearing. There were to be no war cries. They were to keep their positions hidden.

Cornstalk was hoping that with the sound of gunfire, the other whites would recklessly run to the aid of their fellow men not realizing that it was too late for them and that they were headed straight into the hornet's nest.

The men from the cabins were only 15 yards away. They had been talking the entire time since they had left the cabins and now Caesar could actually hear what they were saying. A couple had just set their rifles against tree stumps when the screech of a hawk split the silence of the early morning. This was Cornstalk's signal. It was answered with the exploding sounds and bright flares of muzzle-flash. Smoke rose from the edge of the woods. Caesar had fired and when the smoke had cleared, he saw that the man that he had been aiming at was lying on his side with red seeping from two chest wounds. None of the six men were standing. There were a few moans, but most of the men were motionless. Not one of the Indians had moved and most had already reloaded their weapons. The woods were silent except for the sounds of the men racing from the cabins with their weapons yelling "Injuns! Injuns!"

They raced haphazardly across the clearing toward the site of the downed men. When they reached the downed men, Cornstalk screeched again. Another volley came from the Indians followed by Cornstalks signal to attack. All of the warriors swept from their hiding spots with cries that split the stillness. The whites all cried out in confusion and terror. Those who had not been hit by the last volley from the Indian's guns ran back toward the cabins. A few of the men were overtaken. Caesar saw one warrior's hatchet bury deep in the back of the head of one of the escaping white men. As the man fell, the warrior cried out in blood lust. There was screaming everywhere. As some of the settlers made it to the doors of the cabins and the doors closed, the sounds of their rifles came with the bright flashes from notches in the cabin walls. One warrior jerked suddenly to his right. He cried out as he grabbed his right shoulder and fell. The Indians were within 30 yards of the cabins as more gunfire erupted from the cabins. Cornstalk gave the signal calling off the attack as he realized that the men who had not been killed or overtaken had made it safely back to the cabins. All of the warriors quickly retreated with bullets spraying the ground near them. Two grabbed the young warrior who had been hit in the shoulder carrying him to the safety of the woods. The firing had stopped as the Indians had neared the wood line. Some however, had stopped and were in the process of scalping the men they had killed. As each man's hair was removed, the warrior who removed it held it high letting out a blood-curling shout as the bloody hair-piece was displayed to all of the others. While the scalping was going on, others gathered the men's guns, powder horns, shot, and knives and stripped the settlers of their clothing. Those in the cabins were helpless and could only watch. They could do nothing.

The battle had lasted only around 10 minutes. The woods had grown eerily silent again. Hidden and protected inside the woods line, the Indians had no fear of the settlers leaving the cabins and attacking. Several of the men attended to the shoulder wound of the young warrior. All of the men were talking amongst themselves. The excitement of the battle had not worn off yet. Caesar was still somewhat out of breath from the run back from near the cabins. He had fired his weapon and had run, screaming with the others, tomahawk in hand. Blue Jacket and Silver Heels came to him and had nodded to him, Blue Jacket, putting his hand on Caesar's shoulder said "You have fought bravely in your first battle. You did not hesitate under Cornstalks commands and this day you have helped us to defeat these whites. We must never let them settle in this Kentucky land."

"We gonna attack them cabins?" Caesar asked Blue Jacket.

"No. We have given them a warning. These lands are ours. There will be no more bloodshed today."

During the day, as the Indians made their way North, Caesar found himself deep in thought. He was sure that he had killed a man. The man he had aimed at went down with the others. He had been scalped and the warrior who scalped him came to Caesar and gave him the man's hunting knife. Caesar had smiled at the warrior and nodded a thank you to him. Caesar was struggling with his emotions. Part of him was proud that he had acted bravely in the attack. Part of him was proud that he had gained some respect as a Shawnee warrior. Another part of him was saddened that he had actually killed a man....a man who probably had a family back in Virginia where he had come from...a man who would never return to

Virginia...a man who would never be heard from, or of again. He was sure that he would just be buried and that would be the end of this man. His wife and children would never see him again. He was gone from this earth...perhaps a memory to some. He wondered how many Indians and other Whites had died out here in this wilderness. Their bones left to bleach and slowly rot away, none of them ever to be heard from. For most, their existence just ceased and there was no memory of them. If he were to die or be killed, no one back where he came from would know. A few of his Indian family would be saddened, but the wife and children that he had left back in Virginia would never know. He couldn't help but wonder what his life or any other man's life was really about. Why had some men been born white and some black, some Indian? Why did the white men think that they were superior to all of the others? They had brought his people to this land as slaves. They now wanted the Indian's land. How much land did they need? At least the Indian's were fighting them. He wondered if his people in Africa had fought to not be taken. Why did they let themselves be taken and used as slaves? Why hadn't they fought like this people he was now a brother of? He knew that the he would probably never have the answers to his questions, especially his biggest. What was it all for?

Chapter 24
October 4, 2012

Zane Shawnee Caverns, Bellefontaine, Logan County Ohio

Professor Stevensen and John Logan had been looking for the "Feather Rock" for over an hour. John had come back down to help the Professor look after he had taken another group of visitors on the cave tour. As he came down the trail to join the Professor, he passed Parker heading up the trail toward the parking lot. He had gotten a real good look at him, but both men had intentionally passed by each other trying not to make eye contact.

"I'm getting a little tired of looking at these rocks," said the Professor.

"Yeah...I know," said John. "It kinda seems to be a waste of time. Especially when we don't even know what we're looking for, or if it really even exists."

As the Professor was moving some brush away from another rock, John happened to glance back down the trail along the creek that they had been following. They had moved over 150 yards down the creek. The large Oak marker tree caught his eye. It was the tree that the young couple had been sitting on as the Professor had come down the creek trail. As he looked at the tree, back almost 100 yards, he suddenly wondered what the tree had been marking. He knew that the Indians had called them "thong" trees because of the way they had bent and tied a sapling to the ground to produce a permanent 90 degree angle in the tree. He knew that the bent saplings had served as trail makers as they grew. That they had been used to mark or point the way.

"Professor," John said excitedly. See that tree back there that has the branch bent over?"

The Professor looked up from what he was doing. "Yeah," he said. "The one that looks like it was damaged when it was young?"

"Yeah...that one," John said. "Well, it wasn't damaged. It was bent to look like that as a marker. That tree when it was a sapling was bent and its upper end was tied to the ground with stakes using strips of animal skin or rawhide. Over time, the rawhide would have deteriorated, but the trees form would have been set and the leader would have turned back up toward the sun and continued growing. As it grew, it formed that horizontal "Z" shape and was supposed to point or lead to something or somewhere. A lot of times it was to the next village. It pointed in the direction you were to go. Sometimes they put rocks on the ground to emphasize even more the direction indicated by the bend. Some of the trees pointed to water. Others were boundary trees. If I remember right, others were called "treasure trees." Come on Professor! That's it. That tree just might be telling us where to look. The letter mentioned a marked tree. What if it meant a marker tree?"

As the Professor and John Logan were practically running back down the trail toward the marker tree, Parker eased from behind the tree that he had been observing them from. After he had passed John on the trail to the parking lot, he had circled around the parking lot and the gift store and had slipped into the woods. He didn't want John and the Professor to know that he was watching them so he had faked leaving. He had made his way through the woods in the general direction that he had last seen the Professor and quietly began to watch the both of them. He wasn't quite sure what they were doing, but it was obvious that they were looking for something. Now, they were moving excitedly back up the trail and he needed to get a little closer to see what they were up to or what they had found.

"I know that that tree isn't pointing toward a village. It's pointing almost due north. The Shawnee and Mingo villages were all west and southwest of here," said John as he pointed in the direction of Bellefontaine. "It's definitely not pointing to the cave entrance either. It's over there and up the hill."

The Professor and John stood at the base of the tree looking in the direction that the bend in the tree was facing. There were no rocks piled near the tree, which wasn't surprising considering how long ago the tree would have been staked out.

"How old is this tree?" said the Professor.

"I'm not really sure," said John. "But it's at least a couple hundred years old."

"Well John. Let's start walking in the direction that the tree is pointing and let's just see what we find," said the Professor, as he pointed in the direction that the trunk was pointing. John followed the Professor as the afternoon shadows began to transform the forest along the creek bottom. It had also become windier and overcast and in the far distance thunder could be heard from an unusual fall thunderstorm. It was still a long way off, but both John and the Professor could feel the changes in the air as the storm was approaching.

"I don't see anything unusual that the tree could be pointing at," said John as he wandered off to the Professors right a few feet.

"Me either," said the Professor. "Everything looks the same as everywhere else down here."

They had gone about 200 yards through the bottom when John stopped at the base of the hill that rose up from the bottom. Just ahead of him about 30 yards or so, was a large boulder. It stood alone on the side of the hill.

"Professor...look at that boulder up ahead." The Professor had been looking down at the ground and looked up to where John was pointing. They both could feel the storm getting closer. It had begun to drizzle and the wind was stronger, swirling through the tops of the trees.

"Let's check it out before it begins to pour. We can always come back, but that's the only thing other than trees that's in the direction that that marker tree is pointing," said John.

"Let's take a quick look at it and then we better get to some cover," said the Professor. "It's gonna start pouring here shortly and being in the woods with this wind and the thunder and lightning's not such a great idea."

Parker was watching the Professor and John. He had watched as both stood near the large misshapen Oak and as John pointed in several directions. Just to the West, the sky had darkened and he had heard the thunder. It had now started to sprinkle and it wouldn't be long before it would start to pour. The wind started to pick up and gusted through the ravine as he watched the two quickly head away from the tree toward the base of the hill. He watched as they headed up the hill in the direction of a big boulder. They stopped and were looking at the boulder from all sides. It looked like both of them were running their fingers on the top of the rock almost as though they were tracing something. A tremendous crack came from behind him, startling him. Out of the corner of his eye he saw the bolt of lightning hit a tree just to his right. He had never seen a lightning strike before and he wasn't sticking around for any more. As he turned to look back at John and the Professor, the rain started to come down hard. John and the Professor were headed down the side of the hill and toward the shelter of the gift shop. He headed the shortest way out of the woods to the parking lot. It was no longer a matter of being seen, but one of being safe. He would come back later that night and check to see what they had been looking at and just what it was that John and the Professor had discovered.

Chapter 25
Summer, 1774

Chalahgawtha on the Scioto River

Caesar and the war party had returned within a few days of their attack on the settlers at Harrodstown. The entire village had greeted them and in the evening around a large fire, the people of the village ate, drank and danced in celebration. All of the warriors told the story of their trip to the Kentucky land to drive the white settlers from the hunting grounds. To Caesar, each and every day was a learning experience. Each day and each new experience he learned more and more about these remarkable people who had adopted him as one into their tribe. These people were not savages as the Whites had portrayed them. To him, they were more caring and loving than any of the Whites that he had been around. Even as a free man, the Whites had never accepted him as an equal.

On this particular warm summer evening, Caesar could not help but notice the continual glances of one young woman during the evenings' celebrations. He knew nothing of the Shawnee customs and the next time that he caught her glancing at him, he boldly approached her and sat beside her. At first she appeared to be embarrassed and she and a few of the other women around her giggled. Caesar looked at her and smiled. She smiled back. It had been a long time since Caesar had been with a woman. He had, of course, thought of the wife that he had back in

Virginia. Since he had left, his thoughts on occasion had wandered to her gentle touch, her moistness, the touch of her breasts, her gentle touch of his manhood and the coupling and climax that they had enjoyed. It was those thoughts and during the times when he had those thoughts that he had felt the most alone. There were times when he was alone that he couldn't help but think of her. His thoughts led to a stirring in his loins and he would become hard and stroke himself to relief.

As he sat next to this young woman, his leg touched hers and she reached over and put her hand on his leg. When her hand touched his leg, he looked at her and she smiled. He placed his hand on top of hers. Her touch had aroused him. Suddenly, she stood and pulled him to his feet. He stood and she quietly led him away from the circle of people down a small trail that led towards the river. She had held his hand tighter as she led him. Neither of them spoke.

When they got to the river, she led him down the trail along the bank until they came to a small clearing. The river took a bend to the right in front of them and had created a small sand bar. She went down the bank and motioned for him to follow. As they stood on the sand she pointed up to the moon that had raised full in the sky above the tree line. The sky was clear and there was a gentle breeze and the only sound was that of the river as it rippled over the stones in a shallow area near the bank. As Caesar stood looking at up at the moon, the woman sat down on the sand and was now pulling him down to sit next to her. Caesar looked at her and into her eyes as he leaned over and kissed her. She returned his kiss. When the kiss was over, she stood and removed her buckskin dress. She was now standing naked. Caesar rose to his feet and put his arms around her waist and pulled her close to him and kissed her again. This time more slowly. As he kissed her, he felt her reach down and grab his now hard manhood and then tugged to move his loin cloth to the side. As she gently stroked him, she pulled him down to the sand on top of her, spreading her legs and inviting him to enter into her. Caesar felt her moistness and warmth as he entered her. Within moments they both climaxed and lay spent in each other's arms. Neither had spoken, but it wasn't necessary.

The next morning, the woman brought Caesar food and they spent most of the day together. Within weeks, Caesar had taken the woman as his wife.

During the hot summer months of 1774, the village under Cornstalk had confirmed what they had learned, that an agent for the royal governor of Virginia, John Murray, the Earl of Dunmore, had taken possession of Fort Pitt, and had renamed it Fort Dunmore. Dunmore had then initiated attacks against local Indian settlements along the upper Ohio. From their Shawnee brothers along the upper Ohio, they heard that the Delaware, under the influence of Moravian missionaries, had kept peace with the whites, but the Shawnee had pressed for war. They also learned that Dunmore had called out the militia of southwest Virginia, creating two armies. Dunmore was personally leading some seventeen hundred men from the north and a General named Andrew Lewis was directing eight hundred troops. Lewis' troops, under the direction of a Major McDonald had left Wheeling and marched to the Wapatomica towns on the Muskingum River. Cornstalk had ordered all of the Ohio River villages north of Point Pleasant to be abandoned and when McDonald arrived he found the villages deserted. He burnt some of villages, destroyed some cornfields, and then returned to Wheeling. Lewis's men then headed to the Kanawha Valley to the point of the confluence of the Great Kanawha and Ohio Rivers to establish a camp and wait for Dunmore's arrival.[lxii]

It was now late September but in the summer months Cornstalk had organized a confederacy of Wyandot, Delaware and Mingo living in Ohio to resist the continued white encroachment into the Ohio River Valley. They had allied themselves to Logan to turn the frontier "red with Long Knives' blood." Cornstalk's name now struck fear into the hearts of the white settlers up and down the Ohio frontier, and he had also gained the respect of all of the other Indian tribes.

After participating in the raid into Kentucky, and after marrying, Caesar felt accepted as a Shawnee. In his mind, his old life was completely gone. The Shawnee treated him as though he had been born a Shawnee. Each and every day he continued to learn their language and their customs. Each and every day, and in every way, he had become a Shawnee warrior.

Throughout the village, there were others who had been adopted into the tribe. There were many white women who were now Shawnee, all traces of their white existence gone. There were two other blacks, both runaway slaves and there were several young white warriors. One day Caesar had approached a young warrior who obviously was a white man. He spoke in English to the man, but the man only responded back to him in Shawnee. He knew no English. He said his name was White Wolf.[lxiii] He had no remembrance of living in the white world. He was Shawnee.

As the summer drew to an end, Caesar felt the urgency of the Shawnee position of defending their land from the white incursion. He listened to Blackfish and Pucksinwah, knew of Logan's pain and understood the words of Cornstalk, perhaps even more than any other warrior. He had spoken against the whites at several council meetings and for war, and now, as Cornstalk spoke to the leaders of the Shawnee, as well as the leaders of the other tribes in the confederacy, Cornstalk's words struck deep into his heart.

"Remember this: now there is no turning back; now the seed of war has been planted and watered and already it sprouts. Whether it thrives and grows or is cut down remains yet to be seen."

October 9th, 1774 "Tu-endie-wie"

Caesar understood as Cornstalk called for Indian unity to stop Lewis before Dunmore could come down the Ohio bringing more militia to come against them. In a few days they would go to the point where the

Great Kanawha and the Ohio joined and they would destroy the militia under Lewis. On October 9th, the army under Cornstalk arrived at the Ohio. Cornstalk's Northern Confederacy was some 800 to 1,000 warriors strong and composed of Shawnee, Delaware, Mingo, Wyandotte and Cayuga. The chiefs under Cornstalk were Logan, Red Hawk, Blue Jacket and Elinipsico. They had crossed the Ohio and had camped in the hills just north and east of the mouth of the Kanawha in the land known by the Indians as "Tu-endie-wie," "the point between two waters." They were up hours before the sunrise readying for their attack and during the night they had been silent and there were no fires. The night before they had come to the Ohio, they held a ceremony of purification. During the ceremony they drank a vegetable concoction that was to give them energy and then they began a fast for the two days before the battle, led by the holy men who summoned the supernatural aid and asked for the assistance of the spirits. All of the warriors painted, feathered and their heads shaven to the scalp lock on the crown of their heads, whooped and danced, falling in behind Cornstalk who led them singing his war song.

The morning of the battle, the weather was beautifully clear and the water was low in the Ohio and Kanawha Rivers. The night before, Cornstalk's scouts had reported that the militiamen had been arriving almost daily and that they were expecting Dunmore to arrive within days. They estimated that Lewis had around 1,100 men. They were all Virginians.

Shortly after daybreak two soldiers by the name of Robertson and Hickman, had left camp without permission and had gone up the Ohio to hunt. They were discovered as they came upon the outskirts of the Indian's encampment and were fired upon. The shots echoed through the hills along the Ohio Valley. Hickman was killed and Robertson ran wildly, hollering as he escaped back to the camp. As Robertson entered the soldiers' camp he was yelling that he had discovered a body of Indians that covered four acres of ground. Upon his arrival all of the soldier's camp was thrown into confusion. Col. Lewis remained calm however, lighting his pipe, supposing that a scouting party of Indians, similar to the ones that had watched their movement since they had left Fort Union had just discovered the men. As Col. Lewis passed his outer guard however, the Indians broke through the tree line and began their attack. There was little breeze and the musket smoke hung low to the ground as the Indians attacked the soldiers whose line stretched across the high ground skirting Crooked Run. The suddenness and fierceness of the attack had startled Col. Lewis and his men and Col. Fleming was ordered to reinforce Col. Lewis immediately, forming a battle line that stretched for just over a half of a mile.

The Indians were spaced no more than ten feet apart as they continued their assault on the soldiers. When the Indians reached the forming line of soldiers, the scene was chaotic. There was the ringing of the rifles and the roar of the muskets, the smoke, the clubbed guns and the flashing of knives along with the screams of the men in hand to hand combat. The death groans could be heard everywhere along with the moans of the wounded. The Indians were crushing through the brush as they advanced upon the soldiers. The soldiers began to retreat with the ferocious onslaught and the Indians pursued them. Pistol shots could be heard, as it became a battle of every man for himself. Throughout the woods there was the shrieking of the whites as Indians, covered with sweat and gore bore the trophies of those they had slain, their knives dripping with blood in one hand and their muskets, bent and smeared with brains and hair in the other continued in hot pursuit of the soldiers.

Col. Lewis was hit in the first hour of the engagement, but hid the mortal nature of his wound and continued to fight alongside his men trying to rally them to keep their lines. Exhausted from a loss of blood, he finally sunk to the ground. A few men carried him among the turmoil away from the battle to his tent, where he died around noon.

The battle continued along Crooked Run with heavy losses as brave men fell on both sides. The soldier's line began to fail around noon and as they were falling back, Col. Fleming made a resolute attempt to rally his troops forward again. As he fought, he was struck down by a tomahawk and as he was dying, was taken from the field. At his death, the troops gave way. General Lewis received word of the break in the troop's line and their retreat and ordered up Col. Field with reinforcements. Col. Field's command met the retreating troops and rallied them back to the battle that had now become a desperate, raging struggle by both the soldiers and the Indians.

Caesar had been up along with the other braves well before sunrise preparing himself for the attack on General Lewis' soldiers. During their trip to the Ohio, he had explained to Blue Jacket and Cornstalk that the soldiers that they were going to attack were probably some of the men he had lived with for a short time. They were called militiamen and many of them had experience fighting against the Indians. He explained that they understood the Indian's fighting strategies and that they were tough, courageous, and seasoned men. Cornstalk explained, "Yes. We know about these men. But we must stop these armies and these whites before they destroy our way of life and take all of our land. All of our people, as well as those that have joined us, are united in this battle. We will surprise this army. We will destroy it and the evil that is upon us. We will never make peace with these whites until they leave our lands. We are strong and will be upon them before the others arrive."

Caesar heard the shots not far to his left, just before sunrise, as he was moving into position for the attack. The braves had been moving into position for almost thirty minutes, forming a line that stretched for at least a half mile just inside the tree line on a small rise that followed a large creek. They had been told that the soldiers were camped just beyond the rise on the other side of the creek. From hill to hill it was only 150 yards. Caesar heard the screams of a man, just after he heard the shots, and almost simultaneously, Cornstalks cry to attack came.

To Caesars immediate right at the beginning of the battle was a young warrior whom he had befriended over the past few weeks. His name was Cheeseekau.[lxiv] His name meant "the Sting." Next to him was his Father, Pukeshinwau. Pukeshinwau was the head of Kispoko division of the Shawnee and was a well-respected war chief. When they heard Cornstalk's cry to attack all three were up without hesitation with all of the warriors and running toward the soldiers. As they rushed headlong towards the soldiers with their constant whooping and cursing, Caesar could feel their terror and rage. He felt the same. He fired his weapon and would duck down behind a fallen log or behind a tree, load, and fire again. He could hear the bullets whizzing past him. Several so close he felt a whiff of air on his neck and his face as the bullets flew by, thudding into trees, sending pieces of bark flying. The soldiers were keeping up a steady fire and Caesar saw many warriors fall, yelling in pain. They continued to move forward however with a remarkable resolution as the soldiers kept up their relentless fire, with a determination as strong as their own. At one point during the struggle, Caesar saw Cornstalk rapidly hurrying through the midst of all of the Indians with no fear, shouting to his warriors to "Be Strong! Be strong." Other chiefs ran continually along the line exhorting their men to "lie close and shoot well. Fight and be strong." Caesar watched as Cornstalk, only 30 yards away, took his tomahawk and with brunt force, laid open the head of one warrior who was showing signs of fear. With Cornstalk lifting the spirits of his warriors, the

Indians continued their headlong rush, sure of success when the soldiers ranks gave way with the initial assault.

Shortly after Col. Field arrived with his reinforcements and under an almost incessant fire, the Indians stopped their assault. It was almost 11 a.m. It was almost as if time stood still in the battle. The smoke from the guns hovered over the ground and through the trees down the battle line for over a mile. Above the trees the sky was a deep blue. Both the Indians and the soldiers stood. On their faces were terror, rage and disappointment. There was an eerie silence with the exception of the moans and cries of the wounded, as the dead and wounded were brought off from the battlefield. Men lay dead and dying everywhere, many with shattered limbs and lacerated flesh, pale, ghastly and disfigured. It was a gory site, their garments covered in blood.

The silence did not last long as the sound of a rifle or a musket was heard and all throughout the day, the Indians loudly cursed the soldiers and continued to pick off their leaders. Some of the Indians who spoke some English yelled at the soldiers "Where are your whistles now?" as they chided the soldiers in regard to the absence of any fifes. The Indians began a slow retreat in the afternoon attempting to draw the soldiers into an ambush, and those soldiers who were foolish enough to advance, were cut down by a barrage of gunfire. Earlier in the day, during heat of the battle, General Lewis had ordered a breastwork to be constructed from the Ohio to the Kanawha, thus severing the camp from the neighboring forest. The breastwork was formed by the cutting down of trees and laying their trunks and branches to form a barrier that was difficult to pass. It was designed to keep the Indians from advancing into the soldier's camp if they were to gain an advantage at some time during the battle, while at the same time to serve as protection to Lewis' garrison within. Later in the day, General Lewis noticing the retreat of Cornstalk's warriors detached three companies commanded by Captains John Stuart, George Matthews and Isaac Shelby. He gave them orders to move quietly beneath the banks of the Kanawha and Crooked run and try to advance on the Indian's rear. The maneuver by General Lewis' men was brilliantly executed and caught Cornstalk and the Indians completely off guard driving Cornstalk and his men into a full retreat around 4 p.m.

During the battle and as the Indians had been falling back, Caesar had kept Pukeshinwau and Cheeseekau in sight. Now, after retreating almost three miles, he lay close to both of them. All three were covered in blood and exhausted. Their faces were covered in sweat-smeared blood, gun smoke, dirt and war paint. They were almost unrecognizable. Suddenly, at the sound of a shot, Pukeshinwau reeled to his left. A bright red spot appeared and blossomed in the center of his chest. Cheeseekau crawled to his father, as Caesar watched. He cradled his father; both looked into the eyes of each other. Blood was filling Pukeshinwau's mouth and dribbled down his chin. His breathing was labored as he spoke to his son. "My son, always keep the dignity and honor of our family and never fail to lead your younger brothers to battle." Cheeseekau, with tears rolling down his eyes, could barely utter his response. It was a simple. "Yes father."

General Lewis and his Virginia militia believed that their victory was complete, but during the night Cornstalk led his army back across Ohio dumping many of his fallen warriors into the river.

Chapter 26
April, 1789

Apple Creek, Missouri
(Present Day, Perry County)

Caesar had arrived with his wife and three children, along with Cheeseekau, Tecumseh and some 100 hundred men, women and children of both the Chillicothe and Pekowi divisions of the tribe. They had left Ohio in the autumn of 1788 after receiving numerous invitations from Louis Lorimier. Lorimier was an Indian trader near Saint Genevieve (Missouri) that had been in contact with the Spanish government after the American Revolution, offering to colonize the Missouri area with Shawnee and Delaware if the Spanish would make land available. He had convinced the Spaniards to provide the land, as it would strengthen their defenses against the Osages to the west and the potential threat from the United States to the east.[lxv] For Caesar and the other Shawnee under Cheeseekau, they only wanted to be far away from the Whites. For the warriors, the move wasn't to get away from the defense of their homeland, but more for the protection of their families. There was no peace and security in the Ohio land for the Indian' and the years following the Battle at Point Pleasant[lxvi] had given no relief to the Shawnee tribes and families that called the Ohio lands their home.

After the Battle at Point Pleasant, Caesar watched as Cornstalk and his tribe of Mekoches agreed to peace and to surrender all prisoners who had been acquired as captives.

He also felt the disappointment, along with many others, as Cornstalk sadly acknowledged the loss of Kentucky. Cornstalk also kept the whites informed of any hostile intentions among the Indians. Unlike Cornstalk however, most of the Pekowis, Chillicothes and Kispokos declared that "they still loved the land and would not part with it, and they watched with a growing bitterness the construction of the first white settlements in Kentucky.[lxvii]

During the next few years, Caesar had fought alongside Blackfish, Blue Jacket and Cheeseekau, as the Shawnee furiously defended their Ohio lands and attacked the Kentucky and Virginia settlers, as well as those coming down the Ohio River. Their efforts, although noticeable, gained only an extension of time for the Shawnee and in 1777 the peace and war factions of the Shawnee parted. Many of the Mekoches under Cornstalk and another chief, Hardman, moved with a few Pekowis to the Tuscarawas River.[lxviii] On the Tuscarawas they joined with neutral Delaware at Coshocton. Caesar and most of the remaining Shawnee abandoned the Scioto and traveled westward to the valleys of The Little and The Great Miami Rivers. [lxix]

In November of the same year, the whites at Fort Randolph [lxx] murdered Cornstalk. His murder inflamed all of the Shawnee, even those at odds with him and his peaceful stance toward the Americans in the war. Cornstalk, a young warrior named Redhawk and another warrior, had made a diplomatic visit to the fort to discuss a rumor that an expedition was being planned by the Americans against the Shawnee in the Ohio lands. During the meeting at the fort with Captain Arbuckle,[lxxi] Cornstalk warned that he would not be able to keep all of the Shawnee neutral, but that he and his own tribe were opposed to joining in the war on the side of the British. However, if pushed, he would "have to run with the Stream." Cornstalk was not aware that the proposed campaign against the Shawnee had been cancelled because there were not enough available men. However, Captain Arbuckle decided to detain Cornstalk, Redhawk and the other warrior as hostages in order to ensure that the Shawnee would stay neutral. Elinipsico, Cornstalk's son had just arrived at the fort on November 10th, the day after the meeting, when the Indians killed an American militiaman outside the fort. The militiaman's companions charged into the fort and shot Cornstalk seven or eight times. Elinipsico was shot sitting on a stool, Redhawk was pulled from the chimney and shot as he tried to escape. The other young warrior was brutally strangled.[lxxii] The bodies of Elinipsico, Redhawk and the other warrior were taken and dumped into the Kanawha River. Cornstalk's body was buried near the fort.[lxxiii]

After the death of Cornstalk, Caesar joined Blackfish on raids into Kentucky in 1777 and 1778. Blackfish, encouraged by the British, harassed stations and attacked straggling settlers. In February of 1778, he captured Daniel Boone and twenty-seven of his companions as they gathered salt on the Licking

River. Boone was actually adopted along with several others, but escaped and went back to Boonesborough. In September of 1778, Blackfish, led some three hundred Indians in an unsuccessful siege of the settlement for several days.

During the winter of 1778 and into the early spring of 1779, Caesar's friendship with Cheeseekau grew. Blackfish had been a strong friend of Pukeshinwau, and, just as he had adopted Caesar, he offered to adopt some of Methaoataaskee's children after Pukeshinwau's death. As a result, Caesar also began to develop a close friendship with the young Tecumseh, offering to help Tecumseh learn English. Caesar, also frequently, took Tecumseh along with him to his favorite hunting grounds in a beautiful valley just southeast of a gorge that ran parallel to the Little Miami River. The gorge and the valley were south of Old Chillicothe and were close to an old game trail that was used to travel north and south. [lxxiv]

Aside from the battles that the Shawnee raised against the encroachment of the whites, Caesar's everyday life was now that of a Shawnee warrior. His past as a slave in Virginia was just a deep memory. His Shawnee family was prospering and his reputation and standing within the Chillicothe people was rising. Like most Shawnee warriors, he was respected because he had earned the respect and confidence of his peers. His life however, would change again with the death of his stepfather in the spring of 1779. He would move closer and closer into a friendship with his adopted brothers, Cheeseekau and Tecumseh.

The night of May 29th, 1779 was dark. There was no moon and the sky was overcast. During the day a cold front had moved through and produced very violent thunderstorms. The darkness and the moisture in the forest allowed the three hundred men to quietly approach Old Chillicothe. A Kentucky settler name John Bowman had marched his men from Kentucky, up the Little Miami, and were hell bent on repaying the Shawnee for all of the attacks the past few years. Bowman's men had slowly been encircling the village when a shot rang out. An Indian scout had gone to investigate a noise, and one of Bowman's men shot him. The entire village erupted into chaos.

Blackfish rallied his warriors and led them in a counter attack against Bowman's men. Most of the women and elderly men had made it to the council house for protection. The fighting was fierce, and Blackfish's warriors were driven back by the heavy fire of the Kentuckians. As Blackfish was scurrying from one cabin to another, rallying his warriors to fall back to a few houses at the center of the town, he was hit with a bullet in his right leg, just above the knee. The bullet ripped upward, shattering his femur and emerged in the middle of his thigh. Caesar and several other warriors had managed to grab Blackfish and pull him to the safety of a house, just thirty yards from the council house. The Indians, once in the shelter of a few houses, put up a steady, defending fire. Outside, the Kentuckians put up a relentless fire and torched the houses of the town. Finally,

Bowman's men retreated, afraid that Indian reinforcements would arrive.

The reinforcements did arrive, but too late. They had ridden their horses hard from Pekowi but when they arrived in the early morning, they found a town with many houses still smoldering. The smoke rose in columns throughout the town, billowing skyward into the clearing blue sky. Many buildings had been damaged, but the town would survive. Seven Indians had been killed or fatally wounded, including Blackfish and the Indians had killed ten whites. Six weeks later, Blackfish died from his wound.

The Revolutionary war years were a time of turmoil among all of the Indians in the Ohio lands. For Caesar and the Shawnee, Ohio had become a war zone. The Shawnee towns were used as bases for the Indians, as well as the British, as they moved to and from the Kentucky and Virginia frontiers. The Shawnee war parties participated in an onslaught upon the frontier that was equally matched by fierce counterattacks, primarily from the Kentuckians. Ohio and Kentucky were bloody grounds. By the end of the war in 1783, the Shawnee had not been defeated, but they had been forced to retreat from their towns on the Little and Great Miami Rivers, further upstream. The Chillicothes went to the headwaters of the St. Mary's and the Pekowis, with the other Shawnee built a town at the source of the Mad River.[lxxv] The Shawnee were weakened and many thought that the end of the war would bring some peace, but it didn't. Caesar knew the White's greed and hunger for land. The Shawnee would know no peace as the newly formed United States would quickly begin an aggressive campaign for all of the Ohio lands, as well as all of the Indian country to the north. It would no longer be a battle against the Virginia and Kentucky militias, but a war against the newly formed nation and it's military.

In 1783, the British, with the Treaty of Paris, ceded their lands south of the Great Lakes and east of the Mississippi to the United States. They did so with little care to the Indian allies who had fought, in many instances, alongside them and who actually occupied the lands. Within a year the Congress resolved to annex all of the territories north of the Ohio and east of the Great Miami River. These were the lands of the Shawnee, the Mingo, the Delaware and the Cherokee. Once again, just as after the 1768 Treaty of Fort Stanwix, where the Indians were robbed of their hunting grounds in Kentucky, the Indians were now being robbed of their homelands, the lands that they lived upon.

Over the next six years, Caesar would fight with the Shawnee, his friendship growing with Cheeseekau and he watched as the young Tecumseh moved from adolescence, to manhood, and became a well-respected Kispoko warrior. He participated as Blue Jacket led his Shawnee people in their defensive war against the white invaders and witnessed as Blue Jacket, defeated in the Battle of Fallen Timbers[lxxvi] in 1794, and believing that his actions were for the for the good of all the people, sought peace in the Treaty of Greenville in 1795.[lxxvii] He had discussed with Blue Jacket the realization that the American's occupancy in Ohio was inevitable. He knew this was true, but, unlike Blue Jacket, he had decided he would never stop fighting the white man. His contempt for the white man continued to grow. His hatred was deep rooted. The Indians had always been free and were fighting for their lands and their freedom. He knew what it was like to be owned, to be controlled and to have no freedom. He would never been ruled again or owned, or live among the white men again. He would leave the Ohio lands and go as far away from the white man as possible or die before he would be owned again.

In 1787 and 1788, Caesar, along with his Shawnee brethren and warriors from the Mingo, Delaware, Cherokee and Wabash nations, launched relentless raids against the flatboats that were carrying more and more settlers, with their livestock and belongings, down the Ohio. On one of the evenings, as the Indians camped after a raid, Caesar watched as the men got drunk on the liquor that they had pillaged from the boat and subsequently tortured, beat and burned to death several of the captives. Tecumseh, who was eighteen at the time and who had no power to interfere with the fate of a prisoner, stood and spoke against the tortures and the burnings. He was opposed to taking prisoners and convinced the others not to torture or burn any more prisoners. Caesar personally felt no remorse for those who had been killed. He could remember back to times in Virginia where he had been made to watch as a fellow slave was whipped close to death for disobedience and to a few mornings where they had found men badly beaten and hanging from a tree. In his heart, he knew that Tecumseh was right. It was just too difficult however, for him to forget and to forgive. He knew, that the relatively few captures, tortures and deaths of the white captives, would only anger the whites more, and that no matter what the Indians did, they would not stop the flood of boats and white settlers from coming down the Ohio into their lands.

Cheeseekau and his followers, shortly after arriving at the Village on Apple Creek, became disillusioned with what had been promised to them by Lorimier. Only a few months after their arrival, some Americans that were passing through, shot at some Cherokee and Delaware hunters and stole their furs. They also found out that just to their south, a few miles below the mouth of the Ohio, a town called New Madrid was being built on the west bank of the Mississippi by a man named George Morgan. They found out that the Spanish were recruiting American settlers to the area, as well as the Indians in an attempt to strengthen their claims on the area. For Cheeseekau and his Shawnee followers, it was a situation that they did not want. They were trying to flee from the white man's influence. They wanted a life free of any American interference. Cheeseekau had spoken with several of his leaders, including Caesar, and the decision was made to cross back over the Mississippi. They would not return to the East however, but head south to join with the Chickamauga Cherokees. Of all the Indians, they were the ones who believed as he and his brother. They had settled in an area that was known as

Untiguhi,[lxxviii] the Boiling Pot, along the Tennessee River and were raging a long guerrilla war against the Americans.

Chapter 27
October 4, 2012

Zane Shawnee Caverns, Bellefontaine, Logan County Ohio

John Parker had gotten to his car and had left the parking lot before anyone had even noticed that there was still a car in the lot. All of the other customers had left just before the storm and the professor and John Logan had raced into the gift shop not noticing the car that was still in the parking lot.

It was now just after 1:00 am. He had decided to wait until the early morning to go back and see what the professor and John had been looking at. He had decided to park down the road from the entrance to the Caverns and walk in without his flashlight on. He figured that there wouldn't be any one up at this time and that he should be able to get down past the gift shop and the cave entrance without any light and that no one would notice.

He waited until he got to the bottom of the steps that led down the path into the ravine bottom before he turned on his flashlight. It was still cloudy and without any moon light the woods were wet and pitch black. Without the single beam from the flashlight, he couldn't see more than a few feet.

He made his way to the old oak and followed it up to the rock where he had last seen the professor and John. As he pointed the light from his flashlight on the rock, he noticed what appeared to be an old carving. It was in the shape of a large feather. It was well worn, but it was definitely a carving of a large feather with a much defined quill. He thought to himself. "OK. So there's a feather carved in this rock. This must be the Feather Rock. What do I do now? I know what they were looking at, but what do I do now?"

As he was thinking to himself, he put his hand into his pant pocket and felt the clay image of the medallion. He pulled it out, remembering what he had overheard about finding a Feather Rock. Something about putting the medallion on the quill of the feather and that it would point the way? "Well," he thought to himself. "This has gotta be the rock." He looked at the medallion and placed it down on the rock with the groove on the back of the medallion lined up with the raised quill of the feather. It was a natural fit. "What now? Ok. The letter said that the Indian would point the way to the silver," he said out loud, talking to himself." The carved Indian on the medallion's extended arm and finger were pointing along the bottom part of the ridge, back toward the cave entrance.

John pointed his flashlight in the direction that the finger was pointing. The beam only went about 30 yards. There was nothing. He put the medallion in his pocket and started to walk in the direction that the Indian on the medallion had pointed, shining the light out ahead and sweeping it about ten feet, from side to side. He had gone about fifty yards, finding nothing. "I don't see anything," he thought to himself. "This' id be a lot easier in the daytime." He glanced at his watch. It was just after 2:15am, and he began to slowly move forward, continuing with his flashlight's sweep in the direction he was walking and that the Indian on the medallion had pointed. It was toward the gift shop and the entrance to the cave.

As he got closer and closer to the cave building, he began to notice that there were more and more rocks strewn about the hillside and along the base of the hill as it ran out to the bottomland. As he walked, slowly weaving his way in between the large, mature trees and the saplings, it suddenly dawned on him that the Indian figure must have been pointing to the entrance of the cave. "Of course," he thought. "Back then, there was nothing here. The cave entrance must have been much smaller...just a hole in the ground. It was probably hidden and only the Indians must have known about it. I'm gonna have to come back in the daytime and go back through the cave. There's gotta be something in there. No one could make all of this up and there not be something. Not from that long ago."

He was now only about 50 yards from the building and cave's entrance. He shut the flashlight off and made his way back toward the stairs that ran down into the gorge and back up to the parking lot. Everything was very quiet. He made his way carefully around the edge of the parking lot and skirted the tree line along the entrance road to the caverns, back to his car, and headed home.

Sunday Morning, October 5th

"Emma," said Will, "I wanted you to meet me here this morning because John called me last night all excited about finding something called the Feather Rock down in the ravine. It's a rock down in the gorge that supposedly has the carving of a feather on it and if you place the medallion in the museum on the rock, lining up the groove on the back on the feather's quill, the Indian is pointing in the direction of hidden silver." John and the professor are coming around 8:00 to go down to the rock. John asked if we would go along."

"Did you know anything about any of these things Will?" asked Emma.

"Emma. You and I are the only ones who know about the secret of this cave and our people, but I don't know anything about this Feather Rock or any silver. Our people's secret must be kept. Here comes John. Please keep quiet and let's see how this plays out."

Emma nodded silently to Will just as John opened the door to the gift shop.

The Professor was up early on Sunday morning having agreed to meet John at the gift shop by 7:00am. Both were eager to get back down to the rock and take a closer look at the rock and the surrounding area. The Professor also wanted to see if they could get the medallion from the museum and see if there was any truth to it fitting over the quill of the carved feather on the rock, and if it would point to something. After all, they had found the Feather Rock in the ravine that was mentioned in the letter.

The lights were already on in the gift shop when the Professor arrived. The door was unlocked and as he came through the door, he saw John talking with Will and Emma.

"Good morning," said John, as he saw the Professor come through the door.

"Good morning," replied the Professor. "Will. Emma. Nice to see you," said the Professor as he made his way over to the three who were standing in front of the counter.

"Professor, I was telling Will and Emma about what we found down in the gorge," John said excitedly. "I believe they are both a little amazed. But they want to go down and see the feather carving this morning before we open."

"Will", said the Professor. "I brought this thinking that you would want to see the letter that we had mentioned to you." The Professor took the letter out of his jacket, unfolded it and carefully set it on the counter. Will and Emma both stepped up to the counter and read the letter.

"What do you think," said the Professor. Emma didn't respond, but her eyes showed her amazement. Will, after looking at Emma, turned and looked at the Professor.

"Well. I'm a little amazed." I'm not quite sure what to say. If all that you and John are saying is true. Then I guess we should get the medallion and head on down to that rock and see what we can find."

Will excused himself, unlocked the door to the museum and in just a few minutes came out with the medallion.

"Let's go see what we can find out," said Will. The Professor, John, Will and Emma all headed out the door, down the steps, past the cave entrance and into Tecumseh's Gorge. In a few minutes, they were at the rock all looking in semi-disbelief at the carving on the rock. Amazed that it was there...surprised that no one knew of it over all the years and that no one had ever found this rock with the carving.

Will placed the groove of the medallion onto the quill of the carved feather. It fit perfectly. Without hesitation, all four looked back to their lefts, down the line along the base of the hill toward the entrance to the cave. The Indian's finger on the carving pointed in that direction. Without speaking, all four began to walk in the direction that the carving's finger was pointing. The letter said that the Indian was pointing toward where the silver was. No one was talking. Just slowly walking and looking at the leaf covered ground.

Will broke the silence. "I don't see anything around here, let alone in the direction the Indian on the medallion is pointing. Either this is really all just a bunch of bull or time has just obscured something, anything that we might be looking for. And we don't know what that is!"

"I know that there is something here," said John. "Everything just can't be inconsequential. We've gotta think differently. What would this all have looked like two hundred years ago?

"I don't think that it would have looked much different than it does today," said the professor. Maybe the question should be what looks different? What down here is out of place?"

Emma, as she looked in all directions, said, "Everything looks the same...leaves on the ground... large trees...small trees...a few moss covered rocks here and there. The only thing that wouldn't have been here is the cave entrance and the steps. So, if I look in the direction of the cave entrance and the steps and imagine that they're not there. All I see is..."

John interrupted her. "We know that there's no silver in the cave. However, that fingers pointing in the direction of the cave's entrance. Two hundred years ago the main entrance was just a sink hole with only a two or three foot wide opening surrounded by a few rocks. It was around a ten-foot drop down to the floor of the cave. When that letter was written, the cave entrance was probably well known to the Indians. If the Shawnee used this cave to hide their silver, that's assuming they had a cache of silver, they weren't trying to hide it from themselves, but from the whites."

"You're right," said the Professor. "At that time, there were only a few whites in this area, and unless they just happened to stumble across the sink hole out here in the middle of nowhere, they probably wouldn't have known that it existed. Caesar said that the silver was hid. They obviously didn't hide it out in the open. If they kept it in this cave they must have hidden it and kept the hiding place a secret just in case someone did stumble upon the cave. Maybe there's another room or area in the cave that's hidden or that no one has found. What I'm thinking is that there is either another cave around here, or at least another entrance into this cave that only a few knew about."

"You may be right, Professor. What if there is another entrance to the cave that no one knows about? I've never heard of any other entrances or of any other caves around here" said John. "Have you Will?"

"No...I can't say that I have. I've never heard of any other caves or entrances," said Will. "When we bought this property and took over this land and the cave, I was told that the cave had been explored and that no other tunnels or entrances had been found. It really wasn't part of a cave system, just a large underground cavern."

"Well," said Emma, "If there is another cave or another entrance to our cave, what would we be looking for?"

"Emma," said the Professor, "typically, a small hole in the ground...a sinkhole just like the original entrance to this one."

"I don't see anything around here but the leaves on the ground and a few scattered rocks," said Emma.

"Wait...hold on a minute," said John. "That's it... if there is another cave or entrance then they must have hid it just as the letter says. The only thing they could have hid it with or covered it with is rocks. Otherwise it would have been obvious. There are only a few scattered rocks around here except for those over there." John was pointing and walking to a small cluster of four or five rocks about ten yards ahead of them. They weren't large rocks. Maybe twelve to eighteen inches in diameter, but they were the only rocks that were not by themselves. They were partially moss covered. They weren't piled, but were in a small cluster about four or five feet in diameter.

When they got to the rocks, John knelt down to take a closer look. He grabbed one of the rocks and rolled it away it away from the others...then another, and another. The soil below the rocks was moist. John took the knife that he carried out of its' sheath. It was a Bowie with a 10" blade and a carved deer antler handle. He stuck it into the ground where the rock had been. It went into the ground about five inches with ease. He was about to stand up but decided to scrape away a few more inches of the soil. He stuck his knife in a little harder and deeper this time. It went into the soil almost to the hilt and struck something solid. It wasn't a rock. It felt more like a root. He scraped a larger area of the soil away. The others were intently watching.

"Hold on a minute," he said. "This isn't a root the knife hit."

Will and the Professor both dropped to their knees and began to help John scrape more of the soil away. Without talking, and almost simultaneously, all three of the men each grabbed the remaining rocks and moved them out of the way. They all began to rapidly and excitedly scrape the soil away with their hands.

"I can't believe it," said the Professor. "There are old boards here. They're all pretty rotten. It's amazing that they still held the weight of these rocks."

"Let's get this dug out further and see how big these boards are," said Will, just as John had pried his knife to the side and under the edge of one of the boards and lifted it up. It was only about three feet long. Each end had been resting on rock that had been covered by the almost 10 inches of soil.

"Oh my God," said Emma. There's nothing under the board.

All four could feel the coolness and the dampness of the hole.

"Help me pull up these other boards," said John excitedly. "I think we have found the entrance we're looking for. This is amazing. I almost can't believe it!"

In just a few minutes, all of the boards had been removed and the four stood, looking at an approximately two to three foot wide sinkhole. All of them peered into the hole but could see nothing but blackness. John took a small rock and tossed it down into the hole. Everyone listened intently. John counted to himself. "One, two, three" and then there was the sound of a splash.

"Sounds like there's some water down there," said John.

"I'm guessing its' at least a good twenty feet to the bottom," said the Professor.

"Emma," said Will as he glanced at this watch. "It's 8:20. You better get on up to the gift shop and get ready to open. Maybe you guys better come on up too. I don't think any one's gonna find this. We're gonna need some flashlights, some rope and an extension ladder. Let's get that stuff and get back down here as soon as we can."

Chapter 28
October 1789

Amogayunyi, Running Water[lxxix]

Caesar was with Cheeseekau and Tecumseh as they met with Tsiyugunsini, Dragging Canoe, [lxxx] in Amogayunyi. He had left his wife and children back in Apple Creek. He and his wife had argued when he informed her that they were not going to stay at Apple Creek, but were going to continue to move South with Cheeseekau. Caesar's wife told him that she was tired of moving and that they would never be able to run away from the whites. The whites would never stop chasing them and wanting their land. She was tired of running and she would stay at Apple Creek with her children. He was free to go. She understood his hatred of the whites and his support of Cheeseekau, but she would remain at Apple Creek. Caesar understood her wishes, but he would never stop fighting against the whites and for his freedom, as well as hers and all of the Shawnee. He would fight as long as he had breath.

When the Shawnee under Cheeseekau arrived in Running Water Town, Dragging Canoe was fifty-nine years old. He was tall and strong. The smallpox that had ravaged him in his younger years had scarred his face. Dragging Canoe had led a dissident band of the Cherokee against the United States in the Revolutionary War. In 1777 he became the principal chief of the Chickamauga, or Lower Cherokee, leading them for over ten years in a series of aggressive conflicts against the whites. He refused to recognize treaties and when he was pressed, he simply withdrew farther down the Tennessee with his followers. From each location he continued his fight. It was easy for the Shawnee under Cheeseekau to understand and sympathize with the Chickamauga of Dragging Canoe. They were both oppressed peoples driven from their lands and peoples who were desperate in their struggles to remain in their lands and to retain their way of life and their identities against the continual encroachment of a culture with which they could not coexist.

During that time, Caesar had grown more and more attached to Tecumseh. He and Tecumseh often spoke in English at Tecumseh's' request. They spoke of many things, but Tecumseh was intrigued by Caesar's past as a slave and questioned him on several occasions about his treatment as a slave. He was amazed at what Caesar had told him in regards to how the Whites wanted to own more and more land, and how they bought the Negroes at auctions and made them work the land for them. Tecumseh could not believe that the black men hadn't joined together and fought against their enslavement. Caesar explained to Tecumseh that the majority of slaves were not allowed to leave the plantations that they worked. He had heard of a few rebellions, but that the whites had crushed them, torturing and hanging those who had resisted their enslavement. They lived their lives in constant fear. He told him that there were others like himself, who just ran. They ran for their freedom. Tecumseh expressed his belief to

Caesar that it was now time for all Indians to unite and become as one people to resist the Americans. If not, he was afraid that the Indians would one day become slaves.

On an early May morning Caesar lay concealed next to Tecumseh on a low bluff overlooking the Tennessee River. Next to Tecumseh were Cheeseekau and ten Shawnee warriors. Next to the Shawnee were twenty Cherokee and ten Creek warriors. They were quietly watching three large bateaux working their way down the river.[lxxxi] Caesar couldn't help but think back to the time he was floating down the Ohio wanting and waiting to be captured. He also thought of the many times he had lay in ambush on the Ohio watching the boats coming and going waiting for the right moment to burst from cover.

The day before, word came to the village of three big bateaux coming down the river. The word was that the men on the boats were not good men. They were land speculators who had come only to steal the land and start an illegal colony on the lower Tennessee. The Creek chief, Alexander McGillivray, said that the bateaux had big guns mounted on them that swiveled.[lxxxii] He had explained that the leader of the men was a man named Hawkins and that they were trying to force their way down the river to the Muscle Shoals region above Bear Creek where they planned to build a fort and trade with the friendly Chickasaws. After a brief meeting that included Chief Dragging Canoe, Chief Attakullakulla, Chief Little Owl, Chief Ostenaco, Cheeseekau and Tecumseh, the Indians decided to attack the bateaux the next day.

In the early morning, Cheeseekau led the warriors to the spot that they were now waiting at. They didn't have canoes, but Cheeseekau had picked a spot where the Indians would be protected and be able to openly fire down upon the boats. The sun was just peaking through the trees over the eastern horizon as the boats came within range of the warrior's guns. Cheeseekau gave the signal to fire and the Indians poured a barrage of gunfire down into the boats. They fired and reloaded as fast as they were able. Their gun barrels were hot from their rapid fire and the smoke from their guns rose into the air, shrouding the small bluff that they were on in a gray cloud. The men in the boat had been caught off guard and could only return sporadic fire, as they hid under and behind any cover they could find on the boats as the Indian's bullets exploded all around them.

Caesar had kept up his fire and had laid a bead on several of the men in the boats. With the smoke, it was difficult to tell if you had hit your target, but it was obvious that one of the boats was taking the blunt of most of the firing and was now out of control and drifting toward the south side of the river where the Indians were.

Caesar and several others were directed by Cheeseekau to go down to the river and board the boat. When they boarded the boat, Caesar counted thirty-two dead or wounded men. The wooden deck of the boat was red with the blood of the dead and wounded men and those that were alive were begging for their lives.

As the Indians were gathering the captives, after killing the wounded and rolling all of the bodies into the river, there was a loud boom that came from the far shore. Just to Caesar' right, the water exploded, spraying Caesar and the others close to him, as a ball from one of the other two boat's canon had been fired. The other two boats had gotten to the far side of the river out of musket range and had turned the swivel of their canons upon the captured boat. All of the Indians, realizing the danger of the small canons fire, forced the captives off the boat and quickly got out of the gun's effective range. No one had been hurt. The Indians, along with their captives, quickly disappeared back into the forest and headed back to Amogayunyi.

Caesar and the Shawnee fought alongside the Cherokee in similar attacks against others coming down the river for the next year and one half. During the summer of 1791, Caesar set off for Ohio with Tecumseh. Over the past two years with the Chickamauga, he had discussed with Tecumseh the expansion of the whites and the continued tribal concessions of the Chickamauga, as well as the growing crisis in the Ohio lands. He had encouraged Tecumseh's belief that the only viable means of defeating the whites and keeping them from their lands would be a confederacy of all of the Indians. He believed that the only way the settlers and the speculators would be stopped was by armed resistance. On the night before they left for Ohio, they sat up late around a fire. Everyone else had gone for the night and the two were left alone to discuss their belief in Indian unity.

They spoke mostly in English, as it was easier for Caesar. Tecumseh pressed Caesar to speak to him in English often. Caesar could not read or write and his English wasn't the best, but he was very intelligent. On this particular night Caesar and Tecumseh discussed their plight into the early hours of the morning.

Tecumseh pointed out that everywhere their people had passed away. They were as the snows on the mountains in May. They no longer ruled the forest. The game was gone like their hunting ground in Kentucky. Almost all of their lands in Ohio were gone. Their campfires were becoming fewer and fewer. Caesar couldn't help but agree. He told Tecumseh that they only way the fires would remain would be if they would draw together.

"Look what the white man has done to our people," said Caesar. Tecumseh replied. "Look what he has done to your first family! We must get the Cherokee to raise their tomahawks with the Shawnee. We must get all of our brothers to think as one and to act as one, or there will be no place for us. Those that befriended them...the Pequot, the Narraganset, the Powhatan, the Mohican, the Pakanoket and the Tuscarora are all gone."

"I agree with you, my friend," said Caesar. "But I am afraid that we're gonna learn with a lot of sorrow that it is better not to war against the whites. They're here to stay and I don't think they're ever gonna go away. But, no matter what I think or believe

Tecumseh, I will walk with you as a brother against them. I know that all you have wanted is to live in peace. As a black man, all I wanted was to be free and to live in peace. There ain't no peace with the white man...there's only lies and oppression."

"The only way to stop this evil is for the red man to unite in claiming a common equal right in the land, as it was first and should be now, for it was never divided," said Tecumseh. "We gave them forest-clad mountains and valleys full of game. In return they have only given us rum, trinkets and a grave. We must try to unite all of our brothers and consider the land the common property of all. It is only in unity that we will find our security."

"Tecumseh," said Caesar, "You're right, but the white man won't keep his promises. They didn't even keep their promises to Jesus. Most of them profess to love him and want to keep his Ten Commandments. You remember when our brothers the Delaware thought that they were safe livin' near the Americans because they believed in Jesus. The Americans murdered all of them. It didn't make any difference. They murdered the men, women and children while they were praying to Jesus. I've seen em go to church all dressed up and listen to the preacher and then leave the church and go hang black men that hadn't done nothin'. They kilt 'em just because they were black and they thought that they broke one of their rules. You can't have confidence in the whites? When Jesus came here on this earth, they kilt him too. The Son of their own God 'cause he didn't believe like they did. They whipped him just like they whipped me...you seen my back. They nailed him up on cross! They thought he was dead, but he wasn't. Only after they thought they'd kilt him did they start to worship him. Then they began killin' their own people who wouldn't worship em. Tecumseh, what kinda people is this for us to trust?

"My brother," said Tecumseh. We cannot sell a country. We cannot sell the air, the clouds or the Great Sea. The Great Good Spirit made them all for us and for the use of all of his people. We will have a great council one-day at which all of the tribes will be present. I am Shawnee! I am a warrior! My forefathers were warriors. From them I took only my birth into this world. From my tribe I take nothing. I am the maker of my own destiny! And of that I might make the destiny of my red people, of our nation, as great as I conceive to in my mind, when I think of Weshemanitou, who rules this universe!" I hear his being speak within me the voice of the ages. It tells me that once, always, and until lately, there were no white men on this entire island, that it then belonged to the red men, children of the same parents, placed on it by the Great Good Spirit who made them, to keep it, to traverse it, to enjoy its yield, and to people it with the same race. Once they were a happy race! Now they are made miserable by the white people, who are never contented but are always coming in! We will unite, my friend!"

"Tecumseh...my heart is with you."

Chapter 29
September 28, 1792

The Creek Crossing Place near Nickajack, TN

The fire was large that night. It was a cool evening at the recently established camp and the forty Shawanese that sat around the fire listened intently to Cheeseekau. Caesar and Tecumseh, along with ten other warriors, had arrived back to the Crossing Place from Ohio the day before. Tecumseh had been invited by his brother to reinforce him for an upcoming battle against the whites. The camp was at the Creek Crossing Place of the Tennessee, a small distance above the shoals, on the south side of Mill Creek as it entered into the Tennessee. [lxxxiii]

Caesar and Tecumseh had only been back to the Ohio lands for a short time. Tecumseh's reputation was growing, but he was only regarded as a minor war leader. He and Caesar's friendship had continued to grow, but it was Cheeseekau whose name was feared throughout Tennessee. He had become known to the Chickamauga and all of their white enemies as Shawnee Warrior.

Dragging Canoe died in March of 1792 and it was an angry Shawnee Warrior that picked up his bloody hatchet and continued attacks upon the white settlements on the Cumberland River, a river the Shawnee had called the Skipakysepe, or Blue River. There were now over four thousand settlers building farms and forts on both sides of the river and Shawnee Warrior led his war parties, along with the

Cherokees and Creeks, in an attempt to stop the increasing number of settlers.

John Watts replaced Dragging Canoe as the principal war chief of the Chickamauga.[lxxxiv] Watts was tall and with the exception of his lighter skin and Caucasian features, he dressed in the fashion of the Cherokee warriors. He chose to be clean-shaven and wore a topknot in his dark brown hair. His breechcloth was made of soft tanned deerskin, pulled up between his legs and secured at the waist with thongs. The ends of the breechcloth hung nearly to his knees in the front and back. He had a deer skin purse suspended from his skin belt in the front and a knife fashioned from a steel file hung on the right side of his belt. His moccasins were short with flaps on either side and his leather leggings went from his ankle to his mid-thigh and were fastened to his belt with thongs. He had a pony tail protruding from his topknot that was pulled through a hollowed bone, with the tip of the ponytail exposed. The tip was well greased and sprinkled with red dust. Tied into Watt's hair were two feathers...a single Eagle's feather and a smaller feather, dyed blood red. His ears were pierced with large metal plates inserted into the holes. He wore a necklace that consisted of a hammered copper plate and bear claws. He was heavily tattooed.[lxxxv]

Watts was a brave, eloquent, and sincere man. He had a deep respect for Shawnee Warrior. They shared similar views when it came to fighting the whites to stop them from taking more of their land. Watts did not have to ask Shawnee Warrior to urge all of the young Shawnee men to go to war against the whites. He did have to fight, on the other hand, the views of Bloody Fellow, Nenetooyah...another Cherokee chief. Watts and Bloody Fellow had a falling out while they were attending treaty talks with the newly appointed Governor in and over the territory of the United States south of the Ohio River, William Blount. Blount was also the superintendent of Indian affairs for the Southern District for United States. In 1789, North Carolina ceded its western lands to the Congress of the United States, which organized the Territory south of the Ohio River that comprised Tennessee. Blount was a friend of Washington and a member of the convention that had just framed the Constitution of the United States. He took up his duties in 1790 and his first act was an attempt to end the Indian war by diplomacy. He announced that he would rectify the wrongs done to the Indians.

The year before, two friendly chiefs, Old Tassel and Abram, Old Tassel being the principal chief of the Nation and John Watt's uncle, were killed while under a flag of truce. They were killed by a band of men under the command of James Hubbard, an Indian hater. John Kirk, whose family had been murdered by Indians, did the actual killing. In Dragging Canoe's camp, the killings seemed to be the stimulus for Old Tassel's brother, Doublehead, to become one of the most bloodthirsty of all the Indian chiefs. Old Tassel's nephew, Benge, who became known to the whites as Captain Bench, took forty-five scalps with his own hands. Many white mothers told their children that Captain Bench would get them if they were not good. John Watts was so upset by the bloody death of his uncle that for years after the death he could not mention it without tears coming to his eyes.[lxxxvi]

Now, on July 2, 1791, near the Holston River[lxxxvii], practically every chief of importance, with the exception of Dragging Canoe, was gathered together at Blount's invitation to join in a treaty that Blount said, "Would rectify all of the wrongs done to the Indians." The Indians that were gathered had come to the parley with the understanding that Blount wanted to remove all of the white settlers from the Indian lands. But, the chiefs were bitterly disappointed when, instead of removing the settlers, Blount proposed to buy the land that had been wrongfully taken. John Watts and Bloody Fellow, who both spoke for the Cherokees, vehemently protested. Watts, still distraught by the memory of his uncle's deceitful murder, left the treaty gathering in disgust.

After Watts had left, Blount offered the Cherokees presents, and an annuity of $1000.00 for the land. Bloody Fellow told Blount that "It would not buy a breech clout for each member of my Nation!" He struggled with his emotions, but under duress and with the growing realizing that his Nation would not stop the Americans, he signed the treaty.[lxxxviii]

Bloody Fellow, believing that he was representing all of the Cherokee, was not happy with the treaty he had just signed. He wanted to meet the President and without speaking with Blount and without any forewarning, he set out at the head of a delegation for Philadelphia. He believed that he could get better terms from the President. His effort and that of his delegation resulted in an increase in the annuity to $1,500.00 per year. Washington also conferred a new name upon Bloody Fellow. He was now called Eskaqua, or Clear Sky. [lxxxix] With his new, less threatening, name, he was now a friend to the Americans.

While Bloody Fellow was in Philadelphia, Dragging Canoe died and John Watts was elected as his successor as War Chief. In September, in Willstown,[xc] Watts announced to his Cherokee warriors, along with the representatives of several other tribes, that "To war we will go together!" He was determined to prove that Indians could "fight in armies," as well as white men. He planned, along with Shawnee Warrior, Talotiskee, Tsal Su Ska called Doublehead [xci] and Middlestriker, a well thought out offensive throwing the whole strength of the Nation against the Cumberland settlements. The Nation would wipe them out, then turn eastward and repeat the process at Watauga. Watts would march against Nashville with Shawnee Warrior and Talotiskee. To block any assistance or word of his coming, Doublehead was sent with a hundred men to lie in wait upon the Kentucky road. Middlestriker, with an additional hundred men, was sent to cover the new Cumberland road. This road had just been opened and was a shorter route from Knoxville to Nashville.

After the frenzy and celebration of the decision to strike the Cumberland settlements, many of the thirty Shawnee lingered around the fire into the late hours of the night. Tecumseh and Caesar were sitting near Shawnee Warrior.

"My Shawnee brothers," said Shawnee Warrior. "I thank you from my heart for coming to be at our sides in the battle." He stretched his hands outward with his palms up. "It is with these hands that I have taken the lives of three hundred men. And now, the time has come, that I shall take the lives of three hundred more. Only then, after drinking my fill of blood will I sit down in peace.

I must tell you now that I have had a sign. It is a disturbing dream that I have had. It is a warning. Tomorrow, we will arrive at a fort. We will attack it in the early morning. If we are strong, we will capture the fort. But, my brothers," Shawnee Warrior put his right index finger on the center of his forehead. "I will be shot here, in the center of my forehead."

Tecumseh rose as Shawnee Warrior spoke, as did several other warriors. One could see in his dark, brown eyes, shock and fear. It was fear of the truth of his brother's words.

"My brother...you must not go into the battle tomorrow." Others shook their heads in agreement.

"No Tecumseh...it is an honor to die in battle just as our father did. I do not want to die at home like an old woman. It is better the fowls of the air pick my bones."

Tecumseh fought back his tears, as he knew his brother's words were true. Their eyes met as only the eyes of two inseparable brothers, whose lives of destiny, could meet. There were no tears...only a deep understanding of the love that each felt towards the other. Tomorrow they would feel an emptiness that every man with a brother would feel. One would depart this life. The other would remain with only the memories of the other to sustain them. Tecumseh's only comfort was a deep understanding that Weshemanitou was in control. In each and every man's life he was sovereign. As he sat down, he remembered what Caesar had told him his mother had said about God, that all men's lives were planned by God, and that God was in control of all things. It was all part of His plan. She had told him that God knew what was gonna happen in our lives, but we had to walk them out, not knowing what the next day would bring. He wasn't sure how Shawnee Warrior knew about his death, but he knew that, like his father, he did.

Tecumseh thought deeply about why Weshemanitou was allowing the Indians to be driven from their lands. If the God that the white's believed in was the same as Weshemanitou, why would he choose to favor one man over another? What were the Indians doing that was so wrong that this God was punishing them? Or was he punishing them? Why would a God, who created all things and who planned all people's lives, make some to be conquered by others? Some to be a slave like Caesar had been. It didn't make sense to him. He had seen good men die and he had seen evil men die. Shouldn't good men be favored over evil men? If God created all men and he planned and controlled their lives, then did he create some of the men to be good and some to be evil? What kind of God would do this?

Caesar was up early in the early morning with Tecumseh, his brother and the other Shawnee. He had had a restless, almost sleepless night. He spoke with Tecumseh as they both prepared, alongside Shawnee Warrior, for the day and the upcoming battle that they knew would come. Shawnee Warrior had painted his face black with red, finger width lines descending down from each eye. He was not speaking and nothing was said to him. Tecumseh told Caesar that he had found it difficult to sleep after his brother had told them that he was going to die in battle. He had tossed and turned, deep in thoughts for most of the night, but now, he must walk in this life, this day. Many men would die this day along with his brother if it we're meant to be, but the whites must be stopped from taking the Indian's land.

The Indians had marched in a column, three abreast, all through the day, as they steadily moved toward the Cumberland settlements. It was near midnight of September 30th when the warriors actually approached Buchanan's Station. [xcii] The station was one of the outlying settlements of Nashville. It was laid out, on rocky, high ground, on Mill Creek, as it meandered through pastures that were filled with cattle. The town itself only had a few blockhouse buildings. The buildings were enclosed by a picket stockade with a large blockade built to protect the front gate as it overlooked the creek. John Watts was leading some 280 Cherokee, 83 Creeks under Talotiskee and 30 Shawnee under Shawnee Warrior. He called a halt to their approach within a half a mile of the station and had called a meeting of the chiefs to discuss the attack on the fort.

The chiefs gathered, along with many of the warriors.

"We have had a long day," said Watts. "It is my opinion that we should move past this station and on towards the fort at Nashville. Our main objective is to attack this fort.[xciii]

Middlestriker and Doublehead will be successful and join us in the morning and united we will attack and destroy this fort."

As Watts finished, Talotiskee looked directly at him and spoke. "No, my brother…Buchanan must be taken first. We cannot leave any white men in our rear."

Shawnee Warrior stood and looked at Watts and Talotiskee.

"I am in agreement with Talotiskee. We are here now and we must destroy this fort. We cannot leave any of our enemies behind us. On our march here, we have seen the sign of the militia that has been patrolling this area. They must know that we are near. If we attack at Nashville, and they are not in this fort, then we will allow them to have this stronghold behind us."

"No my brothers, it is my decision," argued Watts. "We must do our best to conceal our numbers and meet Middlestriker and Doublehead without letting the Americans know our strength. If we attack here, we risk the word will reach Nashville that we are near."

Tecumseh started to stand, but Caesar grabbed his legging and pulled him back down.

"Tecumseh," whispered Caesar. It is not your place to speak. Cheeseekau will speak for us and make the right decision."

Tecumseh looked at Cesar and nodded as he sat.

Watts looked hard at Shawnee Warrior and at Talotiskee. He turned slowly and as his eyes surveyed those that had gathered, he weighed their words and realized that they were correct. He consented.

"Ok. We attack tonight. It is a station, built like a cow pen. We will destroy it tonight and wipe it and all of these white settlers from our land."

What Talotiskee and the others did not know was that traders had already alerted Tennessee's Governor Blount that the Chickamauga were planning on sending a large force to wipe out the Cumberland settlements. Blount had warned James Robertson in Nashville and Robertson had not only immediately called out the militia to patrol the area but had gotten word to about 15 families who lived near the station to get to the station for security and to help defend the station. Inside the station there were 15 able-bodied men, who were well armed with plenty of ammunition for their flintlocks. The station had been built like a small fort. It may have looked like a cow pen, but it was sturdily built to withstand an assault until reinforcements from the fort at Nashville, just 4 miles away, could arrive. The settlers were prepared for the Indians assault. The station had been built strategically with defense in mind and in anticipation of an attack the settlers had positioned expert sharpshooters in the blockade's openings with good views in all directions.[xciv]

Caesar and the other Shawnee were about ten yards to the right of Watts and several of the Cherokees. All of the Indians had quietly moved undetected through the clearings and small stands of timber that surrounded the station. The sky was clear and the moon was full. It brought an unusual brightness to the woods and the station's buildings. The Indians could see to move silently and the sharpshooter's eyes, once accustomed to the amount of light, were able to see out almost twenty to thirty yards.

Caesar, as usual, was anxious, but ready. It was a warm night and he could feel the sweat as it formed on his body. He had done this before. He wasn't afraid to die, but, just as any warrior, as any man, he knew that it could happen. This night, he wondered what Cheeseekau's thoughts were? Could a man really sense that he was going to die? Could he be given a vision of his death? He'd never had a vision. He had never seen any fear in a Shawnee warrior that was preparing for battle. They must have fear he thought to himself. Every one's gotta have fear. He had heard some singing death songs prior to other battles, but the songs were not signs of fear. He hadn't heard any death songs this night as they were instructed to remain quiet. He wondered about the silence and if there were any of the warriors singing songs to themselves. He could remember what Blackfish had told him about dying. "Never let the fear of death enter your heart. Live your life so that it can't. If and when it is your time to die, sing your death song and die like a hero showing that your life had purpose."

Suddenly, a few cattle, frightened by the Indian's approach, took off running. The running of the cattle alerted the sharpshooters in the blockhouse and shouts could be heard from them as they saw the Indians had advanced and were within ten yards of the gate. One of the men, John McRory, settled his gun through a porthole at his position and fired. Caesar saw Cheeseekau's head jerk violently backward. A bullet had slammed into the middle of his forehead and half of the backside of his head was gone. He collapsed. His right leg jerked several times and then he never moved again. He lay on his back with his eyes open.

A bullet slammed into the side of the tree that Caesar was hiding behind spraying pieces of bark in all directions. He felt the sting of the pieces as they hit his face and his thoughts snapped back from what he had just witnessed. Chaos broke out all around him. The Indian's had been discovered and were returning a very heavy and constant fire, aiming at the portholes of the blockade.

Tecumseh, as with many of the others fired, reloaded and fired, as the men in the blockhouse returned the fire. Caesar and a few of the other Shawnee warriors had now reached the blockhouse and were attempting to put fire to it. One warrior had climbed up on the roof with a torch. As he tried to torch the roof, he was shot, and fell to the ground. Other warriors attempted to fire the bottom logs, and several were killed. The battle raged on for over an hour with the flash of the settler's guns, shattering the darkness as they fired at the screaming shadows of the warriors as they raced around all the edges of the blockade. The air was quickly filled with the smoke from the guns on both sides, as it rose slowly into the night sky forming a surreal cloud over the station.

John Watts was hit in his right leg and the bullet passed through and entered his left leg. He grabbed his right leg as he stumbled and fell. Several warriors grabbed him and carried him to safety out of the line of the gunfire, thinking that his wounds would be fatal. Another Chickamauga chief, Chiachattalla, had reached the walls of the Blockhouse and had climbed to the roof and was trying to set it on fire. Caesar was only a few feet from him as he was shot and fell to the ground. Caesar bent over him and saw blood oozing from his chest just as he felt the sting of a bullet hit him in his left arm. It spun him around, but he was able to keep his feet, as he grabbed his arm. He raised his gun and fired with one arm at a figure near the top of the stockade and then turned and ran. He was useless with one arm. As he ran, he looked back and saw Chiachattalla climbing back onto the roof with his torch. Chiachattalla fell and as he lay dying, he still tried to light the fort's wall. With his last breath, he shouted encouragement to the other warriors to continue to attack.

The fighting went on for just over an hour. On the inside of the fort during the heaviest of the fighting, the ammunition began to get scarce and Nancy Mulheron, the sister of Major Buchanan, melted pewter plates and dishes and molded them into bullets. She carried the hot balls in her apron around to the men fighting. On the outside, the Indians were beginning to retreat. As Caesar ran back through the trees, with his left arm dangling uselessly, he helped grab a wounded warrior and drag him back to safety. As he looked around, he saw dozens of dead and wounded Indians. Blood was everywhere. He fell to the ground and scooted up with his back to the base of a fallen tree. All around him he heard the moans of the wounded. Some were leaning up against trees. Others were just lying, sprawled, bleeding on the ground...many with life slipping from them. Caesar saw Talotiskee lying motionless at the base of an oak. He had been killed leading his Creek warriors in a hard charge. He saw Little Owl, the brother of Dragging Canoe, lying dead on his back. He had been hit in the chest and in the neck and blood continued to flow from both wounds and trickled out of the corner of his mouth. He saw Tecumseh with his lifeless brother and as he made his way to them, he saw another warrior dragging the lifeless body of Unacata, John Watt's brother.

Caesar was on one knee, next to Tecumseh. They were both by the side of Cheeseekau. The bleeding from Caesar's arm had stopped, but not the pain. The pain, however, that he felt for the loss of Cheeseekau was far greater than the pain in his arm. It was difficult for him to imagine how Tecumseh felt. Cheeseekau was not only his brother, but after the death of their father, he had been his teacher, his guide, his best friend and most importantly, his life had been an exemplary life that Tecumseh had measured his own goals and standards by.

He watched as Tecumseh was getting his brother's body ready to take with them so that he could have a Shawnee burial and as he watched he found himself distant from the activity of the retreat and deep in thought. He was now beginning to understand some of the spiritual beliefs that he was being taught by his Shawnee brothers. It was difficult to break from some of the Christian beliefs that were ingrained in him by his mother, but the closeness of death always seemed to make him think more about understanding and respecting the feelings and cultural beliefs of other people, even if they were different from what you had been taught. He could only think of the similarities of what he was taught about God and the harmonies between those teachings and what the Shawnee were teaching him. He was now beginning to understand that all of life was spiritual and that in this world, everything and each person, went through seasons or cycles. Death was just one part of the cycles. He didn't fully understand how the earth could be regarded as a person's mother, but he did understand that all people must live in harmony with the earth; with everything on the earth, the plants, the animals and especially other people. He was beginning to see and to understand that everything had been created by God and that under God's sovereignty all things were linked though the seasons, beginning with birth and ending with death. All was under God's control and plan. He didn't understand it all, and was confused about the harmony however, and how and why men, in the name of their God, could believe that they were superior over others and because of that that they could take the others land...the place where they lived. He saw it when he was a slave and now as a Shawnee, he had come to know and believe that the land could not and should not be owned. It was still difficult for him to understand that if God created it all, good and evil, bad men and good men, how did God choose who was going to be good and who was going to be evil. What were his criteria? Who was going to be a black man? Who was going to be white? Who was going to be an Indian? It seemed that the more he thought at times, the more he would become confused, but at other times it seemed that all of a sudden he would understand something. Some things would become clear to him. Was that part of God's plan too? Just give him a little at a time.

In the distance, they heard the single boom of a cannon echoing over the land It came from the direction of Nashville and all of the Indians realized that the firing of the canon was the signal from the fort that help for the station was on the way. The fight was over. The Indians were in full retreat, removing all of the wounded and dead from the battlefield. The only body that was left behind was that of Chiachattalla. He was lying so close to the fort that no one dared to go after him.[xcv]

Chapter 30
April, 1798

Near Present, Old Town, Ohio

James Galloway had brought his family and settled near the abandoned village of Old Chillicothe. He was born in 1750 in Pennsylvania and served in the Revolutionary War for 18 months as a hunter, providing game for the soldiers. While living in Pennsylvania he married Rebecca Junkin. He had served with Gen. Roger Clarke on his second expedition against the Indians at Old Chillicothe when Clarke burned Old Chillicothe and several other Indian villages. Now, he was returning with his wife, four sons and one daughter to the land that he had fallen in love with. He had felt some remorse as he participated in destroying the Shawnee village on the land and vowed to himself to return to the area and make his family's home there once the Indians were gone.

On this particularly cool, spring evening, he was sitting with his family after supper when the door to their cabin burst open. There had been no knock and all had been quiet as the family sat near the fireplace and listened as Rebecca read from the Bible. With the abrupt intrusion, James quickly grabbed for his gun that was propped up against the table. But, as he reached for the gun, the Indian that stood before him spoke in English to him

"We are not here to harm you or your family. This cabin that you have built is close to my peoples destroyed village and this is the land that I was born on. You will not need your gun. I only want to see the white man and his family that has come to live upon my family's land...my birthplace."

James stood up and looked into the eyes of the Indian that spoke to him. "Your English is good. I am impressed that you can speak to me in English. But, you have no right to come into our home as you have. My family and I have done you no harm."

"No," said Tecumseh. "Perhaps you are right. We should have announced that we were coming."

"You say that you were born on this land?" asked Galloway. "Are you Shawnee? Did you live in this village? What is your name?"

"My name is Tecumseh. This is Caesar," said Tecumseh. "At one time we did live in this village, but not now. I was born near here and my heart is dear to this land."

Galloway turned and looked at Caesar. "Caesar...you are Negro aren't you?"

Caesar looked directly at Galloway. "I am Shawnee...but, you are correct. At one time, I was a slave in Virginia. That life is gone. I am Shawnee."

Off to the side of the room, Galloway's wife and children huddled as far from the door as possible. They had moved quickly when Tecumseh and Caesar had come through the doorway. The tension in the room had quickly died when all the members of the Galloway family heard the two Indians speaking in English and announcing that they meant no harm. The daughter, Rebecca, had fixed her eyes upon Tecumseh. She had always wondered about wild

Indians. In Kentucky, before they had moved, she had only seen a few who had come to the town that they were living in. She had never been this close to one, and when these two spoke English, any fear that she had quickly disappeared.

As her father motioned to Tecumseh and Caesar to sit in the chairs at the table, she couldn't help herself and spoke to Tecumseh.

"I don't know if I really believe you when you say that you don't want to hurt us."

"Rebecca," said Galloway, rather sternly. It is not your..."

Tecumseh interrupted him. "No, please allow her to speak. As I said, we mean you no harm and I am interested in speaking with you and your family. Please, speak."

"If you don't wanna kill us," said Rebecca.

"Rebecca!" said Galloway. "Watch your mouth."

"No, it is all right." Tecumseh said, "Please let her speak."

Galloway relaxed and sat back in his chair as he looked to his wife. "Would you kindly get us some coffee?" He looked at Tecumseh and Caesar. "Would you like some coffee?" They both nodded back.

Galloway's wife got up and took three cups from the cupboard and placed them on the table. She took the pot of coffee that was already brewed and heating over the flames of the fire in the fireplace over to the table and filled the cups.

"Rebecca, would you kindly get the sugar?"

Rebecca brought the sugar to the table and as she put it down, she looked at Tecumseh and said.

"Are you a chief?

Tecumseh looked at her and smiled. "Yes. I am a chief. I am a war chief."

"Have you killed a bunch of white people?"

"Rebecca! That's quite enough," said Galloway.

"Rebecca," said Tecumseh. "I have only done what I have had to do to protect my people and the land that we live upon. I am Shawnee. I am a warrior. I would ask you and your father...all of your family. How can I trust in your promises? How can I have confidence in your promises? How can my Indian brothers ever have confidence in the white people? When Jesus Christ came upon the earth, I am told that you killed him, the son of your own God, you nailed him up! What kind of a people is this for me...for my people to trust?

Rebecca said nothing. The room was silent.

"Tecumseh," said Galloway. "I have seen war. I have seen its bloodshed. I am sorry to say, but I have killed men and I have seen what the white men can do to one another in the name of their God. "

Tecumseh looked at Rebecca and then back to her father. "I speak only truth to you. I have declared myself freely to you about my intentions. And I want to know your intentions. I want to know what you are going to do about the taking of our land. You ask why I am here. It is to hear you say that you understand. I want to be at peace with the whites. Tell me brother...I want to know now because it appears that the whites do not want peace with me"

"Tecumseh," said Galloway, "your speech is eloquent. It is correct. I only want peace. We mean you and your people no harm. There has been enough killing. I only wish to live with my family in peace upon this beautiful land. You say that this is the land that you were born on. I make a promise to you today, as a white man, but more importantly, as a man, to protect and respect this land. Your Weshemanitou and my God, I believe that they are the same and that God, as our creator, controls all aspects of our lives. You were born here and you lived on this land for a time. It is now my time to live on this land and to respect it as a gift. It is only mine to enjoy for a season. Tecumseh...Caesar...I hope that we can become friends this day and for all days. You are welcome in my house at any time and I hope that I would be welcome in yours. Only next time you come, please let us know that you are coming."

Tecumseh and Caesar rose at the same time and both, with a nod of their heads and a firm handshake, said in unison "You are our friend." Tecumseh said further "We will protect you and your family as we would our own families. No Indian will do you or your family harm."

Caesar and Tecumseh left the Galloway homestead. They were both comfortable with this man and his family. As he walked away, Caesar's thoughts quickly switched from the kind whites that he had just met, to the six years that had quickly passed after the death of Cheeseekau.

Caesar and Tecumseh had returned to Ohio within a few weeks of Cheeseekau's death. Tecumseh had brought his brothers body back to Watt's village and prepared him for a Shawnee burial. Their mother had come, as well as one of their sisters.

Tecumseh, with the help of his mother, prepared Cheeseekau's body. They kept it covered inside of the house that Cheeseekau had lived in while with the Cherokee for a half a day after Tecumseh had brought the body back to the village. Cheeseekau's body was dressed in his finest clothes, including his feathers, his items of honor and his favorite weapons. Before his burial, gifts were brought and Tecumseh and his mother redistributed them.

Cheeseekau's grave was dug about four feet deep and had an east-west orientation. His grave's interior was lined with stone and bark. His body was wrapped in a bearskin. Poles were laid across the top of his grave and bark was laid over the poles, and the earth taken from the grave was piled over the bark covering. For three nights a fire was lit on the top of his grave and each night anyone who wanted to speak, including the elders of the Cherokees, related myths and legends until dawn. Each night, songs were sung and the people danced. Many speeches recollecting and honoring Cheeseekau were given. Tobacco was burned in a small fire made near the grave, as it was a Shawnee belief that the smoke created by the tobacco being thrown in the fire would take the words that had been spoken upward to the dwelling place of the spirit. Food was also placed on Cheeseekau's grave each night during his journey to the other world. It was believed that his spirit would depart the earth on the morning of the fourth day. With his spirit departed, food for a feast was set near his grave. A small house was constructed over his grave. His name would never be spoken again.

Chapter 31
October 5, 2012

Zane Shawnee Caverns, Bellefontaine, Logan County Ohio

Emma opened the gift shop at 9:00 and in the short time from when they had come out of Tecumseh Gorge, Will, John and the Professor had gotten three flashlights, two Coleman propane lanterns, a 30 foot section of yellow nylon ski rope and a 20 foot extension ladder.

The campground wasn't full and there were no special activities planned on this early October weekend so they were not expecting to be very busy this Sunday morning. The first cavern tour was scheduled for 11:00 a.m. and as typical for a Sunday morning, Emma wasn't expecting many people, if any for the morning tour. Most of the registered campers had toured the caverns on Saturday and were always preparing to leave on Sunday morning. She had to have the gift shop and store open however, as a lot of the campers came for coffee and a paper on Sunday mornings. Sunday mornings, with the exception of holiday weekends were normally quiet. Typically, they would have day visitor's show up on Sundays for the 1:00 p.m. tour. She was alone and it was difficult to not just close up the store and head down to the sinkhole that they had discovered.

It was 9:20 and the sun had just started to appear through the trees down in the gorge when Will, John and the Professor arrived back at the sinkhole entrance.

The Professor turned on his flashlight and shone it down into the hole. All three looked down into the hole.

"There's definitely some water down there, but it doesn't look very deep," said the Professor.

"Well," Will said, "let's get that ladder and head down. It can't be more than fifteen feet and we have plenty of ladder."

John extended the ladder and slowly eased it into the opening. The legs went into the water only a few inches, and were solid. He leaned the ladder at a slight angle against the side of the opening. It wasn't going to move.

"Who wants to lead the way?" asked the Professor, as John had already turned around and had his foot on the first rung.

John had his flashlight in his left hand and began to climb down the ladder. The Professor held the top steady as John went down and Will just shined his light down into the hole. John reached the bottom and stepped off the ladder.

"It's only a couple of inches deep," said John. "It's pretty solid. No sand or anything...just rock."

The Professor headed down next as Will steadied the ladder. His flashlight was in his jacket pocket and he had one of the lanterns in his hand. As soon as he reached the bottom, Will headed down with the other lantern.

At the bottom, all three had turned on their flashlights and were shining their lights in all directions, sweeping them from side to side. From the small opening to the surface, they were now standing in what appeared to be a small, but open area of about 20 feet in diameter.

"Look," said the Professor, as he picked up wet pieces of rotting wood, "this looks like part of a ladder."

"Makes sense", said Will, "they had to get in and out somehow. Looks like whoever was here last, left the ladder down here and not up top. They were not planning on coming back."

"Whoever it was," said the Professor, "hid this place pretty good and certainly didn't want anyone to get down here easily."

"Forget the ladder," said John. "Where's this place go?"

"Hey," said the Professor, "we left the rope up top."

"Too late now," said John. "We probably won't need it."

"Yeah...well," said Will. The water is coming from over there under that small ledge. I don't think that were gonna get under that ledge. The water's not running very fast." He shined his light and everyone followed with theirs. "It heads over there...its gotta go somewhere and if it were just dropping deeper, it would be running a lot faster than it is. It must be pretty level down here...at least in this area of the cave."

Will headed out of the small opening and into a narrow passage that angled slightly downward. The passage was only about two shoulder widths wide.

"Let's go", said Will. He started down the passage that paralleled the direction that the water was flowing for about 15 feet. The others followed, with all three shining their lights in the direction they were walking.

"Are we headed in the direction of the cave's entrance?" asked John.

"Yeah...I think so," said the Professor.

"Look! Look!" said John, shining his light ahead and just to the right. The water goes that way, but there's an opening going off to our left. It's heading up a little."

"Look up there," said the Professor, "there's an old candle up on that rock ledge."

"Be careful," Will said to John as John headed off down the passage to the left. "Slow down a little...not so fast. Don't get so far ahead of us. You don't know what's in here and it's real slippery. All we need is for one of us to fall and get hurt."

As the three slowly moved forward they left the open area and found the ceiling lowering to the point they had to stoop to go forward. The walls of the cave narrowed to just shoulder width. It was as though a path had been cut through the rock, but it was natural. They continued for almost thirty yards before the ceiling began to rise again and they could fully stand. They were still on a very narrow path through the rock, but just ahead they could see that the path opened up into a large chamber, and as they got closer they could hear the sound of running water.

You guy's gotta see this," said John as he made his way into the opening and shone his light around. Will and the Professor weren't far behind him.

"Unbelievable!" exclaimed the professor. "Look at this place...it's huge!"

"Whew!" said Will, as he and the others were shinning their lights all around the chamber they had just entered. It had to be 30 yards in diameter and the ceiling was at least 30 feet high. On the side opposite from where they stood, was a series of large stalactites coming down from the ceiling of the cave. They were of all different sizes with the largest being around four feet in diameter. There were corresponding stalagmites that rose from the floor of the cave and several large columns where the stalactites and stalagmites had joined. The entire floor of the cave on the opposite side was flowstone and from the ceiling grew one large drapery that was almost 15 feet across and hung down ten to fifteen feet. The white, differing shades of brown and rose colors that the light revealed on the formations was stunning. Adjacent to the drapery formation was what appeared to be a large ledge and a good stream of water about four feet across fell almost 15 feet into a crystal clear pool below. It appeared that the cave opened up behind the drape and the other formations.

"Let's get those lanterns on," Will said, "they'll give us a lot more light than these flashlights."

As John primed and lit the two lanterns, Will and the Professor just stood in awe of what they were seeing.

"Ya know Will," said the Professor, "I'm no cave expert, but I would imagine that what we've just found is pretty spectacular. And it's easily accessible. I can't believe that no one knew of this? Are you sure that there's no other entrance other than the one for the tour? There's got to be a vast tunnel or cave network down here."

The lanterns lit the entire chamber and it was more fantastic than any of them could imagine.

Will hesitated before answering the Professor. "No...I've never been told of any other cave entrances," He was thinking to himself about the size of the cavern they were in, in comparison to the show cavern that tours were led through. This was a gold mine for tourists. He couldn't believe that no one had found it before. He hadn't lied to the Professor and John about another entrance to the cavern, but he did know of another sinkhole that had been sealed long before the Remnant Band purchased the caverns. He had been sworn to secrecy about the entrance and what was in another smaller section of the caverns. He had never been there as it was sealed long before he was born. Only two people knew of the entrance and the cave's secret and they were to pass it down to two others, but the secret must be kept for the sake of the Shawnee people. Emma was the other one who knew of the cave's secret.

Will thought to himself, *I've got to continue here, but the cave system here must be much greater than people originally thought. If there was any silver, it must have been put in this abandoned part of the cave, years before the caves other secret was hidden and never spoken of.* He wondered where this section of the cave went. Hopefully, nowhere near the other sealed section of the cave. What would happen if they came across...?

"Will! Will! Hey...snap out of it! "What the heck are you thinking about?"

"Sorry...this place is just so amazing."

"Come on," said John. "Let's see what's up behind that waterfall."

As they got closer to the waterfall, the rocky cave floor that they have been walking on became somewhat muddy. As they shined their lights ahead, they could see footprints in all directions.

"Whoever made these footprints was wearing moccasins," said John. "Who knows how old they are and who made them, but they seem to follow this trail and disappear into the waterfall." They all looked at each other and before anyone could say anything, John had already stepped through the water and was on the other side.

"A little water never hurt anyone...sure as hell is cold though! You guys aren't afraid of melting are you?"

Will and the Professor looked at each other and stepped through the water. It was cold!

The trail went about another 15 yards and split to the right and left.

"There's a few more old candles over there," said John. There aren't any more footprints either...any suggestions on which way to go?"

"Let's follow one until we can't go any farther and then come back and follow the other," said the Professor.

"Sounds like a plan to me," said John.

"Hold on a second," said Will. "Look over here. There's something carved on the rock at the head of this path. As Will held the lantern closer to the carving, all three men just stared at the carving of a feather.

"Looks like we're going down this tunnel," said John.

"Not so fast. I don't think you're going anywhere," said John Parker. He startled all three of the men as he pointed a handgun in their direction. He had gotten to the Caverns just before 9 am, thinking that the first tour was at ten. After finding out that the first tour was at 11:00, he decided to head down to the gorge and look around. Once in the gorge, he heard the others over at the opening of the sinkhole. He watched from behind a tree as they disappeared one by one into the sinkhole. He was sure that he had not been noticed and eased his way over to the entrance. He had waited four or five minutes until he couldn't hear their voices any longer and felt that it was safe to go down. Once he was down into the cavern, he pulled his gun out and cautiously followed the other three, staying well back. It was dark but he could see the lights ahead from the flashlights and then the lanterns and they had provided him enough light to slowly ease his way. He had waited for an opportune time to play his hand, as he thought. That time was now! He would let the others lead him to the silver. He wouldn't kill them. Just tie them up with the rope they had so conveniently left for him. He would leave them. It would be a long time, if ever, before they would be found. He would be long gone with the treasure. No one knew who he was, and no one would find him.

The professor stared hard at John in disbelief, suddenly recognizing him.

"You're that attendant from the nursing home that hit my father?"

"I didn't mean to hurt him. I thought he was out for his walk and went into his room to take at look at the letter. I saw him looking at the impressions of the medallion and the letter. We got into a struggle over them. I shoved him away and he hit me with his cane. I hit him pretty hard.

"None of that matters now...give me one of those flashlights."

The Professor gave him his flashlight and kept hold of the lantern he was carrying.

"Let's go find that silver...lead the way," he said, waving the gun.

Chapter 32
August, 1812

Old Town, Ohio

William Stephenson used his home just east of Rushsylvania as a stop on the Underground Railroad. His house had a secret door to a basement underneath the front of the house. He also kept slaves in an upstairs room of his house, underneath a rock bridge on his property, and in a cave in the farm's rock quarry. Slaves went from his house to stops further north in Ohio. Only a few locals knew that he was harboring slaves and helping them as they made their escape. One of the families that helped him and at times kept some of the runaway slaves as they made their way through Ohio and on to Canada were the Galloways.

As the Indians moved further West, and more and more white settlers came to occupy the lands in the Ohio territory, Ohio became a hotbed for runaway slaves escaping north for their freedom. The Stephensons had an occasional relationship with the Galloways, but, it was the Galloways, with their clandestine relationship with the Shawnee's, in particular, Caesar, who discriminately aided the Stephensons with the runaway slaves. On this hot, late summer night, Caesar, accompanied by Tecumseh, was sitting only with James Galloway. James' wife and daughter, Rebecca, and the other children had left the men to themselves after dinner. James, Caesar and Tecumseh were discussing the war that had begun between the British and the Americans. The conversation had gone from religion and the politics of the young country, to the confederacy of the Indian nation that Tecumseh was trying to build. Tecumseh explained to James that he was going to lead his warriors against the Americans and fight on the side of the British. He had failed in his attempt to unite all of the tribes, partly because of his brother's failure, but also because the earlier defeats at Fallen Timbers and Tippecanoe had all but destroyed any hopes of the Indian unity. He would never give up his struggle for the land of his birth and the land that Washemoneto had given his people. It was a struggle now however, for his freedom and the freedom of all of his Indian brethren. It was a struggle for a way of life. He knew that it may cost him his life, but he would never give it up. He had discussed his freedom and the freedom of all Indians many times with Caesar and he would continue his fight as a free man and would never become enslaved or allow his people to become enslaved.

James Galloway understood. As a white man, he empathized with Tecumseh. His values were more of the Indian's than the Whites. Even as an American, he would never betray Tecumseh and his cause. His spirit was one with Tecumseh's, and with Caesars. They were free men, accepting what God had provided for them and having a respect for all men. Tecumseh had seen the slaves that had been escaping for their freedom, just as Caesar had done. He would never give up his fight for freedom and he was in agreement with Caesar about helping any men to be free, especially other blacks like Caesar...men, women and children just wanting to live. If the Shawnee silver could help them, and help those that were helping them to freedom, then it should be used. It was of no good hidden. Caesar had asked for Tecumseh's permission to tell the Galloways of the silvers location and Tecumseh was in agreement with Caesar's idea on the use of the silver. It was no surprise that Caesar used this last meeting with the Galloways to give them a letter in regards to where the Shawnee silver was hidden.

The letter provided detailed directions to an abandoned, hidden cave and a cache of silver that the Shawnee had hidden. Caesar knew that to the Galloways the silver was meaningless. They had come and settled on the land because of its beauty. They had vowed to Tecumseh to protect the land and cherish it as the God given gift that it was. Both Caesar and Tecumseh trusted the Galloways and knew that they would only use the silver, if it were needed, to help any runaway slaves on their struggle to freedom.

"Understand," said Caesar, as he spoke to James. "This is more than tellin' you where some silver is so you can get it and use it for money. While the silver's got value as money and it can help any of the slaves that come through this way, it's also got another value. This silver is a history of who the Shawnee people are. You are our friends. We trust you with this silver. We trust you with this knowledge. The silver's yours to use. We know that you don't have no personal use for it. We just want you to understand the real value of the silver. As money, it'll help you help these men, women and children. They'll need cash. This is good, but the silver's real value is that someday its' gonna tell of a people's history. Where they come from and who they truly are."

"I think I understand," said James. "You're my friends, and I'll never tell anyone about this silver and its location will never be known to anyone. I don't need the silver for myself or my family. We got everything we need. It'll only be used as you ask, if at all. The money don't mean nothin' to me. I'm not sure though what you mean about it being able to tell about who the Shawnee are?"

"James," said Tecumseh, "My people are descendants of the Mayan people of the land of Mexico. We have not always lived in these lands. Like all people, our people migrated to this land many years ago. Much of the silver was brought with the ancestors of our people as they journeyed through time and came to these lands. I have been told that they came by boat, after abandoning their towns, and fled to avoid being conquered by another people. When they fled, they brought very few of their possessions with them with the exception of some of their silver. They knew of its trade value and over the years it helped the people from time to time to purchase needed things for the benefit of the people. Also, many of the silver coins came from the Spanish who were defeated in battles in what is called Florida. Some of the silver was taken from many of the white settlers who brought it down the Ohio with them and also from the Kentucky settlers...silver forks, spoons and such. Over the years, some of it has been melted down and made into armbands and earrings, but most of it has only been kept. It was hidden in the cave and most have forgotten about it over the years. It is rarely spoken of among our people and has remained hidden. Most of the Shawnee do not even know that it exists."

"Well, we better git going," said Caesar as he stood. Tecumseh and James Galloway both stood and all three men looked at each other. None spoke. They just looked into one another's eyes. Each man, in his own way, understood the importance of the silver. To Tecumseh, it was his people's history. To Caesar, it was a means of helping his black brothers to escape their history of enslavement, and to James Galloway, its importance was in the trust that had been given to him from two men. Their places in history separate and not yet understood, but, as their eyes met, each man nodded his understanding to the other, and their places in history were now joined and sealed in this moment.

Chapter 32
October 5, 2012

Zane Shawnee Caverns, Bellefontaine, Logan County Ohio

The three men began down the section of the cavern with Parker, gun in hand, following. No one spoke. After going about 200 yards through an area that was open for about 10 yards to either side of the path, with a ceiling around 20 feet high, the path narrowed abruptly to only around two feet wide. The open area had been strewn with medium to large rocks that had fallen from the ceiling, but John now stopped and shown his light ahead.

"Looks like a large rock has fallen just up ahead of us and is blocking the path."

"Is there any way around? Can you see anything?" asked Parker.

"I don't know," said John, shining his light on the blocked path. "It looks like we may be able to keep going if we climb up and over. It looks like there might be an opening up on top."

"Keep going then," said Parker, "And don't try nothing funny."

John, the Professor and Will all climbed the rock one by one with Parker following.

"The path continues down there," said John. "Looks like this large rock must have fallen at some time."

"Just keep going," said Parker as all of the men scrambled down the far side of the rock and back onto the path. They all stopped at the bottom, with the light from the lanterns illuminating the path ahead. The path was still very narrow with an almost shear rock facing on the left about 15 feet high. On the right, for about five feet was a pile of smaller rocks that rose up about ten feet or so. Just past the rocks, it appeared that they were once again in a narrow tunnel, with shear rock sides, but open on the top.

"Are you sure that you want to keep going?" Will asked. "We're getting pretty far in. I really don't think that there's anything in here."

"What's a matter there chief?" Parker asked, "You getting scared?"

"No...I'm not scared. I just think we're on a wild goose chase. There's nothing down here. Will wasn't sure, but the rocks that they had just past on the right didn't look to be naturally fallen. To him, it had appeared that they had been piled purposely to conceal something. He was hoping to distract the others attention, especially Parker's and hoping that they hadn't noticed what he had about the rocks. He wasn't sure of anything at this point, but if the rocks had been piled there, someone had put them there on purpose to seal off the part or section of the cave. Whoever sealed it probably wasn't aware of the path on the other side of the fallen rock. It must have already fallen before they sealed the section. They didn't know that it existed. He wasn't exactly sure where they were under the ground. He knew that the section of the cave that had remained a secret had been sealed and that no one knew of it. He hadn't been to it, but what if they were heading from another entrance into the sealed off section of the cave.

"I really think that we..." He was interrupted by Parker shoving the gun in his back.

"I think we should keep going," said Parker as he pressed the gun into Will's back.

"What do ya think Chief?"

"John...Professor" said Will. "Keep on going, just be careful."

"Good choice Chief," said Parker. "Who knows what were gonna find up ahead."

All four had traveled another one hundred yards when the path opened suddenly to a room that was approximately 20 feet in diameter and had a ceiling of about 20 feet. There was a small stream on the left that ran the entire length of the room. It was about 5 feet wide with crystal clear water. The path followed parallel to the stream and angled off to the right as the tunnel narrowed again at the far side of the opening.

The group went about ten feet further down the path when John suddenly stopped. He had been shinning his flashlight out in front of the lantern's illumination.

"Oh my God!" exclaimed John.

"What?" Parker asked, still holding his gun and pointing it in the direction of the others.

"Oh my God!" exclaimed John again, as Will and the Professor pressed around him and shined their lights ahead.

Up ahead, just passed the light of the lanterns, the beams from the flashlights were illuminating a closed, wooden chest. There were a few silver coins scattered to the sides and in front of the chest. Everyone, including Parker, panned their flashlights around the small room they had just entered. The room was full of silver. Everywhere they looked they saw coins, forks, spoons, goblets, bracelets and platters. There was a small silver statue of a panther. All of the flashlights however, after panning the room, focused on the stack of silver ingots that were piled off to the left. There had to be over 20 of them. And then suddenly, everyone's attention focused on the small platform in the far right corner of the room. It rose about 6 feet.

Will's heart sank. All of the men just stared at the raised wooden platform with the body of a man laid out on top of it. The wood appeared to be somewhat rotten, but it had not collapsed and the temperature in the cave had helped to preserve the body and keep it from total decay.

Parker lowered his gun and focused with the others on the body. John, the Professor and Will all moved slowly toward the body...Parker followed. What they looked upon was incredible. The body was that of an Indian. His hands were crossed upon his chest. The man's shirt showed the stains of blood. The man was dressed in deerskin leggings and had a sash around the waist. His face was painted black and red and there was a bandage around one arm. Around the man's neck was a British medal.

John grabbed the edge of the platform, with weak knees.

"Will!" John exclaimed.

"Do not speak the name," said Will.

"What? What's going' on?" Parker asked.

"Parker," said the Professor. "If I'm right, you are looking at the body of Tecumseh."

"Tecumseh? You gotta be kidding."

Will turned and looked at both the Professor and Parker. "The man you are looking at is who you have said. What I know is that my people secretly brought his body here after he was killed at the battle of Chatham in 1813. They put his body here and sealed this place. No one has spoken of it or ever thought that this burial place would ever be found. We are in a sacred place for the Shawnee people.

For a few minutes, no one spoke. The two lanterns and the flashlights created an almost surreal view as they cast shadows in all directions.

"Let me show you something else," said Will, as he pointed his flashlight at the head of, and just to the left of the platform. There was an old, worn, leather bag that hung from a pole. The bag was suspended and tied off with a leather strap around its top and the ground around the pole appeared to be swept clean in a four or five foot diameter.

"That is our Messawmi...or Sacred Bundle," said Will. Each of our five tribal divisions or septs; the Thawikila, Pekowi, Kispoko, Chalahgawtha, and Mekoches were given a Messawmi from Kuhkoomtheyna, Our Grandmother, before she moved beyond the Sky World. We are of the Chalahgawtha. In that Messawmi are the various elements prescribed by Our Grandmother."

"Do you know what's in it? Parker asked.

"No," said Will. "Sometimes items that represented certain events that were particularly significant for a sept were placed in the Sacred Bundles. Other items could be reminders of special blessings, sacred beliefs, or powerful totems critical to the survival of the Shawanese. I was told that our shamans kept, among great medicines, feathers of the thunderbirds and a bit of the flesh of the King of the Great Horned Snakes in the bundles. Women in the time of their moon were not allowed to pass within sight of where the bundles, were kept.[xcvi]

I have been told that the sacred bundle also contained an ancient tomahawk, with its head shaped like three leaves and that the sacred bundle directed the Shawnee people on how to take care of themselves, how to hunt, how to build houses and how to find spirit helpers, who would teach them how to make sick people well. Grandmother also taught the people how to have ceremonies and dances to entertain her and honor her, and how to be good and worthy. She gave each sept its song to sing, and provided the Shawnee codes to living."

Suddenly, John turned to Will. "Will...Did you hear that?"

"What?"

Will waved his hand. "Quiet!" he whispered.

John bent down on one knee as he stared at the Messawmi. It seemed as though he had lost all of his strength. He could hear a hum. Almost like the sound of a swarm of bees coming from the bundle.

"You feel it to don't you Will?"

"Yes," said Will. "Do you see it as well?"

"Yes," said John.

Parker looked at both Will and John. "What do... Oh my God. I see it!"

The Professor saw it too and all four men now heard the increasingly loud hum and looked as the sacred bundle took the shape of a giant white bird.

"It is a Manito sent by Grandmother," whispered Will.

"This is indeed a sacred place and I have directed the four of you to this place. My people must no longer be divided. You must bring the knowledge of this place and show it to all Shawanese. Not only Shawanese and to all Nations, but to all men. All Shawanese and all Nations were instructed to live, multiply and follow the sacred laws, prophecies, ceremonies and dances. This man died in an attempt to unite all of the Nations. He did not do it in life, but in death and now, at this time, it is meant for the Shawanese and all Nations to rise again as one and be a strong people in this land. They are to become a proud people and help give a renewed strength to the people who live on this land.

You must understand that all that is done under the heavens, even the experience of evil, has been given to the sons of humanity to humble them. You must understand that this humbling is primarily for you inwardly. If you take it as outward only, you will miss what is important in this message. Cleanse first your inward self so that the outward may also be cleansed.

All that has happened to the Shawanese and all the Nations by the notoriously evil men in the world was caused. You must see that each of you were created evil...for your own day of evil within you. If you think that evil was only outward, then it will have no personal value for you. If you think that I speak only of others, you are wrong. I speak primarily of that which is within you. The inward is always first. Cleanse first yourself and then the things which are without will take care of themselves.

All men's lives have been predestined according to the purpose of the Creator who has created them according to His own will. Understand this, and that all men's days were written and ordained for them when they were not. That all men are called, not according to their works, but according to the Creators purpose that was before the world began.

Understand this and understand that all men throughout creation, of all ages, of all Nations, are of the earth. Do not worship them or any of the divinities that man has been allowed to create. There is but one Creator. I am only an outward manifestation of this Creator."

Just as suddenly as the giant white bird appeared and they had begun to hear the sound and the voice, it faded and disappeared. All that was left was the hanging leather bundle. All four men stood completely silent. Their thoughts however were the same. What have I just seen? Was this real? Did the others hear what I heard? Did they see what I saw?

Parker broke the silence. He looked at Will, John and the Professor and suddenly took his gun with the butt forward and handed it toward the Professor. As he did, he spoke to the others.

"Please take this. I am sorry for doing what I've done. I don't even really know what I was doing. I'm not a bad or evil person and I've never taken anything from anyone in my life. I know in my heart the importance of what has been found here. What we have just seen and just heard. The silver is amazing, but I now understand more of the man who lived and whose body lies there. I think I now understand more of myself. We were given real treasure. All of this was meant to be and whether Caesar knew or not, he was an instrument in leading us to this moment. This moment is truly Caesar's silver. I could never take any of this. Please forgive me?

No one knew what to think. The Professor took the gun from Parker, not really knowing what to do with it.

Will glanced briefly at the Professor and John and then looked directly at Parker.

"I can only forgive you as you have been blessed to see, with all of us, a Thunderbird. It was believed that the Thunderbird was a good force that guarded the door of the house of Heaven. When they beat their wings, they made thunder and their flashing eyes made lightning." [xcvii]

"It looked similar to a large white dove to me," said the Professor. "The white dove is symbolic of the Holy Spirit in Christianity."

"I think that we should leave this place and go back up to the office to decide what and how we should do what we know must be done. Everything must remain as it is and we must begin to make the plans for introducing what we have found and what we have been shown," said Will.

Will, John, the Professor and Parker all took one more glance around the room and then turned to head out and back toward the surface, each with a new, profound, inward understanding of themselves and what they had experienced. Not knowing what the others were thinking as they walked in silence, Will's single thought was back to what he had heard as a child. He couldn't remember who had said it.

"Do not kill or injure your neighbor, for it is not him that you injure, you injure yourself. But do good to him; therefore add to his happiness as you add to your own. Do not wrong or hate your neighbor, for it is not him you wrong, you wrong yourself. But love him, for Moneto loves him also as he loves you. My love is your greatest treasure and I have given it to you and to all men."

Reference Notes

i

Braddock's Road was the first road to cross overland through the entire Appalachian Mountain range. It roughly followed what was Nemacolin's path. Nemacolin's path was a Native American trail between the Potomac and the Monongahela rivers, going from the junction of Wills Creek and the Potomac River, Cumberland, Md. to the mouth of Redstone Creek, where Brownsville, Pa is situated. It was blazed and cleared in 1749 or 1750 by Nemacolin, a Delaware chief, and Thomas Cresap, a Maryland frontiersman. The path then traversed a series of mountain peaks through endless forest to the Forks of the Ohio, the meeting place of the Allegheny, Monongahela, and Ohio Rivers (now Pittsburgh, Pa.).

The Nemacolin Path became "Braddock's Road in 1755 in honor of British Gen. Edward Braddock who led a costly expedition against the French Fort Duquesne at the Forks of the Ohio. Braddock engaged as many as 3,000 troops in clearing about a 12' wide road for 110 miles for his army of siege guns, field pieces and 200 wagons. Today, Route 40 roughly parallels Braddock's Road.

ii

The Classic Mayan civilization was unique and left us a way to incorporate higher dimensional knowledge of time and creation by leaving us the Tzolkin calendar. The Mayans invented the calendars we use today. The present calendar ends in the year 2012.

By tracking the movements of the Moon, Venus, and other heavenly bodies, the Mayans realized that there were cycles in the Cosmos. From this came their reckoning of time, and a calendar that accurately measures the solar year to within minutes.

The "Calendar Round" is like two gears that intermesh, one smaller than the other. One of the 'gears' is called the Tzolkin, or Sacred Round. The other is the Haab, or Calendar Round.

The Tzolkin consisted of 13 months each 20 days long, and the Haab of 18 months each 20 days long, and five rest days, thus making 365 days. The date was written using both rounds. For example, "6 lk 10 Camber" might be the same as if we wrote "20 June 30 Gemini." (Haab - Calendar round / 20 June, and Tzolkin - Sacred round / 30 Gemini.) As both these wheels turned so passed the Mayan years. Every 52 years the cycle began again. It was on one of these auspicious years that Cortez landed, thus giving credence to his god image.

Archeologists claim that the Maya began counting time as of August 31, 3114 B.C. This is called the zero year and is likened to January 1, AD. All dates in the Long Count begin there, so the date of the beginning of this time cycle is written 13-0-0-0-0. That means 13 cycles of 400 years will have passed before the next cycle begins, which is December 27, 2012. The new cycle will begin as 1-0-0-0-0.

A day was called a "kin", and still is today. A 20 day month was a "uinal", one solar year was a "tun", 20 tuns a "katun", and 20 katuns were a "baktun", 13 of which take us back to the August 13, 3114 B.C. date.

Source: http://www.crystalinks.com/may.html

iii

The Toltec were fierce warriors that occupied the Northern Reaches of the Valley of Mexico. They were master craftsman. The Toltec went to war with the Mayans and eventually defeated them, creating a cross Toltec-Mayan religion and society. They are believed to have developed the art of smelting metals like silver and copper. By 1400, the Mayans had splintered and disappeared.
http://casademexico.com/prehispanica.html.

iv

Taken from "The Legend of Swift's Silver Mine" by James A. Dougherty "Geographical Approach to the Legends of Silver Mine." The material was made available by the courtesy of the Historical Society of Southwest Virginia and Rhonda Robertson. File://F:\Swifts Silver Mine.htm

v

<u>Shawano</u> <u>illeni</u> or <u>Shawanwa</u> <u>hileni</u> 'Shawnee man'; historically, <u>Shawano</u> appears, but the contemporary form is <u>Shaawanwa</u>. From the stem <u>shawa</u>- 'warm, moderate (of weather)': <u>shawaki</u> 'southerner, southwind person', <u>shawani</u> 'it is warm, moderate weather'; <u>shaateni</u> 'it is moderate weather'.

vi

The Shawnee Woodland Native American Museum is dedicated to the memory of George Drouillard.

Drouillard was a mixed blood Shawnee who was chief hunter, guide and interpreter for the Lewis and Clark Expedition.

vii

Present day Lighthouse Point, Fla. This is at the mouth of the Ochlocknee River where it enters into Apalachee Bay, just south of present day Tallahassee, Fla.

viii

The Apalachee lived between the Aucilla River and the Ochlocknee River, at the head of Apalachee Bay. They spoke a now-extinct Muskogean language. They lived in towns of various sizes, or on individual farmsteads of ½ acre or so in size. Smaller settlements might have a single mound and a few houses. Large towns of 50 to 100 houses may have had several mounds. Their villages and towns were situated by lakes. The largest Apalachee community was at Lake Jackson on the north side of present-day Tallahassee, Florida. This community had several mounds, some of which are now protected in Lake Jackson Mounds Archaeological State park. The Apalachee grew corn, beans, squash, pumpkins and sunflowers. They gathered wild strawberries, the roots and shoots of the greenbriar vine, greens such as lamb's quarters and the roots of aquatic plants. They caught fish and turtles in the lakes and rivers, and oysters and fish on the Gulf Coast. They hunted deer, black bears, rabbits and ducks.

ix

Anhaica was also known as Iniahica and Yniahico. It was an Apalachee Indian town and the capital of Apalachee Province. Its location was near present day Meyers Park in Tallahassee, Fla. Anahica's population was approximately 30,000. The total population of the Province was around 60,000. Anhaica had 250 buildings when Hernando De Soto set up camp in the town in October of 1539, forcing the Apalachee to abandon the village.

x

After Pontiac's War, Fort Pitt was no longer necessary to the British Crown, and was abandoned to the locals in 1772. At that time, the Pittsburgh area was claimed by both Virginia and Pennsylvania, and a power struggle for the region commenced. Virginians took control of Fort Pitt, and for a brief while in the 1770s it was called Fort Dunmore, in honor of Virginia's Governor Lord Dunmore.

xi

The Treaty of Fort Stanwix was an important treaty between the North American Indians and the British Empire. It was signed at a conference in 1768 at Fort Stanwix, located in present-day Rome, New York. It was negotiated between Sir William Johnson and representatives of the Six Nations (the Iroquois). The purpose of the conference was to adjust the boundary line between Indian lands and British colonial settlements set forth in the Royal Proclamation of 1763. The British government hoped a new boundary line might bring an end to the rampant frontier violence, which had become costly and troublesome. The Indians hoped a new, permanent line might hold back British colonial expansion. The final treaty was signed on November 5 with one signatory for each of the Six Nations and in the presence of representatives from New Jersey, Virginia and Pennsylvania, as well as Johnson. The Indians received £10,460 7s. 3d. Sterling. The treaty established a Line of Property that extended the earlier proclamation line much further west. The Iroquois had effectively ceded the Kentucky portion of the Colony of Virginia to the British. However, the Indians who actually used the Kentucky lands, primarily the Shawnee, Delaware, and Cherokee, had no role in the negotiations. Rather than secure peace, the Fort Stanwix treaty of 1768 helped set the stage for the next round of hostilities along the Ohio River, which would culminate in Dunmore's War.

xii

In the summer of 1774 the situation exploded into a full-blown war. Troops from Virginia and Pennsylvania were sent west. A punitive expedition was planned against the Indian towns of the Shawnee and Delaware. Native raiding parties swept south and burned settlements in Kentucky and West Virginia. The terrible fighting that summer would become known as Lord Dunmore's War, named after the Governor of Virginia.

xiii

Now, Sistersville, West Virginia

xiv

Sinkholes are usually but not always linked with Karst landscapes. In such regions, there may be hundreds or even thousands of sinkholes in a small area so that the surface, as seen from the air, looks pock-marked, and there are no surface streams because all drainage occurs sub-surface. Karst topography is a landscape shaped by the dissolution of a layer or layers of soluble bedrock usually carbonate rock such as limestone or dolomite. Due to subterranean drainage, there may be very limited surface water, even to the absence of all rivers and lakes.

Less than 2 percent of the Ohio landscape includes Karst terrain. The percentage is low because most near-surface carbonate bedrock in Ohio is covered with a thick mantle of glacial deposits that greatly impede or preclude active Karst-forming processes. In addition, the abrasive work of Ice Age glaciers is believed to have destroyed much of the Karst terrain that had developed in Ohio prior to glaciations.

The Bellefontaine Outlier in Logan and northern Champaign Counties is an erosion resistant "island" of Devonian carbonates capped by Ohio Shale and surrounded by a "sea" of Silurian strata. Though completely glaciated, the outlier was such an impediment to Ice Age glaciers that it repeatedly separated advancing ice sheets into two glacial lobes - the Miami Lobe on the west and the Scioto Lobe on the east. The outlier is the location of Campbell Hill - the highest point in the state at an elevation of 1,549 feet above mean sea level. Although it is not known for having an especially well-developed Karst terrain, the outlier is the location of Ohio's largest known cave, Ohio Caverns. The greatest sinkhole concentrations are in McArthur and Rushcreek Townships of Logan County, where the density of sinkholes in some areas approaches 30 per square mile. Sinkholes here typically occur in upland areas of Devonian Lucas Dolomite or Columbus Limestone that are 30 to 50 or more feet above surrounding drainage and are covered by less than 20 feet of glacial drift and/or Ohio Shale. Division of Geological Survey http://dnr/state.oh.us/geosurvey/

XV

This is the Cumberland River. It is 678 miles (1,106 km) long. It starts in Letcher County in eastern Kentucky on the Cumberland Plateau, flows through southeastern Kentucky before crossing into northern Tennessee, and then curves back up into western Kentucky before draining into the Ohio River at Smithland, Kentucky.

In 1748, Dr. Thomas Walker led a party of hunters across the Appalachian Mountains from Virginia. Walker, a Virginian, was an explorer and surveyor of renown. He gave the name "Cumberland" to the lofty range of mountains his party crossed, in honor of Prince William Augustus, Duke of Cumberland whose name became popular in America after the Battle of Culloden (Stewart, 1967). Walker's party pursued their journey by way of the Cumberland Gap into what is today Kentucky. Finding a beautiful mountain stream flowing across their course they called it the "Cumberland River." Walker's journal entry for April 17, 1750, reads in part: "I went down the creek a-hunting, and found that it went into a river about a mile below our camp.

This, which is Flat Creek and some other join'd, I called Cumberland River."

Previous to Walker's trip, the Cumberland River had been called *Warioto* by Native Americans and *Shauvanon* by French traders. The river was also known as the *Shawnee River* (or *Shawanoe River*) for years after Walker's trip.

Important first as a passage for hunters and settlers, the Cumberland River also supported later riverboat trade which reached to the Ohio and Mississippi Rivers. Villages, towns and cities were located at landing points along its banks. Through the middle of the 19th century, settlers depended on rivers for trading and travel.

From Wikipedia

xvi

Ponce de Leon died a few days after his return to Cuba. He was buried in Puerto Rico, the epitaph on his sepulcher reading, "Here rest the bones of a valiant LION [León], mightier in deeds than in name."

xvii

Sisters and Pike Island.

xviii

The name Wheeling supposedly is derived from a Delaware Indian term meaning "head" or "skull," a reference to the beheading of a party of settlers.

The Wheeling Settlement

An entry in Washington's journal, for October 23, 1770, made during his memorable trip down the Ohio River from Pittsburgh to Point Pleasant and return, contains his only reference to settlers at this place: ". . . About three miles or a little better below this place, at the lower point of some islands which stand contiguous to each other (Sisters and Pike Island) we were told by the Indians with us that three men from Virginia had marked the land from hence all the way to Redstone . . ." The three men referred to were doubtless Ebenezer, Jonathan and Silas Zane who, in the previous year, 1769 had come from the South Branch Valley, Virginia, had marked trees to establish tomahawk claims to the land, and made further preparations for permanent settlement. The land marked covered most of the present site of Wheeling, including Elm Grove. Soon afterward others came. In historical accounts some of the names listed are: McCulloch, Wetzel, Biggs, Shepherd, Caldwell, Boggs, Scott, Lynn, Mason, Ogle, Bonnett, McMechen and Woods.

(Published by West Virginia Archives and History) Story of Fort Henry ,By A. B. Brooks Volume I, Number 2 (January 1940), pp. 110-118

xix

Intelligence of the Indian troubles all along the western frontier of Virginia had been conveyed in almost daily letters and reports to the capital at Williamsburg. June 10, 1774, Governor Dunmore sent a circular letter to all the county lieutenants, who were the official heads of the local militia, ordering them to muster the militia and to take such measures for defense as the situation required, including the erection of small forts in the exposed settlements. One of the important points to be occupied and fortified was the mouth of the Kanawha River, and the governor recommended that the forces there should co-operate with the garrison at Fort Dunmore in patrolling the intervening country along the Ohio. About the same time [John] Connolly [in Pittsburgh] was preparing to send a force down the Ohio to build a small fort "at the mouth of Wheeling." This course was approved by the governor, who recommended that Captain William Crawford proceed to Wheeling and from that point carry on a campaign into the Indian country.

Thus, early in June, 1774, Captain Crawford with about two hundred men from Fort Dunmore came to the mouth of Wheeling and began the erection of Fort Fincastle, or, as it was later known, Fort Henry.

There are no contemporary documents that afford any descriptive picture of Fort Fincastle. The fort disappeared before the close of the century, and only the recollections of old men and women, or second-hand accounts, furnished the details on which existing descriptions were based. But there was a plan that seldom varied in the construction of these frontier posts, and had the Wheeling fort differed conspicuously the fact would probably have been handed down in tradition or the early writings. Hence it is possible to accept the usual statement that the fort was rectangular in form, with its four stockade walls consisting of upright pickets eight or ten feet high. Some of these forts had two blockhouses, located at diagonal corners, and others had a blockhouse at each corner. Fort Fincastle is said to have been of the latter kind. These blockhouses extended a few feet beyond the lines of the walls, so that a lateral fire could be directed against any who tried to scale the pickets. And the second store of each blockhouse also projected beyond the wall of the first, so that the enemy was exposed at every point outside of the fort. The traditional accounts state that the fort occupied about half an acre of ground. Governor Dunmore recommended the construction of "a small fort" at this point, and this size would agree with such specifications. The fort was probably about 175 feet long by 125 feet wide, or about one quarter the area of a city square. On the inside of the stockade were rows of cabins, comprising the barracks for the garrison, the store houses, etc.

While the exact lines of the fort could not be traced in the modern topography of Wheeling, the approximate site can be defined with certainty. In 1774, and for many years later, the ground between present Main Street and the river, and about Eleventh Street, formed a prominent elevation or bluff, considerably higher than the highest point of the present hill. On the river side, there was a steep declivity, and for years afterward, early travelers spoke of the difficult approach from the river landing up to the center of the village. On the south the hill fell off abruptly to the lower levels of the bottomlands towards the creek. On the north and east there was a gentler slope from the height chosen for the fort to the general levels of this bench land between the river and the hills. This situation made the fort nearly impregnable from any ordinary Indian attack. No attacking party could successfully assail from the river or from the grain fields in the bottomlands to the south. The ground below the fort on the east and north was likewise cleared, and only a few scattered cabins afforded protection to a foe approaching the fort from those directions.

FORT HENRY from History of Greater Wheeling and Vicinity, Charles A. Wingerter Chicago: Lewis Publishing, 1912. p. 78-100

Another description of the fort was provided in the West Virginia Archives and History. "The fort was in the shape of a parallelogram, with wooden towers or bastions at each corner, which projected over the lower story and which were pierced by port holes for the use of rifles and muskets. In case of attack the fighting was carried on almost entirely from these bastions. Between these bastions was stretched a strong and closely-connected line of oak and hickory pickets, surrounding entire enclosure, within which were located a magazine powder, barracks and cabins for sheltering those who sought refuge within the stockade. On the roof of the barracks7 was mounted a swivel gun captured during the French and Indian War by the British. There was also a well of water within the stockade. On the west side of the Fort outside of it was a never-failing spring of pure, limpid water. The main entrance was on the east side, which was closed by a strong wooden gate. The ground in the vicinity was cleared, fenced and cultivated, extending to the base of the hill on the east, about an eighth of a mile distant.

"From the bluff on the south side of the fort extended the bottoms to the bank of Wheeling Creek. The expanse of ground was a level stretch of land and was used for a cornfield. As late as 1810 no buildings of consequence occupied it.

Story of Fort Henry, A. B. Brooks. West Virginia Archives and History Volume I, Number 2 (January 1940), pp. 110-118

XX

The American Indian leader who came to be called Logan was born in Pennsylvania around 1725. His father was a Cayuga Indian named Shikellamy. Shikellamy later renamed his son after James Logan -- a prominent Pennsylvanian and old friend. Logan grew up in Pennsylvania and came to view many whites as his friends. Chief among them was David Zeisberger, a missionary of the Moravian Church. Logan eventually married a Shawnee woman and moved to Ohio around 1770. He settled in Yellow Creek, a village of Mingo Indians. He became a war leader but continued to urge his fellow natives not to attack whites settling in the Ohio Country.

"Chief Logan", *Ohio History Central*, July 1, 2005

xxi

The name "Shawnee" is an English adaptation of the term *Shaawana*, by which the Shawnee Indians named themselves in their own language. In the Ohio Journal of Science 60(3): 155, May, 1960 an August C. Mahr in an article entitled "Shawnee Names and Migrations in Kentucky and West Virginia" states that Voeglin (1938-40): 318 lists *Saawaanwa* 'Shawnee (tribe or individual),' adding *Saawanwaki* beside *Saawanooki* 'the Shawnee (plural).' Another white adaptation is *Savannah*, name of both the city and the river in Georgia, where in the 1600's, Shawnee Indians were first encountered by Whites.

xxii

On a map as late as 1720 (Moll, 1720) is the mouth of the Cumberland marked as Cherokee territory, and an Indian settlement there, as 'Savannah Old Settlement'; indicating that the Shawnee have definitely left.

(Hodege, 1907,1910:535)." Shawnee Names and Migrations in Kentucky and West Virginia, August C. Mahr, The Ohio Journal of Science 60 (3): 155, May, 1960. P. 160.

xxiii

Across the Ohio River, at the mouth of the Scioto River, the Shawnee had established by 1730 a settlement known as 'Shawnee Town.' The Shawnee that traveled through this area referred to the area as *Skaalaappiye*. In present day Lewis County, Ky., this Shawnee name exists as a neighborhood name, *Eskalapia*, surviving in *Eskalapia Mountains, Eskalapia Hollow*, etc. The name was an indication in its meaning that the trail, at a long stretch, traversed a weed-covered, soggy terrain; in brief, that the land was unfit for a stopover and the planting of corn.

There is evidence, however, that some western Shawnee bands of about 1740 continued their migration from *Eskippakithiki* in a general NEE direction as far east as the Great Kanawah valley in present West Virginia.

Shawnee Names and Migrations in Kentucky and West Virginia, August C. Mahr, The Ohio Journal of Science 60 (3): 155, May, 1960. P. 162.

xxiv

The Savannah and the Shawnee were probably the same tribe. Their removal from South Carolina was gradual, beginning about 1677 and continuing at intervals through a period of more than 30 years. The first Shawnee seemed to have left South Carolina in 1677 or 1678 when about 70 families established themselves on the Susquehanna adjoining the Conestoga in Lancaster County, Pa. At the mouth of Pequea Creek. Their village was called Pequea, a form

of Piqua. The Chief of Pequea was Wapath, or Opessah. He contends that another large part of the Shawnee probably left South Carolina about 1707. In 1708, Governor Johnson of South Carolina reported that the "Savannahs" on the Savannah River occupied 3 villages and numbered about 150 men.
(Shawnee Indian Tribe History accessgenealogy.com)

XXV

The Alligator as a totem. The Alligator is one of the oldest reptiles and animals known to man. They are known in many myths and lore as the keepers of ancient wisdom. By nature, they only eat when they are hungry and do not consume food unnecessarily. Thus, their character teaches one not to waste what they have been given. Their food is also digested slowly indicating that those with this totem should remember to digest and assimilate all experiences thoroughly before moving forward in haste. The eyes of the alligator are positioned high on their head allowing them to remain relatively hidden beneath the water and still see above it. Symbolically this hints to clairvoyant abilities. Their ability to hide in the water ties the alligator to the emotional body of man. The alligator holds the teachings of the discovery and the release of emotions that are locked beneath the surface. Alligators dig deep burrows when the water is high so that during the dry season they can have a wet alcove to retreat to. These alcoves serve as reservoirs from which other animals can get water. Water is the essence of life. The sharing of these reservoirs indicates the alligators respect for all life forms. The power of alligator is its power to survive. They have no known predators. It is believed that if an alligator shows up in one's life or in one's dream time that it might be telling them to take care of themselves and to secure their basic need to survival needs. Alligator's come together only for reproduction. They have distinct individual personalities. Thus, those with this totem are usually loners and only join together in groups when mandatory. Alligator people can be great leaders. They know how to survive in any situation and are strong enough to hold their ground. Alligators teach the art of patience and appropriate timing. They know when to hide beneath the water, peak above it, or take action and snap.

xxvi

James Galloway, Sr. was one of the 1st pioneers to settle in Green County, Ohio around 1797. He was a soldier in the Revolutionary war and an Indian fighter and companion of Daniel Boone. He came to the Little Miami Valley with his family from Kentucky in 1797. He settled in Old Town – Chillicothe – Just North of present day Xenia, Ohio.

xxvii

Near present day Steubenville, Ohio.

xxviii

Scholars agree that Logan was a son of Shikellamy, an important diplomat for the Iroquois Confederacy. Shikellamy has been identified as a Cayuga or Oneida. He worked closely with Pennsylvania official James Logan in order to maintain the Covenant Chain relationship with the colony of Pennsylvania.

Following a Native American practice, the man who would become Logan the Mingo took the name "James Logan" out of admiration for his father's friend.

xxix

Near present day Wellsville, Ohio along the Ohio River.

xxx

Greathouse was born in Frederick County, Maryland, one of 11 children of Harmon and Mary Magdalena Stull Greathouse. The Greathouse family moved from Maryland to Virginia about 1770 and Daniel owned 400 acres of land at Mingo Bottom in Ohio County, Virginia. Daniel married Mary Morris, and they had two children, Gabriel and John.

xxxi

Cornstalks village was near present day Circleville.

xxxii

American Archives, fourth Series, Vol. 1. p. 479.

xxxiii

For the intentions of this book and to facilitate the anger that Caesar may have had for the whites and to help to see that in Blue Jacket some reasoning for Caesar to want to become a Shawnee, I have taken the traditional position that Blue Jacket was white. That he was Marmaduke Van Swearingen, born on January 2, 1753, on a thousand-acre farm in Fayette County, Pennsylvania. This is the traditional position of many historians for over a century. However, one must note that today, there is significant evidence that Blue Jacket was not a white man.

Two distinctly different origins have been ascribed to the great Shawnee war chief Blue Jacket who played a pivotal role in the early history of southwestern Ohio. By one very popular account, he was a captured Caucasian who embraced the ways of the Shawnee and came to lead their warriors in a campaign that unified all the Indian tribes of the Ohio River Valley against the United States of America.

In contrast, modern day Shawnee Indians who still bear the Blue Jacket surname suggest that the legendary War Chief was unequivocally a Native American. Y-STR haplotyping of six living, direct male descendants of Chief Blue Jacket and of four direct male descendants/relatives of the Caucasian family that has become intertwined with the history of the Shawnee tribe is described in this study.

Barring any questions of the paternity of the Chief's single son who lived to produce male heirs, the "Blue Jacket with-Caucasian-roots" is not based on reality.

OHIO J SCI 106 (4):126-129, 2006

The "Blue Jacket-with-Caucasian-roots" legend portrays him as Marmaduke Swearingen, a son of John Swearingen (1721-1784) (Eckert 1967, 1969). Marmaduke is said to have been captured (along with his younger brother Charles) by the Shawnee Indians during a hunting expedition during the time of the American Revolutionary War. The raid that led to the capture of the then seventeen year old Marmaduke is alleged to have taken place near the Swearingen family home, which was northeast of the junction of the Monongahela and Cheat Rivers, west of Morris Crossroads (northeast of present day Point Marion in southwestern Pennsylvania)(Ellis 1882). Marmaduke is said to have negotiated his own naturalization into the tribe in return for the release of his younger brother. According to this oral tradition, the name Blue Jacket stemmed from Marmaduke's wearing of a blue linsey blouse or hunting shirt at the time of his capture (Larsh 1877). Written and oral accounts have claimed that the young Marmaduke became quite enamored with and dedicated to the way of the Shawnee, garnering him great popularity and admiration and ultimately designation to the status of Chief of the Shawnee by the age twenty-five (Bennett 1943).

However, the "Blue Jacket-with-Caucasian-roots" narrative is inconsistent with verifiable historical records in several ways. While no written record of Chief Blue Jacket's birth is known to exist, historians have estimated the date of his birth to be between 1738 and 1740 (Bailey 1947; Sugden 2003). In contrast, Marmaduke Swearingen's birth is documented in the Swearingen family Bible as occurring on 2 January 1763 near Hagerstown, MD (Whyte 1999). During the mid-1750s and almost ten years before the recorded birth of Marmaduke, Blue Jacket was a recognized trader who was noted in the logs of store keepers in the Ohio River Valley. Specific notations pertaining to Blue Jacket are likely to have been made due to his having been granted credit, an extravagance only afforded to exceptional Indians at the time (Jones 1971). Similarly, in 1765, when Marmaduke would have been only two years old, the

Shawnee tribe returned all of their captives in compliance with a prisoner exchange program at the cessation of the French and Indian War. One of these prisoners, Margaret Moore, claimed that she had been the wife of Blue Jacket and that he was also the father of her infant son Joseph Moore and her soon to be born daughter, Nancy Moore. Between 1810 and 1824, several land grants recorded with the State of Ohio name both Nancy and Joseph Moore as the "half-blood" children of Chief Blue Jacket. One land grant dated 13 July 1824 records that the same Nancy Moore was "one Nancy Stewart (married name), daughter of the late Shawnee Chief Blue Jacket" (Logan County, OH). Blue Jacket's second marital union was said to have been with a woman of French and Indian decent, "Métis" Baby, and resulted in two known sons, James and George I, born in 1765 and 1770, respectively. Marmaduke would have been only two- and seven-years old at the time of these births. In addition, by 1773, when Marmaduke would have been only ten-years old, a town located on a tributary (Deer Creek) of the Scioto River in Ohio was already popularly known as "Blue Jacket's Town" in honor of the Shawnee chief (Bailey 1947). Despite these seeming historical inconsistencies, the Swearingens have vigorously avowed their shared lineage with Chief Blue Jacket (Kansas State Historical Society 1908; Whyte 1999).

However, if it is accepted that George I was Chief Blue Jacket's son, it can be reasonably concluded that the famous Shawnee war chief was in fact a Native American and that the popular story surrounding his relatedness to Dutch settlers is without merit.

CAROLYN D. ROWLAND, R. V. VAN TREES, MARC S. TAYLOR, MICHAEL L. RAYMER, AND DAN E. KRANE, Forensic Bioinformatics, Inc., Dayton, OH 45324; Fairborn, OH 45324; Technical Associates Inc., Ventura, CA 93003; Department of Computer Science and Engineering,

Wright State University, Dayton, OH 45435; and Department of Biological Sciences, Wright State University, Dayton, OH 45435

xxxiv

Pequea Creek (pronounced *peck-way*) is a tributary of the Susquehanna River that runs for approximately 40 miles (65 km) from the eastern border of Lancaster County and Berks County, Pennsylvania to village of Pequea, about 5 miles (8 km) above the hydroelectric dam at Safe Harbor along the Susquehanna River in Lancaster County, Pennsylvania. The name of the creek is Shawnee for "dust" or "ashes", referring to a clan that once dwelt at the mouth of the creek.

xxxv

Hokolesqua or Cornstalk (c.1720 – November 10, 1777, was a prominent leader of the Shawnee people. He was probably born about 1720 in western Pennsylvania. Historians today speculate on his early years, but believe that he migrated to the Ohio Country with his family when he was about 10 along with many other Shawnee as they were pushed West by the expanding white settlements in the 1730's.

I have chosen to use the name Hokolesqua as it seems to be the most popular name in Ohio. His name in his own language meant "blade of corn", there are however, other references to his names as: Wynepuechsika, Keigh-taugh-quah-qua and Colesqua. Some have identified him incorrectly as Taminy Buck, who was a well known chief in Pennsylvania and was probably associated with him only by the similarity of the name. (Probably taamini-, 'corn' + po'k- 'mashed"; also Tomenebuck; Tamene

Buck; Tokmene Buck; Domini Buck). In C.Hale Sipe's *Indian Chiefs of Pennsylvania* he goes by the name of Tamenebuck, or Taming Buck. In the Draper manuscripts 3 Dxviii, the Indian name of Cornstalk is Keigh-tugh-qua signifying a blade (or stalk) of the maize plant.

xxxvi

De lisle's map of 1700 places the "Ontouagannha." which here means the Shawnee, on the headwaters of the Santee and Pedee rivers in South Carolina, while the "Chiouonons" are located on the lower Tennessee River. Senex's map of 1710 locates a part of the "Chaouenons" on the headwaters of a stream in South Carolina, but seems to place the main body on the Tennessee. Moll's map of 1720 has "Savannah Old Settlement" at the mouth of the Cumberland (Royce in Abstr. Trans. Anthr. Soc. Wash., 1881), showing that the term Savannah was sometimes applied to the Western as well as to the eastern band.

The Shawnee of South Carolina, who included the Piqua and Hathawekela divisions of the tribe, were known to the early settlers of that state as Savannahs. (Barnwell, 1715, in Rivers, Hist. South Carolina, 94, 1874).

xxxvii

The Munsee were one of the three principal tribes of the Lenape or Delaware. The Delaware were a confederacy, formerly the most important of the Algonquian. They occupied the entire basin of Delaware River in east Pennsylvania and south New York, together with most of New Jersey and Delaware. They called themselves Lenape or Leni-lenape, equivalent to 'real men,' or 'native, genuine men'; the English knew them as Delaware, from the name of their principal river; the French called them Loups, 'wolves,' a term probably applied originally to the Mahican on the Hudson rivers, afterward extended to the Munsee division and to the whole group. To the more remote Algonquin tribes they, together with all their cognate tribes along the coast far up into New England, were known as Wapanaehki, 'easterners,' or 'eastern land people of "grandfather,"

xxxviii

The Little Muskingum River.

xxxix

The Big Muskingum River is four miles downstream from the Little Muskingum. It is approximately 250 yards wide at its mouth. It is the site of today's Marietta, Ohio.

xl

"May 19 - Sailed down the river 16 miles to Bland, an exquisite island. This island was but lately celebrated for its elegant buildings and other improvements of taste. Its former owner, Mr. B., was enticed away by Iron Bull and shortly afterward its buildings were burned to the ground. Only the stacks of chimneys remain as sorrowful monuments of their former greatness. From this place, we sailed down 5 miles to Little Hocking River, which is about 80 yards wide at its mouth. From this, we sailed down 5 miles to the Big Hocking River."

www.dianneandpaul.net/DianneGenealogy/d0000/g0000089.html
"IV. AN EPIC JOURNEY IN THE NORTHWEST TERRITORY BY RODOLPHUS DERRICK - APRIL 30, 1820 TO MARCH 31, 1821.

One of the most fascinating records left to posterity in the Derrick archives is a diary kept by Rodolphus Derrick during his travels down the Ohio River to the Illinois country in 1820 and 1821. Undoubtedly the trip was motivated by a similar journey made a couple of years earlier by Rodolphus' sister, Elizabeth Kellogg, and her husband, Capt. Elisha Kellogg. No doubt Rodolphus wished to see this new Illinois country for himself prior to undertaking any move from his old homestead at Clarence Hollow, New York. Rodolphus consumed an entire year in this expedition, while his wife Loranda remained at Clarence, perhaps to tend the store as well as care for two small children, Rodolphus Frederick and Harriet. The younger child actually was born only a few days after his father had left on his long journey to the West. (According to my (DZS) reading of the record, this statement is incorrect. Baby Harriet was born 4 Apr 1820 and her dad left 30 Apr 1820.)"

The author can find no other mention of this island but from the description, the location described and the fact that the home was burnt in 1811, one would have to believe that it is today's Blennerhasset Island.

In 1797, Harman Blennerhasset and his wife moved to Marietta, Ohio, where they purchased 174 acres of land on an island in the Ohio River. The land formerly belonged to George Washington. The island is located near Belpre. The Blennerhassetts intended to make the island their home. For the first several years that the Blennerhassetts lived on the island, they resided in a blockhouse. In 1800, they moved into a mansion. In their new home, the couple lived the life of the wealthy. Harman conducted scientific experiments, formed an extensive private library, and paid detailed attention to his agricultural fields. The couple became well known for their hospitality, and many travelers down the Ohio River stopped at the Blennerhasset home. The couple's most famous guest was Aaron Burr, a former Vice President of the United States. In 1805 and 1806, the Blennerhassetts assisted Burr in his scheme to break away the western part of the United States to form a new country that he would lead. The United States government heard rumors of the uprising and sent a detachment of Virginia militia to seize the Blennerhasset's island. Harman Blennerhasset was in hiding. His wife was away in Marietta. When she returned, she discovered that the militiamen had ransacked the home. She fled with her three children. Her husband was arrested a few weeks later, but he quickly gained his release. The Blennerhassetts briefly returned to their mansion, but now destitute from Harman's support of Burr, they sought their fortunes in Mississippi. The Blennerhasset's' former home, now under new ownership, burned in 1811. During the 1980s, the mansion was reconstructed on its original foundations. The island is now a West Virginia state park.

xli

The Little Hocking River.

xlii

The Big Hocking River.

xliii

"Sailed down the river 30 miles to Standing Rock or Rock of Antiquity. This is seen standing in the water's edge on the right shore of the river. It is called the Rock of Antiquity on account of its ancient engravings that show themselves on its smooth and almost perpendicular front. On it is represented the huge figure of a man smoking. He is sitting with his elbows on his knees, which seem to meet his breast. His shoulders and head are leaning forward and his pipe is in one hand. There are likewise a number of other engravings partly defaced by time and the friction of the water of the Ohio."

www.dianneandpaul.net/DianneGenealogy/d0000/g0000089.html
"IV. AN EPIC JOURNEY IN THE NORTHWEST TERRITORY BY RODOLPHUS DERRICK - APRIL 30, 1820 TO MARCH 31, 1821.

This "Rock of Antiquity" does exist and has been a prominent landmark on the river at the small village of Antiquity located in Meigs County, Ohio since the area was first settled in the 1790's. The carvings on the rock have long disappeared due to erosion, but I can remember the old timers talking about them. Antiquity is located on State Route 124, halfway between the towns of Racine and Letart Falls, my birthplace.

Steve Badgley
Badgley Publishing Company

xliv

This is the Kanawha River that enters into the Ohio at today's Point Pleasant, W. Va.. Point Pleasant would become the seat of Justice for Mason County, Virginia.

xlv

Tu-Endie-Wei State Park, W. Va. Information from the history of the Battle of Point Pleasant. www.tu-endie-weistatepark.com/battle.htm.

xlvi

This was the site of today's Gallipolis, Ohio. It is the seat of justice for Gallia County, Ohio. Mostly French emigrants would settle it in the early 1800's.

xlvii

The Ohio runs south from today's Pittsburg and makes a big swing to the North just past today's Huntington, W.Va. near where the Big Sandy River enters into the Ohio.

xlviii

The site of today's Portsmouth, Ohio and the confluence of the Scioto and the Ohio Rivers. Portsmouth would not be founded until the 1790's. The Scioto River is a major river in central and southern Ohio. Its headwaters are located in Auglaize County. The river then flows to Columbus, the capital city, and then in a southerly direction to Portsmouth, where it flows into the Ohio River. It is more than 231 miles in length. "Scioto" is an American Indian word meaning "deer."
www.ohiohistorycentral.org/index.php

xlix

Chalahgawtha (or, more commonly in English, Chillicothe) was the name of one of the five divisions (or bands) of the Shawnee. It was also the name of the principal village of the division. The other four divisions were the Mekoche, Kispoko, Pekowi, and Hathawekela. (All five division names have been spelled in a great variety of ways.) Together these divisions formed the loose confederacy that was the Shawnee tribe.

The village where the chief of the Chillicothe division lived was also known as "Chillicothe". When this principal village was relocated, often as a result of war or the expansion of European-American settlement, the new village would be again be called "Chillicothe". Not all Shawnee living in the town belonged to the Chillicothe division, and some residents were from tribes other than the Shawnee. There are numerous Shawnee Chillicothe villages in the historical record.

The Chalahgawtha cited here was also known as Lower Shawnee Town. It was a large Shawnee town on the Ohio River, founded about 1738 by Shawnee. The name of the town was not recorded, but scholars believe it may have been "Chillicothe". The town grew to be a major trading hub in the years leading up to the French and Indian War. Members from most, if not all five Shawnee divisions lived in the town, as well as an assortment of other Native Americans, Europeans, and Africans, with an estimated total population of 1,200 or more people. Lower Shawnee Town was abandoned after the fall of Fort Duquesne in 1758.

The next Chillicothe (1758–1787) was one of seven Shawnee villages on the west bank of the Scioto River, near Paint Creek and the present U.S. city of Chillicothe, Ohio.
(Wikipedia)

I

Logstown stood on the land, now the property of the Harmony Society, at Economy, PA, a short distance below the town, and on the right or north bank of the Ohio. While the Iroquois Indians claimed this land, members of the Delaware and Shawnee Indians lived at Logstown beginning in the 1720s. Members of several other tribes also resided in the community, including the Mingo Indians, the Miami Indians, the Mohawk Indians, and the Wyandot Indians. Because of Logstown's location on the Ohio River, the village became an important trading center for both natives and Europeans.

Ii

This was the culmination to an amazing migration. There is much documentation that leads one to believe that there were two separate migrations from the Carolinas and the Cumberland Valley in Tennessee to the Ohio territory. However, the history of the Shawnee people, prior to 1690 is very sketchy and at best historians have only been able to speculate as to why the Shawnee people seemed to have ended up in two distinct locations in the Eastern US. Their history from the early to mid-1820's is well documented.

lii

Chillicothe (1758–1787) was located on the west bank of the Scioto River, near Paint Creek and the present U.S. city of Chillicothe, Ohio. In 1774 it is estimated that there were around 900 Shawnee living in the village.

liii

The women raised Shawnee traditional houses. They were constructed of bark fixed around a framework of posts. Some enclosed rectangular floor plans. At this time, some of the Shawnee houses demonstrated European influence, and were made from logs and had chimneys instead of holes in the roof.

liv

Shawnee towns usually occupied high ground and overlooked fertile bottomlands that the women laid out in crops. The council house dominated every village. It was a large strong building in which public and ceremonial business of all kinds was transacted.

lv

Blackfish (c. <u>1729</u>–<u>1779</u>), known in his native tongue as Cot-ta-wa-ma-go or Mkah-day-way-may-qua.

lvi

This is the start of what history has called Dunmore's War (1774). It resulted from competition between American Indians and white colonists for control of the trans-Ohio region. Tensions between Virginians and Pennsylvanians, who vied for possession of the fort at Pittsburgh, fueled the conflicts. Early in 1774 an agent of the royal governor of Virginia, the Earl of Dun-more, took possession of Fort Pitt, renamed it Fort Dun-more, and initiated attacks against local Indian settlements. The Delaware, under the influence of Moravian missionaries, kept the peace, but the Shawnee pressed for war. On June 10th the governor called out the militia of southwest Virginia, which, under Gen. Andrew Lewis, prepared for an expedition to the Shawnee towns beyond the Ohio.

lvii

Tarhe was born near present-day Detroit, Michigan, in 1742. He was a Wyandot Indian and eventually became one of the leaders of his people. Tarhe was also known by the nickname "The Crane." Some accounts state that this name is in reference to his tall, slender build.

Like most Indians, Tarhe opposed white settlement of the Ohio Country. He fought to prevent the invasion of Indian land. In 1763, the British, in the Proclamation of 1763, told their colonists not to move west of the Appalachian Mountains because the land belonged to the Indians. Few settlers listened. As more settlers moved onto Indian lands, fighting increased between the two groups. In 1774, the governor of Virginia, John Murray, Lord Dunmore, sent troops to attack the Indians. Tarhe assisted Cornstalk, a leader of the Shawnee Indians, against the whites. The colonists emerged generally victorious from Lord Dunmore's War.

Following Lord Dunmore's War, Tarhe generally supported peace between the Indians and the white settlers. He eventually led the Wyandots into battle again at the Battle of Fallen Timbers in 1794. General Anthony Wayne led the American forces and defeated the Indians. Once again, Tarhe supported making peace with the settlers and signed the Treaty of Greenville. Even after the Treaty of Greenville, other Indian leaders, including Tecumseh, were calling for the natives to unite against the settlers. Tarhe advised the Wyandots to honor the treaty that they had signed.

In 1812, the British and Americans went to war again. Although Tarhe was in his seventies, he joined in the conflict as an ally of the American troops and was present at the Battle of the Thames in 1813. After the War of 1812, Tarhe settled near Upper Sandusky and remained there until he died in 1818 at the age of 76.

From Ohio History Central. An On line Encyclopedia of Ohio History

lviii

Chief Moluntha's village was on Mac-o-chee Creek just east of present West Liberty, Ohio. Moluntha or Malunthy (c. 1692 - November 1786) was a chief of the Shawnee people following the death of Cornstalk.

He fought at the Siege of Boonesborough on the side of the British in 1778. In 1786, threatened with war by Richard Butler and George Rogers Clark, he was among the Shawnee leaders who signed the Treaty of Fort Finney.

Immediately before Logan's Raid commenced, Benjamin Logan ordered his men not to kill any of the Shawnee that might choose to surrender. During the battle, Moluntha was cornered by William Lytle and surrendered to him. Moluntha was brought into the custody of Hugh McGary, and Logan reiterated his order that the prisoners not be harmed. McGary, who was bitter about his defeat at the Battle of Blue Licks, asked Moluntha, "Were you at the defeat of the Blue Licks?" The chief misunderstood the question and answered in the affirmative. McGary immediately killed Moluntha with an axe. Logan relieved McGary of command and court-martialed him.

Moluntha had a son, Spemica-Lawba, who survived the raid. He was raised by Benjamin Logan, and eventually became known as Captain Logan. Chief Moluntha,
Wikipedia.

lix

Blue Jacket's Town was established around 1777. The Shawnee war leader Blue Jacket (Weyapiersenwah) built a settlement near what is downtown Bellefontaine, Ohio. It was known as Blue Jacket's Town. An historical marker identifies the site in Bellefontaine. Blue Jacket and his band had previously occupied a village along the Scioto River, but with the coming of the American Revolutionary War to the Ohio Country, Blue Jacket and other American Indians who took up arms against the American revolutionaries relocated in order to be closer to their British allies at Detroit. Blue Jacket's Town was destroyed in a raid by Kentucky militia in

1786 at the outset of the Northwest Indian War. The expedition was led by Benjamin Logan, namesake of Logan County. Blue Jacket and his followers relocated further northwest to the Maumee River.

Wakatomika was the name of two 18th century Shawnee villages in what is now the U.S. state of Ohio. The name was also spelled Wapatomica, Waketomika, and Waketameki, among other variations, but the similar name Wapakoneta was a different Shawnee village.

The first Wakatomika was located along the Muskingum River, near present-day Dresden, Ohio. In August 1774, during Dunmore's War, Wakatomika and four other Shawnee villages in the area were destroyed by Virginia colonial militia in an expedition led by Angus McDonald.

After Dunmore's War, the residents of Wakatomika resettled further west. A new Wakatomica was established by 1778 on the Mad River in present-day Logan County. This village was destroyed in 1786 during an expedition led by Benjamin Logan at the outset of the Northwest Indian War.

lx

Wapatomika was also spelled Wapatomica, Waketomika, Wakatomika and Waketameki. The first Wapatomika was located along the Muskingum River, near present-day Dresden, Ohio. In August 1774, during Dunmore's War, Wakatomika and four other Shawnee villages in the area were destroyed by Virginia colonial militia in an expedition led by Angus McDonald.

After Dunmore's War, the residents of Wapatomika resettled further west. A new Wapatomica was established by 1778 on the Mad River in present-day Logan County. The village was located between West Liberty and Zanesfield just off of present day U.S. 68 in the Mac-o-Chee Valley. This village was destroyed in 1786 during an expedition led by Benjamin Logan at the outset of the Northwest Indian War.

lxi

Harrodstown became the first permanent settlement west of the Alleghenies in what would become Central Kentucky. Today it is known as Harrodsburg. Old Fort Harrod State Park is a park located within the town and encompasses 15 acres, including Pioneer Cemetery, the oldest cemetery west of the Allegheny Mountains.

lxii

Colonel Andrew Lewis, cousin of Meriwether Lewis of Lewis and Clark fame.

lxiii

White Wolf was John Ward. He had been captured by the Shawnee at the age of 3 and raised as a Shawnee and fought as a Shawnee against the whites. Ironically, James Ward III, his father, was killed during the Battle of Point Pleasant. His son William was a member of his company, and John, White Wolf, actually fought for the Shawnee Indians

in that same battle. White Wolf was killed at Reeve's Crossing, Paint Creek, near Bainbridge in Ross County, OH during a small skirmish with a white party that included his brother James IV.
Libby Preston Genealogy.(Libby@Libby-Genealogy.com)

lxiv

Cheeseekau was the eldest son of Pukeshinwau. He was probably born in 1760 or 1761 in a small village up Paint Creek from Chillicothe. At that time the town of Chillicothe occupied both sides of the Scioto near a ford. There were a few houses situated on the east bank, opposite the mouth of Paint Creek, but most of the Shawnee lived a mile or so up Paint Creek. (Voeglin, Tanner *Indians of Ohio and Indiana Prior to 1795.* 2 vols. New York, 1974.) His mother was Methoataaskee (A Turtle Laying Her Eggs in the Sand). She had a daughter, Menewaulaakoosee or Tecumapease (Flying Over the Water, or Wading Over), and another son, Sauawaseekau (Jumping Panther) prior to giving birth to Tecumseh (I Cross the Way or A Panther Crouching for His Prey) March of 1768, and four more boys. The first was Nehaaseemoo, and then a set of triplets that were born in the winter of 1774-75 several months after the Battle of Point Pleasant. One of the three died at birth. The other two were Kumskaukau (A Cat That flies in the Air or A Star Which Shoots in a Straight Line Over Great Waters) and Laloeshiga (A Panther with a Handsome Tail). Laloeshiga would later disgrace himself and take the name of Tenskwattawa, which meant Open Door. As a child he grew up with another name – Lalawethika. This name signified a noisy instrument such as a rattle. (Sugden, *Tecumseh a Life,*

Holt & Company, New York, 1997.) Cheeseekau is believed to have died in a raid at Buchanan's Station in 1792.

lxv

The following is a summary by Missouri Department of Natural Resources historian Jim Denny of Meriwether Lewis's journal entries for Nov. 25-26, 1803. It is taken from *The Journals of the Lewis and Clark Expedition, Vol. 2* (Lincoln and London: University of Nebraska Press, 1986).

"November 25, 1803: to a point on the larboard side just above Grand Tower. Lewis´ estimate for total miles traveled was 9 miles [actual mileage closer to 16.7 miles]. Lewis thought the land on the larboard side of the river that he was now viewing was even higher than the uplands he had seen the day before.

In many places there were sheer cliffs that rose straight up from the water's edge; in some places the bluffs even projected forward. The rocks seemed the same as those he saw November 24, except that there was more flint; it seemed to lay in strata layered with limestone. All the bedrock he had observed appeared to lay in horizontal layers except where the strata were carried from their original beds by the eroding action of the river current.

The party continued to work its way upstream past high country on the larboard side, with a few small stretches of bottom, and land on the starboard side that seemed low and subject to overflow. How far inland these low bottoms flooded was a subject Lewis had not informed himself about. After passing several insignificant creeks, the party noticed a small creek on the larboard side (today's Indian Creek). Above this creek was a cluster of Shawnee huts and tents.

A few miles farther upstream, the party encountered the mouth of Apple Creek on the larboard side. They stopped here while Lewis took meridian altitudes of the sun. He noted the usual error in the sextant. Lewis considered Apple Creek to be the largest stream he had yet seen on the Mississippi. Just below the mouth of the creek was a large flat rock, now visible, but concealed during high water.

Indian creek was once known as Table Creek because of a projecting rock on the south side of that creek that resembled a table. River men called the rock the "Devil´s Tea Table". The large flat rock that Lewis describes as being just below Apple Creek was probably just below Indian Creek.

On this date, very little water from Apple Creek found its way to the river, although when the water was high the creek could be navigated for several miles. Lewis noted that Apple Creek was similar to other small to medium sized creeks along the Mississippi in appearing to be smaller at their mouths than they really were. The mouths of such creeks were constricted and virtually cease to flow as a mud depositing eddies formed at the point where their feeble currents came up against the powerful waters of the Mississippi.

Eddies on these streams deposit thick layers of mud that can extend back several miles. When the Mississippi dropped, only a small channel could cut its way through the deposits of mud in order to reach the Mississippi. This trickle presents the appearance of a much smaller flow of water than the stream actually had.

In any event, Apple Creek extended a good distance back into the country, 40 or 50 miles by

Lewis´s estimation, where it headed with the waters of the St. Francis River.

Lewis recorded that a Shawnee village was located 7 miles up Apple Creek. He did not know how many Shawnee resided in this village, but he knew enough about the village to know that this settlement of Absentee Shawnee deserved the name "village" more than any other Indian settlement in the region. In the same year Lewis was making his observations, Nicholas de Finiels described the Absentee Shawnee villages, of which the one at Apple Creek was the largest, as systematically and solidly constructed, far above the norm for Native American construction, and surrounded by cleared fenced land. The Spanish land claim at the mouth of Apple Creek belonged to Pierre Menard, the well-known Kaskaskia trader, who hoped to build an Indian trading house at the mouth of Apple Creek.

Opposite the mouth of Apple Creek, on the east shore of the river, Lewis noticed an island (known as Big Muddy Island). Concealed behind this island was stream that Lewis said was known as Muddy River, and alternately as Cow River, or River Avaise (it is today's Big Muddy River). According to Lewis, this river could be navigated for 30 or 40 miles in high water. He understood Muddy River to head into extensive plains with tributaries of the Ohio and Great Wabash Rivers (the Saline and Little Wabash Rivers, respectively)."

http://tower-rock-winery.com/lewis.htm

lxvi

The Battle of Point Pleasant was considered a precursor of the American Revolutionary War and was a turning point in the war against the Indian uprising in western Virginia. It was declared the official first battle of the American Revolution in 30 May 1908 by unanimous vote in the 60th Congress of the United States under Session I, Chapter 228, Section 32. During the battle, one-half of General Lewis's commissioned officers, including his brother Charles, were killed, as were seventy-five non-commissioned soldiers. Another one hundred and forty soldiers were wounded. The actual number of Indians engaged or killed in the battle is not known.

lxvii

Louis Lorimier was the son of a French colonial officer. At the time of his offerings to the Shawnee, he was around 40 years of age. He spoke French, English and a number of Indian languages and was known among the Indians as an honest man. He had traded with the Miamis, Shawnee and Delaware and had fought alongside them in the Revolutionary War. By 1788, he had a son and a daughter by his wife, Pemanpich, a woman who was Shawnee and French and related to a Blackbeard, a Shawnee chief. It is likely that he had discussions with Cheeseekau and Tecumseh and had lured them to the territory with the promise of land and with their despair in finding peace with the whites and in securing a safe home in the Ohio lands.

Tecumseh a Life Henry Holt and company, Inc., NY, NY 1997 p. 52

lxviii

The Tuscarawas River is a principal tributary of the Muskingum River, 129.9 miles (209 km) long, in northeastern Ohio in the United States. Via the Muskingum and Ohio Rivers, it is part of the watershed of the Mississippi River, draining an area of 2,590 square miles on glaciated and un-glaciated portions of the Allegheny Plateau.

lxix

The Great Miami River (also called the Miami River) is a tributary of the Ohio River, approximately 150 miles long, in southwestern Ohio in the United States. The Great Miami flows through Dayton, Piqua, Troy, and Sidney. The river is named for the Miami, an Algonquian speaking Native American people who lived in the region during the early days of European settlement. The region surrounding the Great Miami River is known as the Miami Valley.

The Shawnee retreated from the Ohio from 1768-1794 abandoning the Scioto, travelling westward to the valleys of the Little and Great Miami Rivers where they built homes that were less exposed to American attack. Notable new towns were: Pekowi: on the northwestern bank of the Mad River a few miles west of present-day Springfield in Clark County, Ohio, Mackachack; a Mekoche village on the Mad River North and upstream of Pekowi, Blue Jackets Town; a Mingo town , Old Chillicothe; (a new Chillicothe) on the southeastern bank of the upper Little Miami near modern-day Xenia. P. 31 Sugden, *Tecumseh a Life*, Holt & Company, New York, 1997

lxx

The first fort stood on the apex of the upper angle formed by the confluence of the great Kanawha and Ohio Rivers; it was built in October and November of 1774 and named Fort Blair after John Blair, by Captain William Russell who was both the designer and builder. Captain Russell evacuated the Fort in June 1775, after those who were wounded in the battle had fully recovered. Lord Dunmore, the Colonial Governor of the British Colony of Virginia, removed the garrison. A Short time later the fort was set afire by the Indians.

Captain Mathew Arbuckle and a company of men were sent from Fort Pitt by General Hand, in 1776, to Point Pleasant to build another fort, here they reared Fort Randolph, a larger fort than fort Blair, a few rods farther up the Ohio River from the point.

Fort Randolph was named for Peyton Randolph, a Virginia aristocrat who was unanimously elected as President of the First Continental Congress on September 4th 1774. Fort Randolph served to guard the "backdoor" of Virginia and was garrisoned throughout the American Revolution.

lxxi

Captain Mathew Arbuckle and a company of men were sent from Fort Pitt by General Hand, in 1776, to Point Pleasant to build another fort, here they reared Fort Randolph, a larger fort than fort Blair, a few rods farther up the Ohio River from the point.

Fort Randolph was named for Peyton Randolph, a Virginia aristocrat who was unanimously elected as President of the First Continental Congress on

September 4th 1774. Fort Randolph served to guard the "backdoor" of Virginia and was garrisoned throughout the American Revolution.

lxxii

An interesting account of Cornstalk's murder is found in a narrative by Captain John Stuart who was present at the murder. A portion of his narrative, as it relates to the murders, follows:

"... two young men of the name of Hamilton and Gilmore went over the Kanahway one day to hunt for Deer. On their Return to the Camp, some Indians had concealed themselves on the Bank amongst the Weeds to view our Encampment, and as Gilmore came along past them, they fired on him, and killed him on the Bank. Capt. Arbuckle and I were standing upon the opposite Bank, when the Gun fired and whilst we were wondering who could be shooting contrary to orders, or what they were doing over the River, we say Hamilton run down the Bank and called out saying: "Gilmore is Killed."

On the preceding Day the Cornstalk's Son Elinipsico had come from the Nation to see his Father, and to know if he were well, or yet alive. When he came to the River opposite the Fort, he halloed over. His Father was at that Instant in the Act of delineating a Map of the Country and Waters between the Shawnee Towns and the Mississippi, at our request, with Chalk upon the Floor. He immediately recognized the Voice of his Son, got up, and went out and answered, and the young Fellow crossed over and they embraced each other in the most tender and affectionate Manner. The Interpreter's Wife, who had been a prisoner with the

Indians and had recently left them, on hearing the uproar the next Day, and hearing the men threatening that they would Kill the Indians, for whom she retained much Affection, ran to their Cabin and informed them that the people were just coming to Kill them, and that because the Indians that Killed Gilmore had come with Elinipsico the Day before. He utterly denied it, declared that he knew nothing of them, and trembled exceedingly. His Father encouraged him not to be afraid, for the Great Man above had sent him there to be killed, and die with him. As the men advanced to the Door, the Cornstalk rose up and met them. They fired upon him, and seven or eight Bullets passed through him. Thus fell the great Cornstalk Warrior whose Name was bestowed upon him by the Consent of the Nation as their great Strength and Support. His Son was shot dead as he sat upon a Stool. Redhawk made an Attempt to go up the Chimney, but was shot down. The other Indian was strangled."

"Narrative by Captain John Stuart of General Andrew Lewis' Expedition Against the Indians in the Year 1774, and of the Battle of Pleasant Point, Virginia," in Magazine of American History, November 1877

lxxiii

In 1794, the town of Point Pleasant was established near the site of the old fort. For many years after, the Indian's grave lay undisturbed but in 1840 his bones were removed to the grounds of the Mason County Court House where, in 1899, a monument was erected in Cornstalk's memory. In the late 1950's, a new court house was built in Point

Pleasant and the chief's remains (which now consisted of three teeth and about 15 pieces of bone) were placed in an aluminum box and reinterred in a corner of the town's Tu-Endie-Wei Park, next to the grave of a Virginia frontiersman that Cornstalk once fought and later befriended. A twelve-foot monument was then erected in his honor. (Wikipedia)

lxxiv

Today, this area is encompassed by what is known as Caesar's Creek State park. The Caesar Creek valley was impounded in 1978 by the Army Corps of Engineers to assist with flood control in the Little Miami River watershed. The 4,700-acre park and adjacent 2,500-acre wildlife area were dedicated that year. The Indian trail, part of which follows the ridgeline on the eastern side of the Caesar Creek valley was later used by white settlers in the early 1800s, who named it Bullskin Trace. Later the trail became part of the Underground Railroad used by runaway slaves to reach safe houses run by area Quakers.

lxxv

The St. Mary's River is a tributary of the Maumee River, approximately 100 miles long, in western Ohio and eastern Indiana in the United States. It is formed in southern Auglaize County in western Ohio by the confluence of the short East Branch and Center Branch. It flows briefly west to St. Marys, approaching to within two miles of Grand Lake before turning to the north. In northwestern Auglaize County it turns sharply to the WNW, flowing past

Rockford and Willshire into Adams County, Indiana. In northeastern Indiana it flows northwest past Decatur, then enters Fort Wayne. It hooks around in its last half mile to join the St. Joseph River from the west to form the Maumee in downtown Fort Wayne. The source of the Mad River is near present day West Liberty, Ohio.

lxxvi

The Battle of Fallen Timbers, August 20, 1794, has been called the "last battle of the American Revolution" and one of the three most important battles in the development of our nation. The decisive victory by the Legion of the United States over a confederacy of Indian tribes opened the Northwest Territory, a five-state region un-ceded by the native inhabitants, for westward expansion and led to Ohio's statehood in 1803.

The battle took place amid trees toppled by a tornado just north of the Maumee River in the present-day city of Maumee. The legion was commanded by General "Mad" Anthony Wayne, a veteran of Valley Forge handpicked by President Washington to oversee the new nation's first professional army. Wayne's force, made up of 1,600 to 1,700 "regulars" and 1,500 members of the Kentucky Militia, marched north from Cincinnati to build a series of forts between the Ohio and Maumee rivers.

Among Wayne's officers was 21-year-old General William Henry Harrison, who would become the ninth president of the United States.

Waiting for Wayne and his men were about 1,000 warriors representing the native confederacy and led by Miami war chief Little Turtle, an old nemesis of the United States. Other leaders of the confederacy included Shawnee Chief Blue Jacket and Delaware Chief Buckongahelas.

One of the most famous leaders of the native resistance, Tecumseh, also took part in the battle. Fewer than 100 men on each side died in the brief battle, but the Legion's victory marked a major turning point in the battle for the western frontier. The victory led to the signing the Treaty Greenville in 1795. Without the treaty, portions of Ohio, Michigan, Indiana, Illinois and Wisconsin might have remained a buffer zone between Indian and settled territory, or even become part of British-controlled Canada.

The Battle of Fallen Timbers The Toledo metro Parks Web page. www.fallentimbersbattlefield.com/

lxxvii

Specifically: "A Treaty of Peace between the United States of America and the Tribes of Indians called Wyandots, Delaware, Shawanoes, Ottawas, Chipewas, Putawatimes, Miamis, Eel-River, Weeas, Kickapoos, Piankashaws and Kaskaskias."

The Treaty of Greenville was signed at Fort Greenville (now Greenville, Ohio), on August 3, 1795, between a coalition of Native Americans and the United States following the Native American loss at the Battle of Fallen Timbers. It put an end to the Northwest Indian War. The United States was represented by General "Mad" Anthony Wayne, who defeated the Native Americans at Fallen Timbers. In exchange for goods to the value of $20,000 (such as blankets, utensils, and domestic animals), the Native Americans turned over to the United States large parts of modern-day Ohio, the future site of Chicago, and the Fort Detroit area.

The treaty established what became known as the "Greenville Treaty Line," which was for several years a boundary between Native American territory and lands open to white settlers, although the treaty line was frequently disregarded by settlers as they continued to encroach on native lands guaranteed by the treaty. The treaty line began at the mouth of the Cuyahoga River in present-day Cleveland and ran south along the river to the portage between the Cuyahoga and Tuscarawas River in what is now known as the Portage Lakes area between Akron and Canton. The line continued down the Tuscarawas to Fort Laurens near present-day Bolivar. From there, the line ran west-southwest to near present-day Fort Loramie on a branch of the Great Miami River. From there, the line ran west-northwest to Fort Recovery, on the Wabash River near the present-day boundary between Ohio and Indiana. From Fort Recovery, the line ran south-southwest to the Ohio River at a point opposite the mouth of the Kentucky River in present-day Carrollton, Kentucky.

lxxviii

The mouth of Suck Creek, as it enters into the Tennessee River, is about 8 miles below Chattanooga. At the mouth of the creek, in the Tennessee, is a series of dangerous whirlpools, known as "The Suck." It is noted among the Cherokee as the place where Untsaiyi, the gambler, lived long ago. They call it Untiguhi, "Pot in the water" on account of the appearance of the surging, tumbling water, suggesting a boiling pot. In 1913, the Tennessee River's water level was raised with the completion of the Hales Bar Dam. This part of the Tennessee River flows through what is known as the Tennessee River Gorge. The Gorge is a 26-mile canyon that has been formed by the Tennessee River. It is the fourth largest river gorge in the Eastern United States and is cut into the Cumberland Plateau as the river winds its way into Alabama from Tennessee.

lxxix

Running Water Town, or Amogayunyi was located 3 miles above Nickajack and was the principal settlement of the Chikamaka. It contained over 100 dwellings and was located on the southern bank of the Tennessee River. It is near present days Hale's Bar. There is a mountain stream that continues to bear its name. It was one of the towns that the Chikamaka under Dragging Canoe settled as his band migrated to the region of today's Chattanooga, Tn. They established several towns, the foremost of which was known as "Tsi Ka Ma Gi" or Chickamauga. It was located in the Brainerd area inside the current Chattanooga, TN city limits. It was settled in 1777 and destroyed by Colonel Evan Shelby in 1779.

Others were:
CITICO/SETICO, Cherokee name of "Ustutigwayi" (meaning, "Big fish there") was about ½ mile west of Tsikamagi. It was settled by refuges of the town of Settico of the Overhills. Shelby's forces destroyed it in April of 1779.
KITUWAH (Cherokee name Gatugiw or people of the Creator) the name used by the Cherokee for themselves: was also located in what is now

Chattanooga, TN. It was settled in 1777 and destroyed in April, 1779 by Shelby under orders of the US Government.

OOLTEWAH, WAS founded by Ostenaco, located on Ooltewah Creek, a.k.a., Judd's Creek.

TELASSEE, OR TALASI, was founded in 1777, it was a village near Chickamauga-Town.

TLANUWA, (meaning "Hawk Hole"): This is the Cherokee name for Chattanooga. Also known as "Chattanooga-Town".

TOQUA, in Cherokee, Dakwai, meaning "Place of the Great mystic Fish". Located inside the current Chattanooga city limits. the village was settled in 1777 by refuges of Toqua of the Overhills. It was destroyed in April, 1779. Shelby.

TUSKEEGE, from the Muskogee (Creek) name, Tuskegee means "Warrior's Place". It was located near Suck Creek, downriver from Chattanooga, on the north bank of the Tennessee River. This island town was also settled in 1777, and destroyed in April, 1779, by Shelby. "Bloody Fellow" founded this town.

AMOYEE, meaning "water place", located near the Hiwasee River and north of Chickamauga-Town.

CHESTOEE or Tsistuyi (Means "Rabbit Place", located at Chestoee Creek in present day Polk County.

HIWASEE. Located on Hiwasee River, north of Chickamauga-town. This is in present day Grundy County, at Sweeten Hill.

OCOEE, OR UWAGAHI, meaning "Apricot Place." This is a word of Muscogee (Creek) origin. It was located east of Chickamauga-Town in the valley settlements of the Cherokee.

CROW TOWN, OR KAGUNYI, located near present day Stevensen, Alabama on the Tennessee River. Settled about 1779.

LONG ISLAND TOWN, OR MAYELIGUNAHITA. Located near the present day Bridgeport, AL, on the Tennessee River. Settled after 1779.

LOOKOUT MOUNTAIN TOWN, OR STECOYEE, "Big Fish There." Located near present day Trenton, GA. This was the town of "Little Owl."

NICKAJACK, OR ANIKUSATIYI, "Old Creek Place." Located near present Shellmound, TN. It contained at least 40 dwellings and was destroyed by Major James Ore on September 13, 1794.
http://www.chikamaka.org/ccwy/

lxxx

Tsiyugunsini, "He is dragging his canoe", was known to whites as Dragging Canoe, (c. 1738 – March 1, 1792) He was an American Indian war leader who led a dissident band of Cherokee (joined by Upper Muskogee, Chickasaw, Shawnee, and Indians from other tribes/nations, along with British Loyalists, French and Spanish agents, renegade whites from the colonies, and runaway slaves, against the United States in the American Revolutionary War and a decade afterwards, a series of conflicts known as the Chickamauga Wars. He was also known as the Tecumseh of the South.

lxxxi

A bateau is a shallow-draft, flat-bottomed boat. The name derives from the French word, bateau, which is simply the word for boat. The plural is bateaux. They were used by the French extensively across North America, especially in the colonial period and in the fur trade. The boats' shallow draft worked well in rivers while its flat bottom profile allowed heavy loading of cargoes and provided stability. The smallest bateau required only one crewman, while larger ones required up to five and reach up to 45-58 feet in length. The largest bateaux could carry two to ten tons of cargo. Bateaux could mount a small sail although the flat bottom was not optimal for sailing. In military records, it is seen that the boats were propelled primarily by oars with one oar being used at the stern as a rudder.

In the southern United States, the term is still used to refer to flat-bottomed boats, including those elsewhere called Jon boats.

lxxxii

Alexander McGillivray (December 15, 1750 – February 17, 1793) was a leader of the Creek (Muscogee) Indians during and after the American Revolution. He worked to establish a Creek national identity and a centralized leadership as a means of resisting American expansion onto Creek territory.
He was born Hoboi-Hili-Miko ("Good Child King") at Little Tallassee in Alabama on the Coosa River. His father, Lachlan McGillivray, was a Scottish trader (of the Clan MacGillivray chief's lineage). His mother, Sehoy Marchand, was the daughter of Jean Baptiste Louis DeCourtel Marchand, a French officer at Fort Toulouse, and Sehoy, a mixed-blooded Creek woman of the prestigious Wind Clan. McGillivray was educated in Charleston, South Carolina, where he learned Latin and Greek. He returned to the Wind clan at the beginning of the American Revolution after Georgia confiscated the property of his loyalist father, who then returned to Scotland.

lxxxiii

The Creek Crossing Place was approximately thirty miles below Nickajack. It was part of a trail used by the Creeks making forays north of the Tennessee.

lxxxiv

John Watts was born in 1750 and became Chief of the Chickamauga in 1792 at Dragging Canoe's death. He had a white father and Indian mother. Watts kept the Chickamauga on the warpath with supplies from the Spanish who were located in Florida. He led them on attacks of Nashville in Sept 1792 and Knoxville in Aug 1793. He was defeated in both (in the Knoxville campaign by John Sevier). When Spain withdrew its support (and two of his five towns were burned by the militia) John Watts and other Cherokee Chiefs signed a peace treaty in 1794.

lxxxv

Cherokee men were often heavily tattooed. The tattoos were made by simply pricking the skin and rubbing the wound with ashes from a fire, to give the tattoo its dark color.

lxxxvi

P. 24 Chronicles of Oklahoma, Volume 16, No. 1 March, 1938, EASTERN CHEROKEE CHIEFS John P. Brown

lxxxvii

The Holston River is one of the major river systems **of southwestern Virginia and East Tennessee. The** North, Middle and South Forks of the Holston originate in southwestern Virginia and have their confluence near Kingsport, Tennessee. From there the river flows roughly southwestward, just north of Bays Mountain, until it reaches its confluence with the French Broad River just east of downtown Knoxville, Tennessee. This confluence is considered to be the start of the Tennessee River.

lxxxviii

The Treaty of Holston was signed by William Blount, governor in and over the territory of the United States south of the Ohio River, and superintendent of Indian affairs for the southern district for the United States and representatives of the Cherokee Nation on July 2, 1791 near the Holston River and proclaimed on February 7, 1792. A monument of the treaty is located at the Knoxville courthouse in Knoxville, Tennessee.

"A Treaty of Peace and Friendship made and concluded between the President of the United States of America, on the Part and Behalf of the said States, and the undersigned Chiefs and Warriors of the Cherokee Nation of Indians, on the Part and Behalf of the said Nation.

The parties being desirous of establishing permanent peace and friendship between the United States and the said Cherokee Nation, and the citizens and members thereof, and to remove the causes of war, by ascertaining their limits and making other necessary, just and friendly arrangements: The President of the United States, by William Blount, Governor of the territory of the United States of America, south of the river Ohio, and Superintendent of Indian affairs for the southern district, who is vested with full powers for these purposes, by and with the advice and consent of the Senate of the United States: And the Cherokee Nation, by the undersigned Chiefs and Warriors representing the said nation, have agreed to the following articles, namely:

ARTICLE I.

There shall be perpetual peace and friendship between all the citizens of the United States of America, and all the individuals composing the whole Cherokee nation of Indians.

ARTICLE II.

The undersigned Chiefs and Warriors, for themselves and all parts of the Cherokee nation, do acknowledge themselves and the said Cherokee nation, to be under the protection of the said United States of America, and of no other sovereign whosoever; and they also stipulate that the said Cherokee nation will not hold any treaty with any foreign power, individual state, or with individuals of any state.

ARTICLE III.

The Cherokee nation shall deliver to the Governor of the territory of the United States of America, south of the river Ohio, on or before the first day of April next, at this place, all persons who are now prisoners, captured by them from any part of the United States: And the United States shall on or before the same day, and at the same place, restore to the Cherokees, all the prisoners now in captivity, which the citizens of the United States have captured from them.

ARTICLE IV.

The boundary between the citizens of the United States and the Cherokee nation, is and shall be as follows: Beginning at the top of the Currahee mountain, where the Creek line passes it; thence a direct line to Tugelo river; thence northeast to the Occunna Mountain, and over the same along the South-Carolina Indian boundary to the North-Carolina boundary; thence north to a point from which a line is to be extended to the river Clinch, that shall pass the Holston at the ridge which divides the waters running into Little River from those running into the Tennessee; thence up the river Clinch to Campbell's line, and along the same to the top of Cumberland mountain; thence a direct line to the Cumberland river where the Kentucky road crosses it; thence down the Cumberland river to a point from which a south west line will strike the ridge which divides the waters of Cumberland from those of Duck river, forty miles above Nashville; thence down the said ridge to a point from whence a south west line will strike the mouth of Duck river.

And in order to preclude forever all disputes relative to the said boundary, the same shall be ascertained and marked plainly by three persons appointed on the part of the United States, and three Cherokees on the part of their nation.

And in order to extinguish forever all claims of the Cherokee nation, or any part thereof, to any of the land lying to the right of the line above described, beginning as aforesaid at the Currahee mountain, it is hereby agreed, that in addition to the consideration heretofore made for the said land, the United States will cause certain valuable goods, to be immediately delivered to the undersigned Chiefs and Warriors, for the use of their nation; and the said United States will also cause the sum of one thousand dollars to be paid annually to the said Cherokee nation. And the undersigned Chiefs and Warriors do hereby for themselves and the whole Cherokee nation, their heirs and descendants, for the considerations above-mentioned, release, quit-claim, relinquish and cede, all the land to the right of the line described, and beginning as aforesaid.

ARTICLE V.

It is stipulated and agreed, that the citizens and inhabitants of the United States, shall have a free and unmolested use of a road from Washington district to Mero district, and of the navigation of the Tennessee River.

ARTICLE VI.

It is agreed on the part of the Cherokees, that the United States shall have the sole and exclusive right of regulating their trade.

ARTICLE VII.

The United States solemnly guarantee to the Cherokee nation, all their lands not hereby ceded. /H/

ARTICLE VIII.

If any citizen of the United States, or other person not being an Indian, shall settle on any of the Cherokees' lands, such person shall forfeit the protection of the United States, and the Cherokees may punish him or not, as they please.

ARTICLE IX.

No citizen or inhabitant of the United States, shall attempt to hunt or destroy the game on the lands of the Cherokees; nor shall any citizen or inhabitant go into the Cherokee country, without a passport first obtained from the Governor of some one of the United States, or /J/ territorial districts, or such other person as the President of the United States may from time to time authorize to grant the same.

ARTICLE X.

If any Cherokee Indian or Indians, or person residing among them, or who shall take refuge in their nation, shall steal a horse from, or commit a robbery or murder, or other capital crime, on any citizens or inhabitants of the United States, the Cherokee nation shall be bound to deliver him or them up, to be punished according to the laws of the United States.

ARTICLE XI.

If any citizen or inhabitant of the United States, or of either of the territorial districts of the United States, shall go into any town, settlement or territory belonging to the Cherokees, and shall there commit any crime upon, or trespass against the person or property of any peaceable and friendly Indian or Indians, which if committed within the jurisdiction of any state, or within the jurisdiction of either of the said districts, against a citizen or white inhabitant thereof, would be punishable by the laws of such state or district, such offender or offenders, shall be subject to the same punishment, and shall be proceeded against in the same manner as if the offence had committed within the jurisdiction of the state or district to which he or they may belong, against a citizen or white inhabitant thereof.

ARTICLE XII.

In case of violence on the persons or property of the individuals of either party, neither retaliation nor reprisal shall be committed by the other, until satisfaction shall have been demanded of the party of which the aggressor is, and shall have been refused.

ARTICLE XIII.

The Cherokees shall give notice to the citizens of the United States, of any designs which they may know, or suspect to be formed in any neighboring tribe, or by any person whatever, against the peace and interest of the United States.

ARTICLE XIV.

That the Cherokee nation may be led to a greater degree of civilization, and to become herdsman and cultivators, instead of remaining in a state of hunters, the United States will from time to time furnish gratuitously the said nation with useful implements of husbandry, and further to assist the said nation in so desirable a pursuit, and at the same time to establish a certain mode of communication, the United States will send such, and so many persons to reside in said nation as they may judge proper, not exceeding four in number, who shall qualify themselves to act as interpreters. These persons shall have lands assigned by the Cherokees for cultivation for themselves and their successors in office; but they shall be precluded exercising any kind of traffic.

ARTICLE XV.

All animosities for past grievances shall henceforth cease, and the contracting parties will carry the foregoing treaty into full execution with all good faith and sincerity.

ARTICLE XVI.

This treaty shall take effect and be obligatory on the contracting parties, as soon as the same shall have been ratified by the President of the United States, with the advice and consent of the Senate of the United States.

In witness of all and everything herein determined between the United States of America and the whole Cherokee nation, the parties have hereunto set their hands and seals, at the treaty ground on the bank of the Holston, near the mouth of the French Broad, within the United States, this second day of July, in the year of our Lord one thousand seven hundred and ninety-one.

William Blount, governor in and over the territory of the United States of America south of the river Ohio, and superintendent of Indian Affairs for the southern district, (L.S.)

Indians that signed:

Chuleoah, or the Boots,
Squollecuttah, or Hanging Maw,
Occunna, or the Badger,
Enoleh, or Black Fox,
Nontuaka, or the Northward,
Tekakiska, Chutloh, or King Fisher,
Tuckaseh, or Terrapin,
Kateh,
Kunnochatutloh, or the Crane,
Cauquillehanah, or the Thigh,
Chesquotteleneh, or Yellow Bird,
Chickasawtehe, or Chickasaw Killer,
Tuskegratehe, Tuskega Killer,
Kulsatehe,
Tinkshalene,
Sawutteh, or Slave Catcher,
Aukuah, Oosenaleh,
Kenotetah, or Rising Fawn,
Kanetetoka, or Standing Turkey,
Yonewatleh, or Bear at Home,
Long Will,
Nenetooyah, or Bloody Fellow,
Chuquilatague, or Double Head,
Koolaquah, or Big Acorn,
Toowayelloh, or Bold Hunter,
Jahleoonoyehka, or Middle Striker,
Kinnesah, or Cabin,

Tullotehe, or Two Killer,
 Kaalouske, or Stopt Still,
Kulsatche,
Auquotague, the Little Turkey's Son,
 Talohteske, or Upsetter,
Cheakoneske, or Otter Lifter,
Keshukaune, or She Reigns,
Toonaunailoh, Teesteke, or Common Disturber,
Robin McClemore,
 (L.S.) Skyuka.

John Thompson, Interpreter.
James Cery, Interpreter.

Done in presence of - -

Daniel Smith, Secretary Territory United States south of the river Ohio, Thomas Kennedy, of Kentucky, Jas. Robertson, of Mero District, Claiborne Watkins, of Virginia, Jno. McWhitney, of Georgia, Fauche, of Georgia, Titus Ogden, North Carolina, Jno. Chisolm, Washington District and Robert King.

lxxxix

The word Eskaqua is from the Shawnee. In Cherokee, Clear Sky would be Galunladi-yiga. P.26. Chronicles of Oklahoma, Volume 16, No. 1 March, 1938, EASTERN CHEROKEE CHIEFS, John P. Brown

xc

Willstown was an important town in the south westernmost part of the Nation. It was located in what is today's DeKalb County, Alabama. The actual site of Willstown was just north of, and now occupied by the town of Fort Payne, close today's Valley Head area. The settlement was commonly called Willstown, after Will Weber. Weber was the head of the town. He was a redheaded man of mixed-race, who was famous for his head of thick red hair. The town was also Wattstown because John Watts used it as his headquarters.

It was founded during the Chickamauga wars, and later served as the council seat of the Lower Cherokee well into the 19th century. Will Weber immigrated to the Arkansas country in 1796.

xci

Chief Tsal Su Ska, Doublehead, was the brother of Old Tassel. He was also known as Dsu-gwe-La-dergi and Chuqualatgue. Talo Tiske means "two heads." He established a town on the Tennessee River at the head of Muscle Shoals in 1790. This village sat at the mouth of Blue Water Creek in Lauderdale County. He was known as a bloodthirsty savage because of his habit of cannibalizing his enemy's bodies after a successful raid. He would cut a piece of flesh from one of his victims and eat it as a sign of conquered impotence. Afterwards, he would demand that his warriors, as a symbolic blood oath, do the same. To enhance his gruesome reputation, he dismembered the body of Captain William Overall, after tomahawking him and carrying him back to his village and in full view of everyone began eating the choicest parts, inviting the tribesmen to join him. "The white man is no more than a dog, a pig in the woods. And should be treated in the same way." He was murdered on August 9, 1807.

xcii

Major John Buchanan's Station *(1783 - 1790's)* A settlers' fort located four miles east of Fort Nashville. The fort was attacked twice. First in the spring of 1783, and also in September 1792.

Major John Buchanan was born at Harrisburg, Pennsylvania, January 12, 1759, and was the oldest son of James and Jane Trimble Buchanan (of Scotch Irish descent). After migrating to near Danville, Kentucky, the Major uprooted his family, and along with his father's family, left Danville and they arrived where Nashville is now located on December 14, 1778. They crossed the Cumberland River on the ice at the mouth of Sulphur Spring branch. Upon their arrival they found General James Robertson and one other man living in log cabins on the bluff of the Cumberland River where the county jail now stands today. The third house erected on the site was built by the Buchanans. As a means of better protection and defense against the attacks of the various bands of Indians, they built a fort on the bluff over the Cumberland River where current day Front Street. In 1781 the Indians invaded the settlement and Alexander Buchanan, brother of Major John Buchanan, was killed by the Indians near the crossing of Market and Broad streets. After staying at the Nashville fort four years, Major Buchanan moved six miles east of the Nashville fort and erected a rude cabin on a stream now called Mill Creek. He later built the first mill at the site that was ever erected in the county. He built what the Indians described because of its simplicity a "cow pen fort" at this site.

(Davidson County, Tennessee Buchanan Memoir, 1999 by Richard White.)

xciii

Fort Nashborough was named in honor of North Carolinian General Francis Nash, who won acclaim in the American Revolution. It was the stockade for the settlement that is today's Nashville, TN. A reconstruction today stands on the banks of the Cumberland River near the site of the original fort.

The first Europeans to arrive in middle Tennessee were French fur trappers and trader Charles Charleville, who established a trading post at a salt lick, and another Frenchman named Timothy Demonbreun, who made his home in a cave on a bluff above the Cumberland River. By the middle part of the century, the area that is now Nashville came to be known as French Lick because of the salt lick.

The Indian Treaty of Lochaber in 1770 and the Transylvania Purchase in 1775 opened up much of the land west of the Appalachians to settlers. Several settlements had already sprung up on Cherokee land in the Appalachians, and these settlements had formed the Watauga Association, a sort of self-government. However, it was not until the late 1770s that the first settlers began to arrive in middle Tennessee. In 1778, James Robertson, a member of the Watauga Association, brought a scouting party to the bluffs above the Cumberland River in his search for a place to found a new settlement. The following year he returned with a party of settlers. This first group, comprised of men only, had traveled through Kentucky and arrived at French Lick on Christmas Eve 1779. The women and children, under the leadership of John Donelson, followed by flatboat, traveling 1,000 miles by river to reach the new settlement and arrived in April 1780. This new

settlement of nearly 300 people was named Fort Nashborough. As soon as both parties were assembled at Fort Nashborough, the settlers drew up a charter of government called the Cumberland Compact. This was the first form of government in middle Tennessee.
_(www.frommers.com/destinations/nashville)

xciv

Most of the defenders of Buchanan's station were identified as living to the east of station. The Shanes lived about 5 miles to the east on Stones River. Sarah Gowen, a widower, had a house about 1.5 miles to the southeast of the station. In a little known, eight-page, first-hand narrative account of the battle, written by 10 year old John Buchanan Todd, who was in the fort at the time of the attack, Todd names the defenders of the station as: Maj. John Buchanan, commander, John McCrary, James Mulherrin, James Bryant, Wm Turbull, Wetherell Lattimore, Robt. Castbolt, Thomas Kennedy, Abram Kennedy, Morris O'Shane, John Tony, Geo. Davidson, Thomas Wilcox, Jos. Crabtree, John Goin, Wm Goin & James Todd.

"The Lyman Draper Papers," Tennessee State Library & Archives, Manuscript Accession No. 29, series XX, Vol. 6, frame 68.

xcv

Knoxville, Wednesday, October 10

"During the whole time of the attack, the Indians were never more distant than ten yards from the Block House, and often in large numbers close round the lower walls, attempting to put fire to it. One ascended the roof with a torch, where he was shot, and falling to the ground, renewed his attempts to fire the bottom logs, and was killed. The Indians fired 30 balls through a porthole or the over-jutting, which lodged in the roof in the circumstances of a hat, and those sticking in the walls on the outside are innumerable.

"Upon viewing the ground next morning, it appeared, that the fellow who was shot from the roof, was a Cherokee half-breed, of the Running Water, known by the whites by the name of Tom Turnbridge's step son, the son of a French woman by an Indian; and there was much blood, and sign that many dead had been dragged off, and litters having been made to carry the wounded to their horses which they had left a mile from the station.

Near the block house were found, several swords, hatchets, pipes, kettles, and budgets of different Indian articles; one of the swords was a fine Spanish blade, and richly mounted in the Spanish fashion. In the morning previous to the attack, Jonathan Gee and Savard[?] Clayton were sent out as spies; and on the ground, among other articles left by the Indians, were found a handkerchief and a moccasin, known one to belong to Gee and the other to Clayton, hence it supposed they are killed. "Annals of Tennessee," copyrighted 1853, pub. 1860, pp. 566-67. "An Account of the 1792 Attack on Buchanan's Station" J. G. M. Ramsey.

xcvi

What's In Those Sacred Bundles?
Martha Ironstar
SASKATCHEWAN INDIAN FEBRUARY 1993 v22 n02 p11

xcvii

The Shawnee hold a unique theological conception of their Creator, a female deity known to them as Kuhkoomtheyna, or Our Grandmother. In various other textual references, she is labeled interestingly by terms that can be translated as the "Creator," "the Supreme Being," "Universe Ruler," "Beautiful Cloud," "Author of Life," and/or "the First Woman."

According to Shawnee mythology, Our Grandmother descended from the world above (Sky World) and created the basis or the foundation of the earth, the turtle. Our Grandmother shaped the world, all bodies of water and tracts of land, and rested her newly created world on the back of the turtle. Our Grandmother performed most of the cosmic creations. At this same time she, with her grandson Cloud Boy and their little dog, rested on the earth.

Shawnee theology proposes four distinct phases, or periods of creation. In each of these phases, Our Grandmother appears actively engaged in the creative process.

The Four Phases of Creation
Phase I: Chaos

Creation occurs from chaos. Our Grandmother creates the universe and elements of matter. Other 'Sky World' figures appear, apparently through the creative hand of Our Grandmother. These include 'Corn Person,' 'Star People,' 'Sun Person,' Her two grandsons, Her little dog and Moon Woman (who lives close enough to Our Grandmother to be her shadow or, in some instances, could be considered an actual reflection of Our Grandmother).

Phase II: Cloud Boy's Contribution

Our Grandmother allows her grandson, 'Cloud Boy' (sometimes also known as Rounded-Side) variant license in creative actions. In this stage, the roots of human weakness and destructive influences appear. 'Cloud Boy' also appears responsible for some comical actions and even foolishness. For example, the Shawnee believe that 'Cloud Boy' shapes clouds into likenesses of animals, people, mountains and other comical shapes to entertain and delight mortals here on earth. He has also been accused of moving objects (articles of clothing, personal belongings, etc) in order to "joke" with the Shawnee people.

Phase III: The Great Deluge

Then, a great deluge came and rising waters destroyed most of the world. Immediately after the flood, Our Grandmother still lived on the earth, having survived the great flood. After she kindled a new fire, she began the task of recreation. Curiously enough, Our Grandmother did not create the Shawnee first, but began with the Delaware. Later, she created the first two Shawnee divisions. Her grandson, 'Cloud Boy,' created two more and finally Our Grandmother brought all of the Shawnee people together and they ultimately numbered five divisions. The Shawnee tribal divisions include Thawikila, Pekowi, Kishpoko, Chalakaatha, and Mekoche.

Phase IV: Final Creative Actions

In the final phase of creation, Our Grandmother gives the acquisition of fire to the people, and instructs them in the proper ways in which to kindle this sacred fire. She assigns guardian spirits, explains and assigns the sacred bundles and sets the ceremonies, rituals and rites to which all Shawnee must comply.

Then she moved to her heavenly home in the Sky World, where she now lives as a spirit-god, and began weaving her 'doomsday net' (skemotah) so that faithful and/or worthy Shawnee can be collected and saved. She is the author of life, the restorer of the earth and the punisher of evil.

According to oral histories and Shawnee stories our Grandmother has eight separate, but discernible message revelation techniques for Her Grandchildren, four for chosen Shawnee individuals and four general message revelation techniques for her grandchildren, the Shawnee people. Her messages are revealed as four social or public revelations and four specific or personal revelations.

Her words have had a powerful impact on the Shawnee people. Message themes include "keep my bundles sacred, observe my prescribed celebrations, keep my laws, and listen for my special prophetic revelation."

Sacred Bundles

The first, and possibly the most important message from Our Grandmother remains: "Keep your sacred bundle carefully." In other words, the Shawnee and, more specifically, the divinely assigned bundle keeper, has to keep the bundle safe, secure and protected from theft, the weather or neglect.

Referred to as the 'Messawmi,' each Sacred Bundle was a gift to one of the five Shawnee divisions from Our Grandmother, given immediately before she moved beyond the Sky World. This bundle contained various elements prescribed by Our Grandmother, or represented certain events that were particularly significant for each division. Often, the items contained in the bundles were reminders of special blessings, sacred beliefs, or powerful totems critical to the survival of the Shawnee.

Our Grandmother can still control them and will inform a chosen prophet if she desires a change in either the contents of the bundle, or a specific ritual surrounding a bundle. Sacred bundles are kept in a special place, regarded and treated like human beings. Sacred bundles are often moved so that they don't become uncomfortable, or cramped.

Though kept and treated with sacred care, the bundles are shrouded in mystery even to their appointed custodians. Immediately preceding the end of the world, Our Grandmother will recall the bundles.

Ceremonies, Rituals and Dances

Our Grandmother reigns as supreme deity of ceremonies, rituals and dances for the Shawnee. Her message to the Shawnee remains, "Keep the dances and ceremonies sacred, so I will be nourished and you will be prosperous."

From the Bread Dance to the Green Corn Dance, the Shawnee gather for symbolic hunts, feasts, and dance festivals in order to honor the Master of Life. These annual ceremonial dances provide a chief vehicle for worshipping Our Grandmother. The annual ceremonial dances are performed in order to worship Our Grandmother, thereby preserving the tribe and the world.

Even if a ceremony is not primarily devoted to Our Grandmother, She will notice and punish any neglect. The dead, as well as the living, must participate in her ceremonies, wear Shawnee paint and dress in the Shawnee manner so that Our Grandmother will not mistake them for white people on the day she brings her grandchildren home to her country.

The many feasts suggested by Our Grandmother provide her opportunities to visit the Shawnee. Though the relationship between feast events and Our Grandmother is indirect, the ceremonies provide opportunities for her to visit with her grandchildren. Our Grandmother constantly observes the Shawnee from her home above, using her well-known 'Sky Window.'

In addition, Our Grandmother makes certain appearances on earth to inspect, or participate in ceremonies at closer range. She has been known to visit the Shawnee during the First Fruits ceremony in order to taste the food set out for her. She has been heard singing above the arbor during the Bread Dances.

Performance of these various ceremonies and dances preserve the Shawnee and the world. Sometimes, mounted warriors ride around the dance ground four times just to amuse Our Grandmother, who comes to earth for the day to view the celebration and dance.

She has even been known to make a visit during the active ballgames of the Shawnee. She smiles in approval when in the speech before the ballgame it is said that the ball games are played because they were ordained by her rules.

All of the major ceremonies of the Shawnee were, and are, believed to have originated with Kokumthena. These moments of contact put the

Shawnee in intimate contact with an ultimate power that shapes their lives, guides their values and provides a sense of control and purpose for the Shawnee people.

Sacred Pouches

Just as the sacred bundles represented the key mediums of relating to Our Grandmother for the five divisions, so the Pawaka (the individual totem bundle) emerged as the personal form of the Messawni. In other words, the Pawaka became the personal sacred bundle. Elements of the Pawaka were earned by worthy accomplishments, personal achievements, and personal preparations rather than by free gifts from Our Grandmother.

Individual Shawnee possess their own personal guardian spirits, identified in adolescence during vision quests where youths fasted and meditated. These tutelary spirits, commonly conceived to be animals, make themselves known through dreams, hallucinations, or some other revelatory event. These experiences are considered personal and supernatural.

Guarded carefully, few Shawnee will speak explicitly about these particular aspects of their religion. Yet, the hidden relationship that exists between the powers sought (or received) and the visionary experience, which affects the individual deeply, brings personal revelation from Our Grandmother.

New ceremonies might originate in an individual totemic vision and could be incorporated into the village patterns.

Witness Ceremonies

Witness Ceremonies are for Our Grandmother to communicate with her grandchildren (the Shawnee) individually. She has created a number of intermediaries known as Tipwiwe. The Tipwiwe may be translated as "Truth bearers" or "Witnesses." The Tipwiwe carry the words of prayer to the Creator and affirm the sincerity of the person offering the prayer.

One important truth bearer is tobacco. In fact, tobacco works as a witness in two ways. In small or minor occasions, the faithful respondent uses only a pinch of true Shawnee tobacco in the private ceremony. A pinch may be placed on the ground right after a successful deer hunt, or a small amount placed on the ground after lifting some herbs from the earth. These minor, but important, observances allow the Shawnee personal communication with Our Grandmother.

During major community events, a Shawnee person can take a palm full of the special tobacco and toss it into the fire. The smoke takes prayers and messages up to Our Grandmother so that she can "notice" the faithful person, family or tribe and know the sincerity of the act.

Other "witnesses" include water, the eagle, fire, the hawk, the four winds and stars. Cedar remains an important component of the fires ignited by the sincere Shawnee worshipper. The sacred fire of the Shawnee alerts Our Grandmother of the intention of a personal approach by one of her grandchildren.

Witnesses allow any one of the Shawnee communities to communicate with Our Grandmother and hear her confirmation of their faith. Our Grandmother confirms her watchful care of the Shawnee through these truth bearers. The truth bearers and witnesses stand ready to assist the faithful Shawnee in ceremony and worship.

The Vision Quest

The Vision Quest is exclusively an individual undertaking; although the expectation remains that prophetic visions will occur. The special message and blessings received on a vision quest are not necessarily for public knowledge. However, if the person receives very potent visions, they could consequently become 'sweat-lodge doctors,' healers, leaders, or prophets.

Both girls and boys were encouraged to engage in the vision quest. Shawnee children started this ritual at around the age of seven, earlier than most other Native American children. Waiting spirits rove about everywhere in the invisible world hoping for a child to find them. If we search long enough, we find them. The spirit sings a song for the child to learn and use when calling upon the spirit guardian.

Guardian spirits provide interpretation and revelation from Our Grandmother. Guardians are especially active during vision quests and at other spiritual revelations or journeys.

In fact, some individuals who have received the assignment of their guardian spirit may relate, in the name of prophecy, the message of the guardian spirit rather than directly quoting Our Grandmother. In this sense, the guardian spirit would presumably act as an intermediary between the Creator and the individual receiving the revelation.

The revelations received in these vision quests are private, unless otherwise prescribed by Our Grandmother. If tribal service is deemed necessary, then the ability to perform 'supernatural' actions becomes communal in nature and generally includes special communication (prayers) with Our Grandmother.

Prayers are offered up to Our Grandmother at first-fruit ceremonies, funerals, naming rituals, annual events/dances, and at the end of the ballgame season.

Special Sounds and Signals

One of the most interesting and distinct manners Our Grandmother uses to communicate with individuals comes in the form of "unique sounds."

Unique sounds are specific signals to good persons among chiefs and councilors, who are created with special insight and able to translate the very thoughts of the Creator. The special sounds that have been mentioned cannot be described. Only the "wise ones" recognize the sounds and signals.

Special signals seem to operate like the sounds that occur over the heads of Shawnee participants during the various festivals and dances. Shawnee believe that the voice of Our Grandmother can be heard above the voices of singers during the festivals.

The chosen person to deliver the special revelations offered by Our Grandmother usually receives the message during a council meeting, bundle ceremony, or other significant festival. The messages may be delivered immediately, or the message medium may take time to translate the thoughts, desires or wishes of Our Grandmother.

This practice is different from prophecies, for there may be no predication, or warning involved. Many times the messages seem to be a confirmation of action, personal insight, or affirmation of leadership ability.

Foreknowledge and Prophecy

Our Grandmother, being the Supreme Being, can deliver prophetic messages through bundle ceremonies, dance ceremonies, Sky World visitations, signs and individual insight. The Creator bestowed the gift of prophecy.

Although revealed to individuals, the prophetic messages are regarded as benefiting the tribe and thus remain communal in effect. These messages are for the entire tribe.

Individuals having prophetic insight do not learn about their own personal future but the future of all Shawnee, or all people, or even the future of the world as a whole. Our Grandmother rather exclusively dispenses this foreknowledge. Since She no longer lives on earth, the Shawnee person must make a journey to her home in order to communicate and receive new revelations from her.

On many occasions, special invitations were issued to individual Shawnee allowing a visit with Our Grandmother. She would entertain the selected representatives in her Wigiwa and deliver a special message for the whole tribe. After the visit, the fortunate human messenger returned to the Shawnee people and delivered the world of Our Grandmother. The Shawnee heard from Our Grandmother through these various revelations and prophecy.

Sacred Shawnee Law

The Shawnee Laws (saawanwa kwteletiiwena), a very important part of the knowledge and instruction received from Our Grandmother, includes twelve precepts. The laws represent a stable part of the

Shawnee culture and provide an insight into life for the tribe before contact with Europeans.

Shawnee laws were handed down during the post-flood creation phase, when Our Grandmother brought all five tribal divisions together to receive her instructions. In the lengthy admonishments, she taught the Shawnee how to take care of themselves, how to live, how to conduct ceremonial dances, how to raise corn and hunt and what kind of houses to build and gave them other laws.

She also gave laws with the assurance that 'manitos' or spirit guides, such as Bear, Wolf, Deer and Eagle, would accompany the Shawnee and give them insight and constant contact with Her. The laws are noteworthy for their extreme length and comprehensiveness of subject matter.

Male laws are taught to young boys and the female laws are to be taught to young girls. The laws were recorded in the first person as though Our Grandmother herself were talking directly to the Shawnee people.

The first law sets forth the origin and purpose of Our Grandmother's precepts and describes the benefits of following her law and the consequences of failing to observe them. Modes of sexual conduct during intercourse are outlined along with requirements of behavior during menstruation and pregnancy.

The second law is general in scope.

The ten remaining laws center on a particular animal such as the deer, bear, dog, birds, wolf, buffalo, raccoon, turtle, turkey and crow. The laws described services the animal rendered to the

Shawnee and the manner in which the animal should be treated.

The number of laws (12) also equals the number of Shawnee septs or clans. Each of the clans used many of the preceding animal totems to represent their particular clan and there were twelve of these as well.

The importance of the numbers four and twelve help provide new insight into the study of Shawnee spiritual beliefs. For example, the Shawnee recognize the "four corners" (four cardinal directions), four seasons, four winds, four levels of the world, and four lives of animals. The Shawnee recognize twelve clans, twelve witnesses, and all feasts, dances and ceremonies are scheduled to last four to twelve day periods.

As with most all other Native American peoples, recognizing balance in the world remains of paramount importance to the Shawnee people.

In the contemporary world of the Shawnee people, Our Grandmother receives few visitors in her actual home. The people received are Shawnee individuals who have prophetic inclinations. Her communication to modern visitors consists chiefly in advice not to deviate from her established ways, or involves special revelations for the future.

Potentially, Our Grandmother reserves the right to create new messages and ceremonies by instructing any of her new visitors, or guests as to what to do when they return to earth. Today, Our Grandmother sits quietly in Heaven watching all people, but especially the Shawnee. She smiles if the Shawnee follow her rules.

She sends 'manitos' to talk with her people, provide guidance, and give them hope. Her messages resound through the sacred bundles, sacred laws, prophecies, ceremonies and dances. Observing these messages, "the Shawnee must live, multiply and follow the manitos on the path to Heaven.

>http://www.aaanativearts.com/cat444.html
Would you tell me, how Shawnee spirits would react to houses being built on a burial site?
~Submitted by Rose M

About the Author

Mark Stonecipher currently lives in Marysville, Ohio. He is an Ohio native. He earned his Bachelor's Degree from Tulane University in 1972, where he graduated with honors in history. He attended the University on a full athletic scholarship for track.

In addition to his full time position as a sales person for Honda Marysville, he also is an administrator and staff writer for OHRunners/Milesplits, the leading High School Track & Field web page in the US. He has published dozens of articles and interviews with many of Ohio's, as well as the nation's best High School Track & Field athletes.

For more great stories, please visit our website.
Thanks and have a great day.

Badgley Publishing Company

WWW.BadgleyPublishingCompany.com

A Special Thanks to Artist Marty Jones

Creator of Caesars Portrait on the Cover and Title page. Please visit this website for more beautiful works of art by an excellent artist.

www.mjarts.com

Made in the USA
Middletown, DE
15 November 2021